THE CHRONICLES OF NARNIA: PRINCE CASPIAN

WALT DISNEY PICTURES AND WALDEN MEDIA PRESENT AN ANDREW ADAMSON FILM "THE CHRONICLES OF NARNIA: PRINCE CASPIAN" BASED ON THE BOOK BY C.S. LEWIS
A MARK JOHNSON/SILVERBELL FILMS PRODUCTION GEORGIE HENLEY SKANDAR KEYNES WILLIAM MOSELEY ANNA POPPLEWELL MUSIC BY HARRY GREGSON-WILLIAMS
COSTUME DESIGNER ISIS MUSSENDEN EDITED BY SIM EVAN JONES, A.C.E. PRODUCTION DESIGNER ROGER FORD DIRECTOR OF PHOTOGRAPHY KARL WALTER LINDENLAUB, ASC, bvk
CO-PRODUCER DOUGLAS GRESHAM EXECUTIVE PRODUCER PERRY MOORE SCREENPLAY BY ANDREW ADAMSON & CHRISTOPHER MARKUS & STEPHEN McFEELY
PRODUCED BY MARK JOHNSON ANDREW ADAMSON PHILIP STEUER DIRECTED BY ANDREW ADAMSON

WALDEN MEDIA   Narnia.com   WALT DISNEY PICTURES

THE CHRONICLES OF NARNIA, NARNIA, and all book titles, characters and locales original thereto are trademarks of C.S. Lewis Pte Ltd. and are used with permission. ©Disney Enterprises, Inc. and Walden Media, LLC. All rights reserved.

Designed by Cindy Vance

THE CHRONICLES OF
NARNIA

PRINCE CASPIAN

THE OFFICIAL ILLUSTRATED MOVIE COMPANION

ERNIE MALIK

HarperCollins Children's Books

JUSTIN 0

CONTENTS

FOREWORD

Back to Narnia

ANDREW ADAMSON

I know I am lucky. I was given the opportunity to take a hugely important childhood memory and show it to people in a way that had previously only existed in our collective imaginings. You're very lucky if that happens once in your lifetime . . . but for me, it has happened again.

When I started to think about the second *Chronicles of Narnia*, *Prince Caspian*, I knew that it would be an arduous and difficult journey to turn this book into a film that would hopefully meet the expectations of my fellow fans. I knew, from the last experience, that it would be a long and exhausting process with many frustrations along the way.

And I leapt into it willingly! Many of the reasons for this are captured in this book.

Like Ernie, I felt that the family we built making the first film was what made so much of the process worthwhile and what made the anticipation of capturing that moment again so exciting.

This new journey would take us from New Zealand to the Czech Republic, from Slovenia to Poland, and finally to the United Kingdom. It would take over 2,000 people and more than two years to complete the film. It would be a journey that would test us all, but once again be full of the comedy and camaraderie that would see us through the difficult times together. That's what makes filmmaking worthwhile . . . well, that, and hopefully making a film that people like!

Ernie's book will hopefully share a little of this journey with you, introduce you to the cast and characters both onscreen and off, and maybe inspire you to grab a few friends and a camera and delve into your own childhood again.

London
October 2007

Douglas Gresham

Ever since I first read about Narnia when I was a small boy, my head has been filled with images of the place and its amazing and delightful characters. Since I was a young teenager, I have dreamed of someday seeing the books made into fine films. A desire that continued as I grew into adulthood. I watched that lifelong dream come true when *The Lion, the Witch and the Wardrobe* exploded onto movie screens around the world in 2005.

And now, we begin the second chapter in my lifelong dream as we continue bringing the Narnian Chronicles to life on the big screen with the next story, *Prince Caspian*.

I was moved and thrilled on seeing *The Lion, the Witch and the Wardrobe* slowly taking shape and then reaching out to the world's public and being embraced all across the planet. I always expected the movie to be a delight and a joy to world audiences, but have been somewhat humbled by its level of success. Success in this business is a bit of a double-edged sword in that having been greeted with such enthusiasm for our first Narnia movie, we have to make very sure that our next one is even more exciting and delightful.

We searched once again for wonderful places in which to film, and spread our efforts from New Zealand to the Czech Republic, Poland, and Slovenia. At times we were frustrated by weather—rain when we needed sun, and sun when rain might have helped—but our amazing set design, building, and decorating teams worked their magic and once again Narnia began to appear in the fields and forests of the world, springing to life as if Aslan himself were singing it into existence.

I have already led a long and interesting life, but having seen *The Lion, the Witch and the Wardrobe* on the screen and now watching the amazing work that has gone into *Prince Caspian*, I am convinced that as good as the first one is, the best is yet to come.

Great sets appeared in wonderful locations in far off New Zealand. Having seen the wonders wrought by the great craftsmen on the first movie, I knew this time pretty much what to expect, but on *Prince Caspian*, my expectations were once again exceeded. I loved the almost circus lifestyle of friendship and camaraderie that developed on location in the deep bush, and then back in the studios, the great fun of the after-work sessions with the plasterers and painters and others who were thrilled to be, once again, visiting Narnia. And I'm delighted that there were many familiar faces back for the second film.

Then, back once again in Prague, the most amazing and fantastic set I have ever seen reached up to the sky and waited for us to film it. Miraz's castle and the Telmarine Village emerged from the studio backlot and challenged us to draw magic from it. We did. Andrew, Walter Lindenlaub, our director of photography, and all the teams of lighting guys, camera guys, greens men, horsemen (and women), all the makeup artists and the vast numbers of others who make up a film unit, plunged into this fabulous edifice and, working by day and by night, brought forth wonders.

Next, Narnia flooded the fields and forests of the lovely Czech countryside, and the raucous shouts of our military trainer, Billy Budd, echoed around the hills of Usti as our Telmarine armies learned the battlefield formations and maneuvers that they would need all too soon when in earnest they would meet the forces of Old Narnia.

Me? I was in heaven, having more fun than a man my age really has any right to, I guess.

Now it's all over. *Prince Caspian* is done. So, further up and further in, let's get on with *The Voyage of the Dawn Treader*!

Malta
September 2007

MARK JOHNSON

In early 2003, I sat down for breakfast with Andrew Adamson, who had just committed to direct *The Lion, the Witch and the Wardrobe*. He and I were discussing this project for the first time, and I had fundamental doubts that the book itself could be translated into a movie that could embrace the imagination and the wonderment of C. S. Lewis's pages.

Andrew had an advantage on me. He had read the book as a 9-year-old boy, and it had been vividly percolating in his mind ever since. I, on the other hand, had read the seven *Chronicles* only as an adult and had the disadvantage of not being able to apply a child's imagination to the world of Narnia. As a grown man, I respected the book *The Lion, the Witch and the Wardrobe* and enjoyed it immensely but somehow failed to have the ability to imagine the look, the feel, and the sounds of Narnia itself. For the next two and a half years, our cast and international crew took me by the hand and showed me with awe-inspiring detail what C. S. Lewis's world could look like on celluloid.

Now, nearly four years later, having just finished the filming of *Prince Caspian*, I realize that the challenge of once again creating the world of Narnia, a different Narnia from the first film, has tested all of us seasoned "Narnians" in a way I never thought imaginable. Instead of a snow-covered landscape we have created a world of dense forests and impenetrable rock mazes and gorges. From locations as far away as the South Island of New Zealand to the storming expanse of a vibrant ravine in Slovenia to the seventy-year-old sound stages of Barrandov Studios in Prague to the quiet, intimate patches of Polish glens, we have once again made real what I so cautiously feared could not be achieved. In *Prince Caspian* the lyrical and magical world of Narnia is once more realized. I wholeheartedly believe that our audience will, in a matter of a few celluloid minutes, completely embrace this new Narnia.

Once again, our magicians in our cast and crew have shown this somewhat skeptical producer what the magical but very real geography, sound, and feel of Narnia has become. Thanks to the book in your hands, you can glimpse the behind-the-scenes talents and efforts of our artists and technicians. And, most important, thank you for allowing us the opportunity to once again imagine and create the world of yet another *Chronicle* in the ever-changing land of Narnia!

Los Angeles
November 2007

"*The main thing I learned in making the last film was to never do this again. This time out, I wanted to do it better.*"
— Andrew Adamson

TOP: *Andrew Adamson (left) sets up a shot with cinematographer Walter Lindenlaub (right).*
MIDDLE: *Director's assistant Alina Phelan and Anna Popplewell enjoying the first day back on set.*
BOTTOM: *Andrew Adamson rehearses with William Moseley.*

THE JOURNEY

Back to Narnia

At 9:43 A.M. on Monday, February 12, 2007, Andrew Adamson found himself back in Narnia. Or at least, well on his way.

This time out, the talented filmmaker would not take his camera into C. S. Lewis's extraordinary world through a magical wardrobe as in his 2005 film, *The Lion, the Witch and the Wardrobe*.

No, this time Andrew entered through a vintage subway-station turnstile at the Strand tube stop near London's Trafalgar Square, circa 1941.

He was, however, a long way from Charing Cross, and nowhere near London.

In fact, at the time of the very first shot on this overcast Monday morning, Andrew stood on production designer Roger Ford's minutely detailed recreation of an English tube station, entirely believable right down to the grime and rubbish caked under the rail tracks, on stage 4 at New Zealand's Henderson Studios.

It was on this exact spot over two and a half years ago that the Kiwi native rolled the first frames of film on his first Narnian adventure, *The Lion, the Witch and the*

Wardrobe, which also happened to be his first live-action film as a director. The movie was a critical and financial smash hit, with three Oscar® nominations, including a win for Howard Berger and Tami Lane for achievement in makeup. It went on to become, at the time, the twenty-second highest grossing film in Hollywood history. (Incidentally, for the record, each of Andrew's three feature films, including the first two *Shrek* movies, ranks among the fifty most-successful films of all time!)

The modest, funny, and determined filmmaker is inarguably one of Hollywood's most successful directors. Along with the Oscar®-winning *Shrek* and its equally popular sequel, *Shrek 2*, Andrew's three movies have earned over $2.1 billion at the global box office, but he keeps things in perspective. When he stepped behind the cameras to guide the next Narnia story, he recalls, "The main thing I learned in making the last film was to never do this again." Countering with his trademark chuckle, he confides, "This time out, I wanted to do it better."

The next story in C. S. Lewis's *Chronicles of Narnia*,

In addition to the dozens of movie technicians and background players, there were four very familiar faces, barely containing their excitement.

and the subject of the book in your hands, is *Prince Caspian*, which begins a year after *The Lion, the Witch and the Wardrobe* with England still in the throes of World War II. On day one of filming, the faux subway platform bustled with activity much as the real one would have done some sixty-five years ago. In addition to the dozens of movie technicians and about seventy-five background players dressed as commuters in English tweeds and uniformed schoolchildren, there were four very familiar faces, barely containing their excitement.

Reunited once again, these faces belonged to William Moseley, Anna Popplewell, Skandar Keynes, and Georgie Henley, better known to fans worldwide as the Pevensie children: Peter, Susan, Edmund, and Lucy. Their first adventure into Narnia, which began with timid steps through the wardrobe, resulted in a spectacular battle to conquer the White Witch's powerful hold over the magical land, freeing Narnia from her icy spell forever.

This time, however, the Pevensies will be called into Narnia as they stand on this very platform, for, as they will come to find, the land they love is in trouble. Thirteen centuries have passed in their absence, and an evil ruler, Miraz, stands on the verge of wiping out every last trace of Narnia. Only his nephew, Prince Caspian, the rightful heir to the throne, can stop Miraz, and he uses the ancient magical horn of Queen Susan to summon the Pevensies, themselves the former kings and queens of Narnia, to restore the land to its former magic and glory.

"It's very close [to the book] in the same way that *The Lion, the Witch and the Wardrobe* was," Andrew says. "What I tried to do on the first movie was imagine the story was real and C. S. Lewis had written a book for children about it. In the first film, I set out to tell the real story so it had a bit more depth, a bit more action, a bit more grit and reality to it. I think that's true with this one as well. Also, this film is probably a little darker and grittier than the last one, partly because the children are older, making the story more adult in nature.

"In the last film, I think we went to some pretty dark places. Aslan's death, certainly, is one of the darkest moments in the film. I think this movie has the potential to be even more sinister. In some ways it's going to be easy for the audience to relate to the villain in this film. Miraz is potentially a political figure, someone who we might actually see in real life, which makes him and the story that much darker."

The second story also had more personal meaning for the director, as he saw in it hints of his own childhood. Although born in New Zealand, Andrew spent his formative teen years in the South Pacific island nation of Papua New Guinea, "which no longer exists as I remember it growing up there from ages 11 to 18. For me, it's a similar experience for these four children as they venture back to Narnia, a world that is not the same as when they went there in the first story."

Before Andrew was even born, C. S. Lewis began *Prince Caspian* with these words:

> Once there were four children whose names were Peter, Susan, Edmund, and Lucy, and it has been told in another book called *The Lion, the Witch and the Wardrobe* how they had a remarkable adventure.

As detailed in the pages you're reading now, Andrew's own adventure back into Narnia, and that of the talented cast and crew of this film, should prove to be every bit as remarkable.

TOP: *Andrew Adamson prepares to lead the Pevensies back into Narnia.*
BOTTOM: *Andrew Adamson, K. C. Hodenfield, Jeff Okabayashi, and others watch the grips lay a dolly track.*

THE STORY

The Second Chapter

"This is the second chapter in a lifelong dream!" Douglas Gresham can hardly contain himself. And with good reason. As C. S. Lewis's stepson and the creative and artistic director of the C. S. Lewis estate (as well as the co-producer of the films), Gresham has worked tirelessly to create this movie franchise for the better part of his adult life, and with *Prince Caspian*, he is overjoyed to see it continue.

Published between 1950 and 1956 and long regarded among literature's most enduring and imaginative classics, the Narnia books have sold over 100 million copies in almost fifty languages, making it the second biggest-selling book series the world over.

The full catalog of the *Chronicles of Narnia* includes seven books, which, in order of publication, are *The Lion, the Witch and the Wardrobe* (1950), *Prince Caspian* (1951), *The Voyage of the Dawn Treader* (1952), *The Silver Chair* (1953), *The Horse and His Boy* (1954), *The Magician's*

Ben Barnes as Prince Caspian.

Nephew (the prequel to the series, 1955), and *The Last Battle* (1956).

The new production, once again a joint venture between the Walt Disney Studios and Walden Media, continues the franchise that kicked off with the spectacular, Oscar®-winning 2005 release of *The Lion, the Witch and the Wardrobe*, one of the most successful movies ever made.

When it came time to decide which of the remaining six books to bring to the screen after the resounding success of the first movie, it seemed that *Prince Caspian* would be the obvious choice. Or was it?

As the first movie approached the end of production, discussions ensued between the filmmakers and the two studios. The C. S. Lewis estate suggested that the film series proceed in the order in which the books appeared over a half-century ago. But first, Andrew Adamson wanted to explore another idea.

"For a brief moment, I thought about combining *Prince Caspian* and *The Voyage of the Dawn Treader* as the next

film," Andrew admits. "One is an epic adventure story set on a ship, very cinematic in scope, which I thought would make a wonderful adventure movie for the audience and a terrific follow-up to the first movie. *Caspian* seemed less cinematic and was proving quite a challenge when working on the script."

Had the filmmakers pursued that tack, they would have followed the course charted by England's BBC television network. Back in 1989, following their own successful, BAFTA-winning presentation of *The Lion, the Witch and the Wardrobe*, they produced their next Narnia adaptations individually (first *Prince Caspian*, followed by *Voyage of the Dawn Treader*) but repackaged the pair on video as one film, dubbed, naturally, *Prince Caspian and the Voyage of the Dawn Treader*.

Logistically, it made perfect sense to film *Prince Caspian* as the second in the franchise. If it were pushed any later, the four young actors playing the Pevensies would likely be too old to reprise the characters of Peter, Susan, Edmund, and Lucy. As it is, in *Prince Caspian*, the four children are supposed to be only a year older than in the first story, but as filming approached in early 2007, the four young talents were growing up fast—already almost two and a half years older than when they first entered the wardrobe back in June 2004.

Would the filmmakers have to recast the siblings with look-alikes if they made *Caspian* later? If, as some camps might suggest, *The Horse and His Boy*, now commonly read in order after *The Lion, the Witch and the Wardrobe* and before *Prince Caspian*, were to be made instead? Thankfully, we'll never know.

"The order in which the books are read does not necessarily bear any relationship to how the movies are made," Gresham says. At Gresham's suggestion (based on a conversation he had with Lewis himself about

TOP: *Caspian kneels before Aslan.*
MIDDLE: *Caspian shows Susan his crossbow skills.*
BOTTOM: *Lucy looks for Aslan.*
RIGHT: *Kings and queens of Narnia: then and now.*

*T*he four children have come back to a place that they've longed to be in, the place they grew up in, which is no longer the same.

the books' proper order) publisher HarperCollins now packages the seven-book series in the order that follows Narnian chronology.

Despite what's in print, however, Douglas affirms, "We are making the movies in the most logically consistent order. *Prince Caspian* follows *The Lion, the Witch and the Wardrobe*, thus dictating the continuity of casting of the same four children. If we follow *Prince Caspian* with *The Voyage of the Dawn Treader*, as is the plan, two of the Pevensies return—Lucy and Edmund.

"That gives us a trilogy of movies with a constant character thread, because Caspian also appears in *Dawn Treader*," Gresham explains. "Then, Eustace, who is introduced in *Dawn Treader*, and a new character named Jill would appear in *The Silver Chair*, the fourth book in order of publication. After that, we'll see how we proceed. Although I must say I am in favor of altering the order by making *The Magician's Nephew* as the fifth movie. That's the one I very much look forward to bringing to the movie screen."

With seven *Chronicles*, there can be literally thousands of different orders of reading them. As a kid, screenwriter Steve McFeely read *The Voyage of the Dawn Treader* first, for no particular reason, and then went back and read all the others. His childhood escape into the literary series has blossomed into a full-time vocation. As filming on *The Lion, the Witch and the Wardrobe* continued into December 2004, Steve and his writing partner, Chris Markus, began breaking down the story of *Prince Caspian* using index cards to plot major story points. It's never as easy as it seems, and they delivered their first draft in April 2006 (the next chapter will delve deeper into their process). Less than a year later, they boarded the *Dawn Treader* project as well, with their efforts well under way as this book is being written.

"*Prince Caspian* is a completely different story from *The Lion, the Witch and the Wardrobe*," explains producer Mark Johnson. "The four Pevensie children are called

The Pevensies discover Cair Paravel's treasure chamber.

Prince Caspian
is about a return to
truth and justice after
centuries of corruption.

Sergio Castellitto as Miraz.

back to Narnia after having been back in England for a year. They've adjusted to a varying degree to being British schoolkids again. All of a sudden, they're brought back to Narnia because they are needed to help save the land once again."

Andrew vividly recalls his first reaction to the story. "When I read *The Lion, the Witch and the Wardrobe* as a child, I remember getting to the end of it and thinking, 'Well, hang on a sec!' These guys were kings and queens. They ruled Narnia for fifteen years. They fought battles. They won wars against giants and now they have to go back to school? Although C. S. Lewis didn't really deal with that a lot in the stories, to me, as a child, then examining it again as an adult, I wanted to see what happened next."

Thus, the challenge for Andrew and the screenwriters was "exploring the effects their experiences in the first

[story] might've had on them," says Chris Markus. "It's an area Lewis leaves mostly untouched, like Andrew says. Lewis memorably examined what it would be like for a 1940s schoolkid to become king of Narnia. However, he doesn't much consider what it would be like for a king of Narnia to *return* to being a 1940s schoolkid."

"Their year back in London must have been awkward at best," adds partner Steve McFeely. "Imagine going from giving orders . . . to taking them. From fighting wars and throwing royal balls . . . to doing homework. Given their different personalities, each Pevensie handles the situation with varying levels of success. Some are resigned, others frustrated, and their sudden return to Narnia pushes different buttons in each."

Before we get too much further, we should probably give a quick refresher course for the unfortunate few who aren't yet familiar with the story thus far.

The Lion, the Witch and the Wardrobe introduces us to the four Pevensies and follows their journey out of

Peter and Caspian outside Aslan's How.

the London blitzkrieg during World War II and into the creaky, labyrinthine country home of the eccentric Professor Kirke, where they were sent to wait out the war. Bored in the countryside, they invent games to amuse themselves, one of which leads them into an enormous, carved wooden wardrobe, where, instead of finding musty old clothes, they find . . . trees. And snow. And . . . Narnia, a once-peaceful land inhabited by talking beasts, dwarfs, fauns, centaurs, dryads, and dozens more creatures. It's now a cold, frozen wasteland, however, cursed into eternal winter by the evil White Witch, Jadis. With the help of a faun and, later, two kindly beavers, the Pevensies trek across the frozen land to find Aslan, the noble and mystical lion who has returned to Narnia to help them fight the White Witch. Summoning legendary courage and faith, the Pevensies overcome Jadis and her icy spell in a spectacular climactic battle, and Aslan crowns each of them kings and queens of Narnia in their palace, Cair Paravel, where they rule

happily ever after . . . until, that is, fifteen years later, when they stumble back through the wardrobe and find our world—and themselves—completely unchanged.

Prince Caspian picks up the story one year later, with our four heroes and heroines in school uniforms, fidgeting on the subway platform we explored in the last chapter, with little idea of what adventure awaits them. "*Prince Caspian* tells the story of Narnia thirteen hundred years later, after the Pevensies left in the first story," Andrew explains. During that time, Telmarines, pirates from the land of Telmar, have come in and taken over Narnia and driven all the creatures into the forest. And Prince Caspian, the rightful heir to the throne, has been ousted by his evil uncle, Miraz. When Caspian blows Susan's horn, that brings our four Pevensie children back to Narnia to save the land from Miraz, the unrightful king.

THE CHRONICLE OF THE CHRONICLES

Is *The Magician's Nephew* book one or book seven? Is *The Lion, the Witch and the Wardrobe* book one or book two? Is *Prince Caspian* book two or book four?

It may take a Ph.D. to figure that one out, but thankfully, Lewis scholar Peter J. Schakel, author of *The Way into Narnia: A Reader's Guide*, has one.

Schakel writes that most reprints from the 1960s through the 1980s did number the books in the order in which they were originally published between 1950 and 1956. However, the first revised numbering (which reflected *The Magician's Nephew* as book one) appeared from Williams Collins & Sons in the Fontana Lions issue of 1980. *The Magician's Nephew*, originally issued as the sixth book, in 1955, is recognized as the prequel to the more well-known *The Lion, the Witch and the Wardrobe*.

According to published reports, the debate over the reading order may have begun when Lewis responded to a young reader's letter that he received in 1957, just one year after the final installment, *The Last Battle*, hit bookshelves.

An American boy named Laurence Krieg argued with his mother over the proper reading order. He opted for the chronological sequence while his mother believed in the order of publication. So the youngster wrote to Lewis and asked him which order he recommended. Lewis's reply, which resides in the collection at Wheaton College's Wade Center, the museum that houses the largest collection of Lewis's writings in the world, reads:

I think I agree with your order for reading the books more than with your mother's. The series was not planned beforehand as she thinks. . . . So perhaps it does not matter very much in which order anyone reads them. I'm not even sure that all the others were written in the same order in which they were published. I never keep notes of that sort of thing and never remember dates.

"Lewis is one of the least proprietary authors I know," states Christopher Mitchell, the Wade Center's director and curator, who visited the *Prince Caspian* movie set in Prague during production. "In fact, [Lewis] once noted that an author doesn't necessarily understand the meaning of his story better than his readers do. At the moment of his writing Laurence, he was happy to side with the boy. But, if the mother were to have written back with the reasons why she felt the published order was better, I have no doubt that Lewis would have affirmed her observations as well . . . and appreciated both views."

ORIGINAL PUBLICATION ORDER

The Lion, the Witch and the Wardrobe (1950)
Prince Caspian (1951)
The Voyage of the Dawn Treader (1952)
The Silver Chair (1953)
The Horse and His Boy (1954)
The Magician's Nephew (1955)
The Last Battle (1956)

CURRENT PUBLICATION ORDER

The Magician's Nephew
The Lion, the Witch and the Wardrobe
The Horse and His Boy
Prince Caspian
The Voyage of the Dawn Treader
The Silver Chair
The Last Battle

"It's a wonderfully nostalgic story," he continues. "Basically the four children have come back to a place that they've longed to be in, the place they grew up in, and the place they've ruled for fifteen years, which is no longer the same. Everything's changed. Cair Paravel is in ruins. The creatures they know have been driven to the wild. Aslan hasn't been seen for over a thousand years. They must come to terms with that while simultaneously trying to restore Narnia as they knew it."

The four children have been summoned back by Caspian, whose life is in danger as his evil uncle, Miraz, plots to eliminate the young Telmarine heir so his own newborn son can ascend the throne. With the help of a kindly Red Dwarf, Trumpkin, a courageous talking mouse named Reepicheep, a faithful badger, Truffle-hunter, and a leery Black Dwarf, Nikabrik, the Narnians, led by the mighty knights Peter and Caspian,

Lucy Pevensie on her first trip into Narnia (The Lion, the Witch and the Wardrobe).

embark on a remarkable journey in which they once again encounter Aslan, rescue Narnia from the tyrant's hold, and restore magic and glory to the land.

"I think the second story has a lot of what the first film had, but now complemented with some great action," Andrew points out. "I think it's a grittier, darker story in some ways than *The Lion, the Witch and the Wardrobe*. But it also has this wonderful sense of nostalgia. This idea of growing up, of ascending from

childhood to manhood, shedding our past, and taking on new challenges, [is] something we all go through.

"I also think it has more pure battle action than *The Lion, the Witch and the Wardrobe*, which is a very emotional story about sacrifice and forgiveness. The last movie was kind of an epic emotional story. The level of sacrifice was so extreme. Aslan was sacrificing his life to save the world. In some ways, this is a more personal story, a story of these kids coming back to a place that they love that no longer exists, rediscovering and rebuilding that place. This is, in some ways, more about coming to adulthood, about growth and adventure. This story gives us a chance to visit the Pevensies again, to see them now in a new light."

"*Prince Caspian* is about a return to truth and justice after centuries of corruption," explains Gresham, who first came to know his stepfather when Lewis was composing the books in the 1950s. "Jack [as Lewis called himself] was also trying to illustrate some of the most important personal . . . and historic concepts so prevalent in the nineteenth century. Things such as honor, loyalty, commitment, personal responsibility, courage, duty, honesty, and chivalry to name but a few, which *are* important but seem more or less discarded in the twentieth and twenty-first centuries. These attributes are vital to the success of the societies of man. All realized and illustrated through myth and fantasy and the great delight of imagination."

CODE NAME: TOASTIE

If you happened to stroll by Male Namesti in the heart of Old Prague in late fall of 2006, you might have seen a strange sign adorning one of the regal medieval buildings—a light blue flag adorned with a regal-looking mouse roasting what looks like a sandwich over a small campfire. In elegant letters below, the single word: *Toastie*.

Toastie joins such enormous productions as *Blue Harvest*, *Blackwood*, and *Jamboree*, whose common dubious distinction is that they adopted pseudonyms to avoid the public eye.

The proliferation of Hollywood screenplays that can be purchased at trade and collectibles shows and, more prominently today, on the Internet, is staggering. To avoid scripts falling into the public domain (be it for private collectors or media wishing to uncover secret story/character details before filming even begins), filmmakers over the years have resorted to secret code names on the screenplay's title page. Thus, *Blue Harvest* for *Return of the Jedi*, *Blackwood* for Rob Bowman's big screen adaptation of Chris Carter's popular television series, *X-Files* in the late 1990s, and *Janbore* for *Lord of the Rings*.

Before choosing the final code name for *Prince Caspian*, the filmmakers had considered a host of titles, including *The Winter Horse*, *Back to Henderson*, *Hobson's Choice* (a cute reference to the Hobsonville air base where the first film was shot, and the title of a popular 1934 movie comedy) and *Prince Capsicum*, the latter entry from associate producer Tom Williams, his tongue firmly planted in his cheek ("capsicum" is the Kiwi

TOP: *Headquarters of Toastie Productions, Prague.*
BOTTOM: *The production logo.*

phrase for green and red bell peppers). One strong possibility was *Wimbleweather*, which proved too revealing, as it refers to the name of one of the Narnian characters in the story.

Some studios organize a contest to name films when shooting under a temporary title, or a title they know is not marketable. The filmmakers had done the same thing on *The Lion, the Witch and the Wardrobe*, calling

> Had the film been shot in Italy, Andrew just might have nicknamed the script Panini.

that screenplay *The Hundred Year Winter* (which, of course, refers to the evil spell cast upon Narnia by Jadis, the White Witch). As they began preparations for the second Narnia installment, production coordinator Lauren Swearingen (the petite dynamo and heartbeat of the production office who returned in that guise on the new film) contacted Walden Media for some suggestions.

After looking at Walden's list of thirty-odd titles, director Andrew Adamson stated simply, "Why don't we just call it *Toastie*."

For those who have never spent time in New Zealand, a "toastie" is the nickname attributed to a Kiwi grilled cheese sandwich, a mainstay on the snack (or craft service) table that sits on the set for cast and crew to graze for nibbles during the shoot day. Two special machines (kind of the Kiwi version of a George Foreman grill) sizzled all day long on the "crafty" table of the first Narnia movie as the locals (and out-of-towners who grew fond of, and fat from, the local delicacy) slathered bread with a variety of cheeses and condiments that included everything from bacon to pickles, from creamed corn to onions. Had the film been shot in Italy, Andrew just might have nicknamed the script *Panini*. And, who

Andrew Adamson.

would ever be able to connect the dots between *Prince Caspian* and *Toastie*? Because most movie titles require a title treatment (an illustration or artistic rendering of the title), the company's art department devised a mouse (Reepicheep?) toasting a piece of bread on his sword held over a campfire.

To add another layer of security to their devilishly clever enterprise (just as they did on the first film), every script was numbered and inscribed (via a huge watermark on the center of all 115 pages of the screenplay) with the name of the cast or crew member who received a copy of the script prior to the start of filming. Thus, if an illegal copy (a script is copyrighted material) was found for sale, the indelible watermark could be traced back to a specific crew member.

And then, that person would be considered "toast" in the eyes of the studio and filmmakers.

FROM PAGE
TO SCREEN

A Word is Worth a Thousand Pictures

On February 5, a week before the first day of filming, Andrew sat down in a screening room in Auckland and watched a preliminary cut of his new movie, *Prince Caspian*.

He had yet to roll even one frame of film on his new Narnian adventure.

Confused?

The process of creating a feature film on the scale of *Prince Caspian*, with its precise and complicated computer-generated imagery (CGI) and its costly budget commitment, goes beyond the ordinary moviemaking process. As with all movies, we begin with the written word—here, a classic book transformed into a script, a series of sequences represented by exposition and dialogue—a verbal blueprint for the movie. But with a film like this one, once a draft of the screenplay is completed, a group of illustrators, called storyboard artists, begins to translate those words into pictures. These are simple pen-and-ink drawings done by hand or, more recently, created on a computer screen. Somewhat resembling comic-book panels, these illustrations, some very simple and some highly detailed, begin to tell the story visually for the very first time. During preproduction, this phase, called visual development, is the first time the project begins to take shape as a picture.

These storyboard drawings are then scanned into a computer and converted into animated panels, or animatics, a more sophisticated way of viewing storyboards that can show camera angles and movement in a two-dimensional environment. A second team of artists and technicians then animates entire sequences of the story using 3-D software similar to that employed in animated films like *Shrek*. This process is called previsualization, or "pre-viz," and by adding sound effects, dialogue, and music, these artists illustrate with great detail how the scenes will look on screen and how the moments will play dramatically and emotionally. Once

LEFT TO RIGHT: *Director of photography Walter Lindenlaub, director Andrew Adamson, and first assistant director K. C. Hodenfield on the Cair Paravel ruins set on New Zealand's Coromandel Peninsula.*

all these elements were assembled on *Prince Caspian*, film editors Sim Evan-Jones and Josh Campbell could piece together a version of the film for Andrew to see. (Concept art, another important part of visual development that helps drive the art department, will be discussed in a later chapter.)

Previsualization helps Andrew through the production phase of the filmmaking experience, ensuring that his vision makes it onto the screen. He can choose the precise camera angles to stage the scenes in the best dramatic fashion, and accomplish this on a tighter schedule and leaner budget—few shots will be wasted, and the crew can consult the pre-viz to help them understand a complicated sequence. Much of this film is shot in a green-screen environment, and the actors and filmmakers must imagine sets and characters that will be added only months later, in postproduction.

But pre-viz is more than just a simple deconstruction, as pre-viz supervisor Rpin Suwannath, a veteran of

Co-producer (and C. S. Lewis's stepson) Douglas Gresham on the Cair Paravel ruins set on New Zealand's Coromandel Peninsula.

the first film, explains. "The way we previsualize these movies isn't just on a shot-by-shot basis. It's on a scene-by-scene basis. We try to give Andrew more of an emotional tool so he can figure out if his scenes are working, rather than just a technical tool for figuring out the shots."

"Andrew comes from an animation background, so he's pretty used to this," observes screenwriter Chris Markus, who first encountered this unusual process on *The Lion, the Witch and the Wardrobe*. "Basically the idea is to film the storyboards, which people have been using on movies forever. Put them in the computer and combine them with what you might think of as video-game sequences, making the characters move. Then we have people in the office do the voices, bringing the process to life."

"It is a different way for us to work," admits fellow writer Steve McFeely. "I mean, we did it on *The Lion, the Witch and the Wardrobe*, so we're used to it now. The usual process is, you write a script, you hand it over, someone films it. Here, we write it, sketchily 'film' it, and do it again and again until we become comfortable with a version of the *movie* instead of just a version of the script."

THE SCRIPT

The early stages of script development on *Prince Caspian* began when writing partners Markus and McFeely visited the set of *The Lion, the Witch and the Wardrobe* in mid-October 2004. It was just days before the company would complete the stage work in Auckland and head south to New Zealand's east coast locales of Oamaru (Aslan's Camp) and Flock Hill (the climactic battle scene).

For *The Lion, the Witch and the Wardrobe*, the writers had inherited a draft of the project, a very literal transcription of the book, to which they contributed their own voices. "When we came in, we were handed a very faithful adaptation of the book in script form," Markus recalls. "But it wasn't living as a movie. It was sort of the book typed out as dialogue. It needed more character than, frankly, the book had. We needed to individualize the four kids and also make all the creatures fully individualized characters.

Curiously, the writers had not yet had any of their own scripts produced when Andrew suggested them as collaborators, based on their original screenplay about the late British actor Peter Sellers. That film, *The Life and Death of Peter Sellers*, premiered as an HBO feature in 2005, with Oscar®-winner Geoffrey Rush in the title role, and went on to earn sixteen Emmy® nominations, including a win for Markus and McFeely for Outstanding Writing for a Miniseries.

For *Prince Caspian*, the duo, who'd worked together for over a decade since their grad-school days at the University of California at Davis, became a trio. "On this one, we all decided to be a three-man writing team," explains McFeely. "We had grown to trust and respect each other. So, from the beginning, we threw things back and forth with Andrew."

"It was nontraditional if you picture a writer going off into a room alone and coming out with a finished product," says Markus. "With three people, two of you can come to an agreement, and the third can arbitrate.

BOTTOM: *Writing partners Chris Markus (left) and Steve McFeely visit with Andrew on the set.*

And it can work, regardless of whichever third happens not to be there. I define the art of screenwriting as a willingness to collaborate."

"In a way, you make fewer mistakes in the long run," adds McFeely. "By myself in a room, I'll think an idea is brilliant, and I'll type it out. If it's a mistake, I won't know for months. But if I have Chris next to me, he'll tell me I'm an idiot pretty quickly. And if I have Andrew next to me, he'll tell us that we're both idiots."

Or maybe savants, as the pair rose to the spectacular challenge of adapting Lewis's second Narnia story. Markus affectionately interprets the tome as "an incredibly charming book about a walk in the woods and camping," meaning no disrespect, of course. McFeely elaborates: "A third of the book is told in flashback by this character Trumpkin about what has happened to

this character named Prince Caspian. The kids enter Narnia, then they disappear for a good third of the book. They return, have a small adventure with Caspian, and solve Narnia's problem.

W e didn't take the events of this book and tell a different story. We're telling the same story, just in a way that allows you to sit in a theater and watch it.

"As writers, the biggest challenge we faced was connecting the Pevensies' story to Caspian. In Lewis's book, there are essentially two separate narratives that come together only near the end. While this is perfectly entertaining to read, it makes for a strangely structured movie where your favorite characters are absent for long stretches at a time. Consequently, we decided to weave the two plots together early, bringing the Pevensies into

Narnia near the start and giving them a greater role in Caspian's journey."

"There's very little interaction in the book between your main kids, the Pevensies, and Prince Caspian," Markus confirms. "They don't really meet the Telmarines, the bad guys, until the end. That would make an oddly shaped movie if you chose to adapt it exactly as written. What we wanted to do was stretch the two halves so that they overlapped, which results in getting the kids to Caspian earlier, thus generating some sparks. It's a more complicated story in that it's operating from three points of view—the four Pevensies, Caspian, and the bad guy, Miraz, who has his own [motivations]."

Those familiar with the moviemaking process know that adapting a book into a film poses specific challenges—what passages and characters in the book must be incorporated into the script, and what leeway can a writer have to make changes without altering the structure and themes of the source material. "If someone were to say that this is not a true adaptation, I would reply it's true in spirit," Markus explains. "I don't think it betrays any of the story or characters. I don't think anybody's a different character than they were in the book, and I think the events have been made possibly more cinematic. But they haven't really been changed."

"What makes these books great, when you read them as a kid, is that your mind is teased into [imagining] what all these things are," echoes McFeely. "As opposed to something like *Lord of the Rings*, which is an incredibly dense, detailed encyclopedia of Tolkien's world, Middle Earth. Lewis lets your fertile ten-year-old brain go to town. We didn't take the events of this book and tell a different story. We're telling the same story, just in a way that allows you to sit in a theater and watch it."

Co-producer and Lewis authority Douglas Gresham, who, it might be said, spent his childhood in Narnia as Lewis's stepson, is very protective of the stories' essence, but agrees about the subtle changes needed to bring the book to the screen.

"We've had to amplify things a bit," he admits. "What you can do in a book very often won't work on the screen. A lot of *Prince Caspian* is walking and talking, which is fine on the pages of a book but doesn't really come across very well in the cinema. So there are things we've had to do to make it a little more lively. Even though we set the bar pretty high on the first movie, this has all the hallmarks to be a faster-moving and in some ways more exciting film than *The Lion, the Witch and the Wardrobe*."

"Because of the way the last film was structured, action was really the button at the end of the film," Andrew Adamson adds. "In *Prince Caspian*, it's more inherent to the story. There are battles all the way through. The [first] movie very deliberately started small until we got to the epic battlefield. We've seen that epic world now. So at the beginning of this movie, we have to start epic and then get more epic. There's a scene we've added that's not in the book—a great raid on Miraz's castle where we've taken griffins and Minotaurs and centaurs and had them fight against human soldiers within the confines of a castle. These are the kinds of images we haven't seen before, so it was fun to get a chance to play with those."

STORYBOARDING

A year and a half after that initial script meeting with Andrew in New Zealand, the writers completed a first draft of the screenplay in early 2006. As they started over the next few days and continued well into filming, their words would be translated into hand-drawn images courtesy of the storyboard department, a group of a half-dozen illustrators who, in the words of senior artist Mike Vosburg, "took the script, or treatment in its initial stages, and translated it into a series of pictures."

Storyboard artist Rico D'Alessandro (top) and senior storyboard artist Mike Vosburg (bottom).

CAM

SOLDIERS

TRACK

"CHASING ASLAN" - PAGE 01

"CHASING ASLAN" - PAGE 02

ARTIST: FEDERICO D'ALESSANDRO   "CHASING ASLAN" - PAGE 03

The old cliché goes, "A picture is worth a thousand words" but for this department, the reverse is true: each line of the script can spawn many, many images, and changes the process of interpreting the story.

"In successful collaborations, the storyboard artist enables a viewer to look at the story rather than read it," Vosburg says. "On *Prince Caspian*, as with *The Lion, The Witch and the Wardrobe*, we boarded the entire film so that it could be viewed on an animatic, which then allows Andrew to watch a test version of the film. He suggested changes . . . so we drew new frames . . . He made more changes . . . we drew more frames. More changes, more . . . well, you get the picture—no pun intended! Andrew's goal was to solve whatever problems there could be in the story and visualization of it before any of the movie was shot."

Vosburg, a veteran of the last film, likens his work to that of "a five-year-old boy on the floor with a box of crayons and a couple of action figures. The only difference is that we're working from a script. One of my mentors once told me, 'Learning to draw is a prerequisite for the job, but the drawing should always be secondary to telling the story.'"

"The idea is to 'watch' the movie before anything has been shot and therefore be able to make decisions that normally come *after* the real cameras have begun rolling," explains fellow board artist Rico D'Alessandro. "It's a powerful way to 'previsualize' a movie. For the artists who make it, it's just plain fun."

The soft-spoken Mike Vosburg hails from Detroit, and the garrulous Rico, who's from Colorado by way of Uruguay, is nearly a whole generation younger. Separated by only a few feet of space in their attic-like Auckland office studio, the pair approach their craft in very different ways. Editor Sim Evan-Jones can even pinpoint which artist drew a storyboard panel on seeing it. (Fellow board artist Tom Nelson is the third member of the team, but didn't make the trip to location.)

Mike, who worked in comic books and animation before moving into film, prefers drawing in traditional pen and ink (although he does use the computer as a necessary tool). Rico combined his academic pursuit of comic book illustration (New York's School of Visual Arts) and screenwriting (Loyola Marymount College in Los Angeles) into the world of commercials before switching over to feature films, and uses the computer much more than the pen to bring his drawings to life.

"Going into the project, I decided that the best approach to the animatic was to not make it like a slideshow—many animatics I've seen are guilty of this—but to fully animate almost every frame," he explains. "This adds to the 'cinematic' effect that an animatic can provide. To do this more effectively, I went to an all-digital approach, doing everything from the drawing to the animating within Photoshop."

The process doesn't stop there, however. The characters may walk, but they still need to talk. Rico notes, "The idea of the animatic is that they take all these scenes with movement and action and they cut it together with sound effects, music and dialogue . . ."

". . . For which *we* are often drafted to be the voices of the characters," Vosburg chimes in, with a gleam in his eye. "Of course I've wound up getting typecast—the professor in the first movie, the tutor Cornelius in this one—while my fellow board artist Rico wound up in the starring role as Prince Caspian . . . maybe because his wife, Coral, also works in editorial!"

As for the big picture, Rico explains that a storyboard artist's imagination needs to go beyond the pen and the page. "To make an animatic that flows well, you've got to think like a director ('what's this scene about?'), a production designer ('what's it all going to look like?'), an actor ('what's my motivation?'). When you make an animatic, you're 'filming' the movie on paper, so you've got to be a one-man production team. That way, Andrew can look at it and basically see the movie before he even shoots the thing and make decisions based off that for the story or for blocking certain scenes, thereby getting certain moments that he wants.

"For any given shot, all kinds of animation could

be happening, from facial expression changes to character and camera movement —sometimes all at the same time." For example, he says, "The script calls for Susan to pull out an arrow and fire it into a bad guy. Rather than simply cover the action, I tried to bring that moment to life by putting on my animator's cap. In a wide shot, I animate Susan whipping around, seeing her expression change from scared to determined. I animate her arm reaching back, pulling an arrow from her quiver and stringing it to the bow as she steps forward, while simultaneously the camera pushes in for dramatic emphasis.

"Now, cut to an angle over Susan's shoulder where I animate the bad guy charging forward. Susan fires, and we see the arrow zip through the air, sending the bad guy sprawling to the ground just in front of her as she dives out of the way. The whole scene will be drawn like this, and after the editors get their hands on it and work their magic, hopefully it'll look and feel like watching a movie."

Rico also claims that storyboards can, either consciously or not, influence the look of the movie. "Since Mike, Tom [Nelson], and I worked on the project at such an early stage, many of the characters had little to no visual description in the script. We were faced with the problem of drawing scenes without knowing what many of the characters looked like. So, at some point we worked on developing their individual 'look' so all three artists could draw the same character in their own styles,

yet have the characters be instantly recognizable.

"Eventually, I think the way we drew the characters became everyone else's mental image of what they looked like. Especially Miraz. At some point early on, we conceived of him with a beard, which Andrew liked. When it came time to cast the actor playing the role, Sergio [Castellitto], his look was strikingly like the first concepts of the character as interpreted by all three artists." Coincidence?

The script lets the artists' imaginations run free, and the results get circulated to every department involved in preproduction—so, the designs that the board artists create may find their way past the simple black-and-white palette. Notes Vosburg, "You're working kind of blind [from the script]. You're trying to create this stuff and come up with your own vision. If it's brilliant, it might wind up being used."

"The idea was to previsualize these shots on the computer so that we could plan out the motion control moves," he explains. "Now, this technology assists and guides such key production personnel as the production designer, the cinematographer, the film editor, and the VFX artists.

"Pre-viz covers animatics as well as something we call 'shot deconstruction.' That process takes the shot and then figures out relative to the ground what the camera position is, what the camera's doing, the lens information, basically creating a diagram that can be used on the shoot day to recreate the [virtual] camera and what the camera's doing in the real world."

PREVISUALIZATION

The next step in assembling the proto-movie we call the animatic is to enter a three-dimensional world, and begin to choreograph precise camera movements, stunts, and visual effects. This immense responsibility falls on the shoulders of another Narnia veteran, Rpin Suwannath and his team of pre-viz artists.

Born in Bangkok, Thailand, but raised and educated in California, Rpin was working part-time on 1995's *Batman Forever* when he first met a young Kiwi visual effects supervisor named Andrew Adamson. Andrew went on to develop feature animation with the *Shrek* movies at Dreamworks, while Rpin began working with a computer animation program called Maya, which came in handy in 1998 when he was hired to work on a horror flick called *The Haunting*.

On his first film, almost ten years ago, Rpin's "team" consisted of himself and a computer console. On *Prince Caspian*, Rpin coordinated and supervised a staff of twelve artists (up from eight on the last film) from three countries, starting almost a year before Andrew commenced principal photography. Even as filming kicked off and carried on, the pre-viz team continued, fine-tuning some scenes not yet filmed and, in some cases, not yet written or storyboarded.

"One of the big sequences for pre-viz on this film was the night raid on Miraz's castle," he explains. "When we started on the project, there really wasn't a finished script. We worked mostly from a treatment and notes. There were no storyboards. And most important, this scene did not exist in the book. So we animated this many times over, which in essence served as inspiration for the screenwriters, who were writing based on what we showed them in the computer."

Once Roger Ford's massive, six-story exterior set (on the Barrandov Studios backlot in Prague) underwent construction, the size and look of the castle then informed the pre-viz artists, who had up to that point been working with a castle designed from a cardboard model. They revised the sequence in the computer so that its final depiction would be as close as possible to what Andrew would begin filming on the night of April 24. It would then take Andrew and his second unit director, John Mahaffie, over a month to complete the film's complicated, thrilling second-act set piece.

With so many storyboard artists and pre-vizzers translating the script into pictures, one might think there would be some overlap between the departments' duties. As technology advances the craft of filmmaking and opens up new avenues for visualizing a scene, is the art of storyboarding becoming obsolete?

Not so, says Rico D'Alessandro. The pen is still faster than the microchip. "Last-minute changes that affect how the director shoots a scene can be quickly re-envisioned with a series of hand-drawn, two-dimensional panels," he explains. "Rpin's computer squad needs to build images and characters in the computer before they animate a sequence. Pre-viz will be factored in quite a bit more as [it] becomes easier, faster, and cheaper to do. But it still takes some time. Storyboards for now are the fastest way to visualize a script. I'll also answer that question with another question: will cell phones completely replace landlines? I doubt it."

Mike Vosburg also cringes when he hears the question. "Let me just add one thing for filmmakers everywhere," he says. "You should never attempt to make a film without storyboards. They're essential for the process. Hitchcock was a prime example of how to put storyboards to good use. It served him both artistically and financially."

Good point, Mike, but what if he'd had a pre-viz department?

THE EDITING

The final puzzle piece in assembling the animatic is the assemblers themselves—the editor, Sim Evan-Jones, and his editorial department, who bring to this rough, animated version the same skills they will use in cutting and fine-tuning the finished film itself. As soon as there were storyboard and pre-viz artists producing images, back in early 2006, Sim was working hand in hand with them, placing them in order and constructing the story, beat by beat.

The amiable, soft-spoken Brit met then-aspiring director Andrew Adamson at DreamWorks in the late 1990s, when both were working on an animated feature, *The Prince of Egypt*. Since then, he's edited every single one of Andrew's movies with wit and precision, and is an integral part of the creative process.

In preproduction, Sim and Rpin collaborated closely as pre-viz sequences were completed, using cutting-edge technology that allows them to work even more efficiently than on the first movie.

"When we did the first film, Rpin would send me his finished sequences as a Quicktime movie," Sim confirms. "Now, he edits his work on the Avid, which is the computer we use to cut the actual movie together. He uploads the material on our Avid site, which I then download and cut into the movie."

Even more so than the pre-viz and storyboard departments, the editors, like the screenwriters, have to keep the big picture in mind, and pay careful attention to the pacing, tone, and overall feeling of the movie. Theirs is a heavy task—to construct the movie without a single frame of film.

"When Andrew watched the [first] previsualization on February 5, the film existed as a 60/40 ratio of storyboards to pre-viz graphics," he explains. "The version we showed Andrew, complete with a music track from not only *The Lion, the Witch and the Wardrobe* but some other scores as well, sound effects, and prerecorded dialogue, *was* the complete film. As we began to shoot the movie, my department edited the processed film footage into the pre-viz version to show the project's progress."

And this becomes the often slow but fascinating process of assembling the movie itself. As scenes get shot and the actors begin to inhabit the locations, sets, costumes, and overall world of the movie, the storyboards get replaced with real live images—sometimes a few seconds at a time, sometimes with a whole scene. At several points during the shoot, Andrew will watch the movie again, and again, with gradually more and more live-action footage included as the shoot progresses, until one day, months later, there won't be a single storyboard or previz frame to be found. But for some, it will still be very familiar.

RIGHT: *Sim Evan-Jones (in the center in the brown shirt) and his crew on the Telmarine Village set.*
BELOW: *Cameraman Greg Lunsgaard (left) controls the motion of the camera to match the previz.*

"When audiences see the film in the cinema on May 16, 2008," Sim notes, "the version they watch and hopefully enjoy is very close to what Andrew saw almost a year and a half earlier, before he had recorded one frame in the movie camera."

136 Days—The Schedule

Filming on *Prince Caspian* came to an end 136 days after it commenced on February 12, 2007. (Production officially wrapped on August 31 in Prague.) During preproduction, the filmmakers worked with the assistant directors to plot out the shooting schedule, based on many variables, especially the project's budget and locations and cast availability. A film cannot proceed without such a key document.

Assistant director K. C. Hodenfield and his key second, Jeff "O" Okabayashi, spent three concentrated weeks breaking down the screenplay into one-line descriptive phrases that mark and identify each scene in the script. Scenes in motion picture screenplays are also assigned sequential numbers. The length of each scene is tallied by the number of pages it occupies, with every page measured in eighths. So, if a scene reads at 2 ½ pages, the schedule reflects that as 2 ⁴/₈ pages.

Once a complete shooting schedule is prepared (containing all pertinent information, such as the number of extras required for a scene, special film equip-

TOP: *First A.D. K. C. Hodenfield with Douglas Gresham.*
BOTTOM: *Second A.D. Jeff "O" Okabayashi.*

ment, etc.), it is duplicated in a condensed version called a one-line schedule.

The bible of any film shoot, the one-liner includes the basic info for each day's shoot. From left to right as it reads on the page, the one-liner includes the scene number, the location and one-line description of the action, the page count, which cast will appear in the scene (identified by numbers accorded them in the scheduling stage), and the date the scene is scheduled to be filmed. Many on the crew reduce the normal page size to a five-by-seven-inch version that they carry in their pockets at all times for quick reference.

So on Monday, July 30, 2007, the company was scheduled to travel back out to Usti in the rural Czech Republic to complete scene 126 ("INT. Miraz's Tent, Edmund offers challenge, Miraz is trapped and accepts"). The scene calls for daylight. (Day and night are always listed on the one-liner as well.) The scene was 2 ¹/₈ pages in length. Cast members on call that day would include Skandar Keynes as Edmund (#4), Sergio Castellitto as Miraz

(#11), Pierfrancesco Favino as Glozelle (#12), Damián Alcázar as Sopespian (#14), Simon Andreu as Lord Scythely (#15), Pedja Bjelac as Lord Donnon (#16), and David Bowles as Lord Gregoire (#17). Those numbers only (not accompanied by the cast names) appear on the schedule.

All that information is then transferred onto the call sheet, the daily work schedule prepared by second assistant director Okabayashi (and approved by first assistant director Hodenfield and the producers). The next day's call sheet is distributed to all cast and crew when filming wraps at day's end. The call sheet includes everything from the aforementioned information to the weather forecast for the day; the call time (when cast and crew need to report to the set and location); the specific location (with an attached map if necessary); the number of extras required; special instructions (livestock on set, effects); and the names of the entire crew and their respective call times on subsequent pages on international film shoots (the call sheet in the United States is a single 8 ½ X 14 page, with filming instructions on the front and crew listed on back).

In subsequent sidebar pieces scattered throughout the book, we'll take a closer look at some of the individual days in the production, to illustrate how each day of filming is unique and unexpected.

A call sheet, one of the essential tools of the trade.

THE LOCATIONS

Where on Earth is Narnia This Time?

One day, while looking for Narnia, James Crowley discovered he had a problem. There was no more room for new stamps in his passport. "All of a sudden, I was getting stopped or delayed as immigration didn't know where to stamp."

This was a problem, because Crowley, the talkative location scout and yet another veteran of the first movie, still had a long way to go before he found the imaginary land.

"I did get twelve new pages added to my passport," he says. "I ended up going to the U.S. Embassy in Prague, where they taped in the new pages. Looked a little sketchy to me, but it bears the official seal."

Crowley's task is one of the greatest challenges on a fantasy film—finding the real-life location to portray a place like nowhere on earth. And while Andrew

The spectacular "Glasswater River" site on New Zealand's South Island, a site that both Andrew Adamson and Anna Popplewell cited as their favorite location during filming.

Adamson would have to make the final decisions on where to shoot, the director was busy with casting and script matters. Which led the experienced scout Crowley, who'd collaborated on a total of six movies with producers Mark Johnson and Philip Steuer, to hit the road on April 4, 2006, with his all-important passport in hand.

He wouldn't return to his hometown of Austin, Texas, until the day before Christmas. In that time, his nine-month global sojourn took him and his local scouts through the United States, to Canada, China, New Zealand, Argentina, Romania, Slovenia, Slovakia, the Czech Republic, Poland, Bulgaria, Spain, Germany, Austria, France, Italy, England, Ireland, Switzerland, and Croatia.

There can't be too many jobs that pay you to travel the globe for the better part of a year. And of course, he had help—a network of scouts in various countries, as well as local film commissioners well-acquainted with their nations' landscapes.

"There was a predetermined feeling . . . certainly about New Zealand," Crowley concedes. It is, after all, the director's homeland and the physical and spiritual home of the first film. "Europe was also discussed, but not where, specifically. Part of this was due to the seasons. For this story, we needed the endless summer as opposed to the endless winter in *The Lion, the Witch and the Wardrobe*. So the seasons and which hemisphere certainly played a huge factor in determining the final locations for the movie."

Despite his connection to New Zealand, Andrew Adamson agrees that the logistics drove the decision. "Once we chose our locations, then we could schedule the shoot based on where summer would appear—February and March in the Southern Hemisphere. We followed the New Zealand shoot with stage work in Europe before going back outdoors for the European summer.

By the time Crowley concluded his world tour in time to crawl down his own chimney on Christmas Eve 2006, the filmmakers had made their final choices of which countries would portray Narnia in the second movie.

Four countries, total. Two continents. Both hemispheres.

To play Narnia thirteen centuries after the events of the first film, Andrew chose New Zealand (both North and South Islands), the Czech Republic (Usti, in the north, Prague, the capital, and the Brdo region, just south of Prague), Poland (Stolowe National Park, in the southwest, and the Kamiencyka Gorge, right on the Czech border), and Slovenia (the river Soca in Bovec, high in the Julian Alps).

Clearly, this would mean quite a bit of relocating for the cast and crew, officially known as "company moves." The whole process is somewhat like the circus packing up the tents to move from town to town. So get out your passports, and pack your toothbrush—the odyssey is about to begin!

Photographs of the key location scout, James Crowley, in three countries—Poland (top), New Zealand (center), and Czech Republic (bottom).

And what did this global search turn up first? For some, the place was all too familiar.

"Imagine, twenty countries, on five continents," jests actress Anna Popplewell. "And we came back to the same places where we filmed the first movie!"

New Zealand

Although three-quarters of the shoot on *Prince Caspian* would take place in Central Europe, Andrew chose to launch the movie on familiar ground in New Zealand. Home of the fierce national rugby team, the All-Blacks, and known to the indigenous Maoris as *Aotearoa*, "land of the long white cloud," the country enjoys a balmy summer from December to March, while most of us in the Northern Hemisphere are shivering away through winter. However, New Zealand was chosen not just for sentimental and logistical reasons, but because the small island nation has so many dazzling locations. Almost 75 percent of the first movie was filmed on soundstages in three locations around Auckland, but this time out, we'd get to do a lot more exploring outside!

The Coromandel Peninsula

Jutting out into the Pacific just east of Auckland is a glorious strip of land marked by grand mountains and proud promontories that plunge down into graceful and unspoiled white beaches, lapped by a gentle surf. This is the Coromandel.

After beginning production on Roger Ford's perfectly detailed grimy tube stop set at Auckland's Henderson Studios, the company awoke early one morning to drive the three hours over the Coromandel mountains to the tiny beach town of Hahei, on the peninsula's east coast. It took a bit longer than the Pevensies' near-instantaneous magical journey onto the beach (and, indeed, longer than the 45-minute daily helicopter trip enjoyed by Andrew, the producers, and the VFX crew), but it was no less spectacular.

The volcanic rock formations rising out of Mercury Bay on the Coromandel Peninsula.

Two breathtaking sites at Hahei, on the peninsula's Mercury Bay, were used for the scenes where the four Pevensie children take their first steps back into Narnia: Cathedral Cove, a popular kayaking beach controlled by New Zealand's Department of Conservation (DoC), and a majestic bluff rising several hundred feet above the ocean waters, where the siblings discover the ruins of Cair Paravel, one of production designer Roger Ford's many handsome set builds.

It was fortunate and perhaps a bit incredible that no film had yet shot a scene at Cathedral Cove, with its unique and distinctive rock formations. It certainly wouldn't have been out of place in *The Lion, the Witch and the Wardrobe*, nor in fellow Kiwi Peter Jackson's *Lord of the Rings* trilogy. And for the *Prince Caspian* scout crew, it was always the first choice.

Because Cathedral Cove is under close DoC supervision, only a minimal number of crew members were allowed to make the steep, fifteen-minute walk down the hill from basecamp to the pristine beach, and the

several tons of equipment were delicately dropped in on cables from helicopters. Over the next two days, the crew would complete scene 20, affectionately summarized on call sheets and shooting schedules as "Pevensies not in Kansas anymore." Right where the translucent blue waters quietly lick the shoreline, a stunning, cave-like passageway with a huge arched ceiling (hence the name Cathedral Cove) rises majestically from the surf.

It is here that Andrew's camera begins following the four children as they make their way through to the sandy shore on the other side, still unaware of their whereabouts.

While scene 20 did not require a set build, Kiwi art director Jules Cook, also on his second journey into Narnia, had his work cut out for him at the second Coromandel location, where he supervised the stunning Cair Paravel ruins set for scene 23 (on the schedule: "Kids realize they're in Cair Paravel centuries later"). The build took Cook's construction crew two months to complete on the hill high above Mercury Bay, not far at all from Cathedral Cove.

Made largely of huge blocks of carved polystyrene (better known as Styrofoam), the set included the remnants of the four thrones on which Peter, Susan, Edmund, and Lucy were crowned as Narnian kings and queens as the first movie ended. Staying faithful to Lewis's opening chapters of the book, Russell Hoffman's greens crew added several apple trees.

The six-day trip for the 250 cast and crew members who descended on the Coromandel, scattered among 28 hotels, motels, and apartments, included a weekend of absolutely flawless weather, perfect for fun-in-the-sun activities that made the shoot take on the spirit of an island vacation. That weekend, most of the cast and crew could be spotted on the local beaches kayaking, surfing, diving, snorkeling, swimming, and sunbathing—and, for those not careful in New Zealand's ozone-depleted sunshine, sunburning—just ask Skandar about his scorching weekend!

Where the siblings discover the ruins of
Cair Paravel, one of the production designer
Roger Ford's many handsome set builds.

South Island

After a brief respite back at Henderson Studios to complete the subway scenes (which bookend the Pevensies' adventures in the film), the company departed for New Zealand's South Island, a magical place that offers some of the planet's most glorious scenery.

"I think the biggest part of the look of *Prince Caspian* was the thought of a deep, ancient wood," explains James Crowley, who worked without the benefit of a finished script early on, and instead took inspiration from Lewis's prose in choosing locations. "When we pick this chronicle up, the Telmarines have forced the Narnians to retreat to the most wild and remote regions of their world. In our scouts, we looked for this hidden part of Narnia that the Telmarines had not been able to penetrate. Andrew wanted deep old-growth forests that would give this impression. This was not such an easy task, especially in an area as heavily populated as Europe."

"The thing that New Zealand offers that a lot of places don't is old-growth forests," Andrew adds. "There's not an area of Europe that hasn't been felled and regrown at some point, so finding an old-growth forest was very difficult. In New Zealand, the whole west coast of the South Island is covered with ancient forests."

Three distinct Kiwi sites were chosen for the two-week trip down south. The first two, spectacular rivers in the country's South Westland area controlled by the DoC, have been given aliases by the production to protect their locations—the "Westland River," a picturesque estuary that dramatically empties out to the Tasman Sea, and the "Glasswater River" (the name used in the book), some 50 miles away.

The effort to conceal the names and locations of these two rivers was mandated "by the conservation folks to avoid a post-filming impact on locations through

---

OPPOSITE TOP: *Peter Dinklage as Trumpkin.*

OPPOSITE MIDDLE AND BOTTOM: *Lucy encounters a not-so-friendly bear.*

increased visitation numbers, which can affect the environment, especially the more sensitive sites, says Kiwi location manager Eric Napier. "During negotiations with the DoC to get clearance for these sites, significant emphasis was placed on the nondisclosure of film locations in the media and film-related publications. This was of key importance for both the conservation of the environment and the benefit of the New Zealand film industry."

The team spent their first weekend in an area called the South Westland, a verdant, remote and rainy spot. The several hundred crew members along for this leg of the journey were scattered in dozens of hotels, hostels, and private homes over a 190-mile radius surrounding an area called the Haast River Valley, from Wanaka in the south to the Fox Glacier area in the north.

This part of New Zealand is isolated from the rest of the South Island by the huge Southern Alps mountain range. This mighty, forbidding terrain extends for nearly 370 miles up the island, and is bigger in area than the entire European Alps. It's no surprise that this isolated region is sparsely populated; in fact, the entire South Island is home to just 750,000 residents, only 20 percent of the country and just over half the population of Auckland itself!

At the "Westland River" location, Andrew staged three scenes ("Soldiers dump Trumpkin; kids hasten soldiers' departure") that marked actor Peter Dinklage's first days of filming. Everyone who needed to be on set at the mouth of the river traveled by helicopter, seven passengers at a time, over a verdant mountain range so dense with trees and shrubs as to necessitate the aerial journey. As the choppers cleared the green peaks, the endless Tasman Sea loomed on the horizon, the blue sky dramatically joining with the aquamarine waters on an infinite horizon.

The flight path descended over the ocean waters down to a makeshift wooden landing pad set up on the sandy shore about a quarter mile away from the working set, which was just a series of pop-up tents (mostly for

ABOVE: *The crew on location, "Glasswater River."*
OPPOSITE: *Anna Popplewell takes in the South Island scenery.*

makeup, and schooling for Georgie and Skandar) and the twelve-foot-square screens and silks to deflect the harsh sunlight that illuminated the mouth of the river where it meets the sea.

Another company move took the crew about 50 miles south to "Glasswater River," where Andrew staged scene 41 ("Trumpkin saves Lucy from a bear; explains changes in Narnia"). The gripping sequence, highlighting Roger Ford's meticulous Telmarine longboat, is another scenic wonder, reminding us all why New Zealand was chosen for the movie.

VIPERS AND SAND FLIES AND TICKS, OH MY!

"Y<small>OU</small> may find Narnia a more savage place than you remember."

So warns Trumpkin, the Red Dwarf, in scene 41, after young Lucy is attacked by a ferocious bear.

But it wasn't bears (or lions or tigers for that matter) that the crew approached with caution during the lengthy film shoot.

In Narnia, it was vipers and sand flies and ticks. Oh my!

The varmints seemed to follow the company on its worldwide journey, from New Zealand (biting, annoying sand flies) to the Czech Republic (encephalitis-infected ticks) to Poland (venomous snakes).

We've said it way too many times: and you thought movie-making was glamorous!

On day 13 (yeah, lucky us), way back in early March, the company camped out for two days at the "Glasswater River" site that was rife with thousands of tiny carnivorous sand flies. Bloodthirsty little suckers!

It was not a major insect bite, but more of an irritant, like that of a mosquito. You felt the initial sting before missing the chance to shoo away the little bugs (the size of the tip of a dull pencil point, they attacked in droves). Then, an aggravating, itchy welt persisted for days, sometimes resulting in a bit of swelling and irritable blistering. Dozens of bites concentrated in a small area (on the hand, arm, or leg) looked like an awful case of acne, hives, and measles combined in some diabolical experiment gone horribly wrong!

A<small>BOVE</small>: *New Zealand's "Glasswater River" location, where pesky sand flies chewed through the scratchy cast and crew.*

And it was not a whole lot of fun as the crew sat on the rocky shores of the crystal-clear water (hence the script name "Glasswater River") trying to eat the catered lunch—balancing a plate of food in one hand, utensils in the other, while combating the tiny flying vampires.

By the severe appearance of the blotched arms on some of the American crew, like DVD videographer Charlie Visnic, the camera twins named Greg (Irwin, the focus puller, and Lundsgaard, the operator), makeup artist Howard Berger, Phil "The Still" Bray, and me, these critters seem attracted to Northern Hemisphere blood (although producer Johnson's assistant, Mark Ceryak, walked away unscathed). Some of the locals, like driver Scotty Brown, did not have a single welt while donning shorts and short-sleeved shirts daily.

Of course, there was always insect repellent, and the company made several different concentrations available to the bespotted crew to ward off these annoying little pests. And the 80 percent version actually worked. The intense formula not only kept the sand flies at bay, but was so powerful that it melted plastic. Just ask those who sprayed their hands, then worked on their computers in the catering tent. The repellent not only erased the markings on computer keys, but actually dissolved the keys themselves!

In between scratching and swatting, there was a film to make, and the actors standing in front of the cameras were not immune to the swarming attacks. During one take, our young Edmund, Skandar Keynes, said he could feel them hovering around his face and tried to blend his irritation into his performance.

Leaving the sand flies behind upon the company's relocation to the Czech Republic, the crew faced another entomological menace: ticks. Everyone was offered an option to receive a series of inoculations to protect against encephalitis, an inflammation of the brain that can result from the bite of an infected tick. Since we would ultimately complete an extended schedule in heavily wooded forests (both in Poland and the rural Czech Republic), physicians offered shots (a series of three) of a medicine called Encepur. While the drug protects against encephalitis, it has no effect on Lyme disease, also a nasty by-product of tick infestation.

Unlike the conspicuous sand flies, a tick bite can go undetected for days, as it is painless. Once a person is infected, a circular red blotch, not unlike a bull's-eye, begins to appear on the skin.

As the days turned into weeks out in Usti in the rural Czech Republic, the tick count continued to tick upward, with crew members reporting that they had found fifty ticks on their bodies.

If the insect world was not invasive enough for crew members, they next encountered a different species of enemy in the rural forests of southwestern Poland. The first sign one spotted near the set in the Stolowe woods read "BEWARE—Viper Snake." Seems the venomous reptile is indigenous to these parts. The warning suggested immediate medical treatment with anti-venom if bit.

Down at base camp, the company had an ambulance on standby, standard procedure on movie sets for emergency injuries in such rugged terrain.

Sure sounds like a prescription for Hollywood glamour to me!

ABOVE AND BELOW: *Safety on set is, of course, the most important concern.*

"TOASTIE"

MEMORANDUM

DATE: April 11, 2007
TO: Everyone
FROM: Production
RE: Ticks and Vaccines

Like other places in the world, some of the ticks that live in European forests and countryside of may be carriers of various diseases. Specifically, tick-borne encephalitis and/or lyme disease.

In light of the fact that we will be filming in areas where these ticks may live, we will be arranging (and paying for) encephalitis vaccinations for all interested crew. Unfortunately a vaccine for lyme disease doesn't currently exist.

Encephalitis Vaccination details: Our doctors say that once the inoculation has been administered, it takes between 3 to 6 weeks to take affect and the vaccination lasts approximately 1 year.

The Plan: Production needs to get a head count of everyone who would like to be inoculated. Once we have a complete list, we'll arrange for the doctor to come to set for the vaccinations and will advise everyone the appointment date and time accordingly.

We are asking that all interested crew please contact the Production no later than Friday, April 13th to be added to the list.

Thank you.

*T*his trunk of a massive oak tree, created
by Roger Ford's artisans in Auckland, served
as the backdrop for the wonderful moment...

With the soaring Hooker mountain range looming on the northern horizon, making for a spectacular vista once the cloud cover lifted off its towering, snow-capped peaks, the site provided a stunning backdrop for a terrifying moment in the story when Lucy approaches a brown bear, expecting a friendly greeting like she encountered with most of the talking animals in the first story. When the bear suddenly attacks, Trumpkin fells the beast with a single arrow.

In between takes, mechanical special effects techie Jason Durey (who handled all the "reel" snow in the first film) took a raft ride up the river for a view of the idyllic canyon where Andrew next staged a scene showing the Pevensies and Trumpkin rowing the ancient Telmarine canoe. Durey equipped the vessel with a hidden motor, not to alleviate the repeated paddling by actor Will Moseley (who's more than capable of the task), but to allow the boat to quickly return to its original position, thus giving Andrew repeated takes without losing time in between.

The dramatic river chasm, which was Anna Popplewell's favorite location in all four countries, is bookended on each side by cascading waterfalls gushing down cliffs that plunge two hundred feet into the glassy waters. The water shimmers so clearly that Anna suspects "audiences won't believe it's real water—it appears to be an optical illusion created by VFX in postproduction."

The final South Island site before the company wrapped its twenty-five day, New Zealand shoot and headed to Europe was Paradise. No, really. The aptly named, privately owned horse ranch about an hour's drive from Queenstown near Glenorchy might look familiar to fans of *The Lord of the Rings*.

Ben Barnes and Warwick Davis, who respectively play Prince Caspian and his sometime nemesis, Nikabrik, were on hand at this location in scene 16, where the fugitive Caspian blows Susan's horn. The trunk of a massive oak tree, created by Roger Ford's artisans in Auckland and then shipped south, served as the backdrop for this wonderful moment, which marked both Ben's and Warwick's very first time before the cameras on the film, a moment each had been anxiously awaiting.

A week later, as we packed our bags to leave in late March, an unexpected snowfall turned Paradise into a winter wonderland—never mind that it was still technically summer! Still, those of us not from New Zealand were reluctant to leave the magic and majesty behind, but a new adventure loomed—Central Europe, which would become our home and workplace for the next five months.

Czech Republic

After a ten-day break in production to relocate scores of crew members and tons of film equipment literally halfway around the world, twelve time zones away, *Prince Caspian* resumed filming on April 1.

Like our first day of production back in February, we returned to London—not on Roger Ford's evocative tube station set, but on the streets of England's famous capital to shoot scene 22 ("Lucy tells Susan about the boys fighting").

By now, you shouldn't be surprised to know we were not actually in London. Prague, the capital of the Czech Republic, is known as the City of One Hundred Spires because of its skyline, dotted with church steeples, castle towers, and sharp, medieval rooftops. For us, however, the collective talents of the art department, costumers, and transportation coordinators transformed 17 Listopadu (which roughly translates to November 17 Street, the date when the Czechs revolted against communism in 1989) into London's Trafalgar Square, circa 1941.

During the company's first shoot day in Europe, thirty vintage cars, trucks, and English double-decker buses rolled up and down the two-block stretch that was closed off to the public until 5:00 P.M. Hundreds of tourists showed up as the day progressed, cameras at the ready. Although the production found thirteen antique vehicles in the Czech Republic, they had to reach out to collectors in the United Kingdom to fill out the caravan of classic cars.

In addition to cast members Anna Popplewell and Georgie Henley, there were 206 locals dressed in vintage threads, which costume designer Isis Mussenden and her associate, Kimberly Adams, brought in from London, as well as from Western Costume, the legendary wardrobe warehouse in Hollywood.

FULL PAGE: *The production brings London to Prague.*
INSERT: *Susan and Lucy.*

BARRANDOV STUDIOS

The legend of Barrandov Studios dates back to 1931. It was home to such modern cinema giants as Milos Forman, Jirí Menzel, and the late Ján Kadár, whose individual works in the 1960s revitalized the studio and the Czech film industry. Its infamous history also includes eighty-two films made there between 1939 and 1945 under the control of Hitler's notorious Third Reich propagandists after the Nazis invaded Prague. Following the war, the studio languished for the next four decades (save for Forman's Oscar®-winning *Amadeus* in 1984). In recent years, Hollywood has rediscovered the landmark Czech studio (one of Europe's largest facilities), filming such productions there as *Casino Royale*, *The Brothers Grimm*, and *The Bourne Identity*, among many other notable titles.

Barrandov

After a day spent in faux-London, the production then moved into what would become our home base for the next few months, Barrandov Studios, the venerable Czech movie studio that has attracted many large-scale Hollywood productions over the last decade.

While two other major film productions were simultaneously shooting in Prague (including a futuristic thriller starring Narnia's own Mr. Tumnus, James McAvoy), Prince Caspian occupied most of the ten sound stages that reside on the hilltop lot about twenty minutes outside the city's Stare Mesto (Old Town) center.

The production appropriated stages 6, 7, 8, 9, and 10 during the five-month stay at Barrandov to house Roger Ford's massive and imaginative set builds, which ranged from the monumental Stone Table shrine in Aslan's How (stage 6) to Miraz's Great Hall, site of his coronation, on the adjacent stage 7.

When a suitable deep-woods locale couldn't be found to portray Lewis's descriptive and enchanting Dancing Lawn setting, where the Narnians gather to plot their attack against Miraz and the Telmarines, Roger suggested his crew build a forest at the studio—inside a soundstage!

Thus, Barrandov's brand-new "Max" stage 8 became an indoor forest, complete with a sophisticated sprinkler system to feed the living lawn until the filming in mid-June. Visitors given a peek of the unique design felt like they were entering a massive greenhouse. While not as large as the Lantern Waste snowscape created by Ford for *The Lion, the Witch and the Wardrobe* in Auckland, the Dancing Lawn cast a magical spell (if not an enticing bouquet) nonetheless.

Roger's pièce de résistance on this production, however, was the mammoth Telmarine castle courtyard built on the studio's backlot. At six stories high with an interior dimension exceeding 23,000 square feet, the magnificent design took two hundred laborers

The Telmarine army at the Usti battlefield location.

(carpenters, painters, sculptors, and more) over fifteen weeks to build, beginning in January, in the dead of a thankfully mild and dry winter.

Barrandov became the anchor for the production's European tour primarily for the economic advantage: the exchange rate on the country's local currency, the Czech koruna, was much more favorable than the continent's primary currency, the euro, which the Czechs had not yet adopted. Additionally, the company chose Prague because of the industry infrastructure. One need only witness the work on display in Roger's stunning castle build to recognize that the Czech Republic boasts a huge, enthusiastic, and skilled talent pool of artistic laborers. The set was a monument to Czech craftsmanship.

Usti

In searching for a site where Andrew could stage the film's final battle and also erect a giant stone bunker to house Aslan's How, location manager James Crowley admits that his goal was "to try to top Flock Hill, the New Zealand location for the battle in *The Lion, the Witch and the Wardrobe*. Not an easy task. When you add up the sheer size of the equipment, crew, and cast that make up these battles . . . wow! That was a tough one. Sadly, the biggest problem was finding a wide-open space in Europe that was surrounded by a hardwood, old-growth, and wild-looking forest. It's a pretty dense population there, so a lot of those woods are long gone. Usti had two out of three components, so the location accomplished Andrew's needs from a practical standpoint."

To be specific, the location they chose was a vast prairie in a small farming village called Neznabohy near the industrial town of Usti nad Labem. A port city of 100,000 people on the Elbe river in the North Bohemia region, Usti is seventy-five miles northwest of Prague, just near the German border. Cinematographer Walter Lindenlaub, who grew up in Hamburg, notes that this area of the Czech Republic was once part of his homeland, Germany.

Caspian and Nikabrik in the forest of ferns near Dobris.

The company made two separate trips to Usti. The first took place over four weeks in late May and early June to stage several scenes prior to the final epic battle between the surviving Narnians and the marauding Telmarines. During the first tour of duty, Andrew directed actors William Moseley and Sergio Castellitto through the paces of a thrilling, exhausting sword duel between Peter and Miraz, which took over a week to film. Sergio called the scene the toughest of his thirty-year career.

After this scene was completed in early June, the filmmakers returned to Barrandov, then packed up for Slovenia, while Roger Ford's crew dug a massive pit in the battlefield prairie in the crew's absence for the towering battle sequence that Andrew staged in early August, one of the film's two epic climaxes.

One More Forest

One more Czech location hosted the crew for a few days, another stab at an old-growth forest locale. Andrew chose an area near Dobris, some thirty miles southeast of Prague, for its thicket of tall pine trees to stage scene 36 ("Meet Reepicheep & Glenstorm's sons").

As the one-liner suggests, this four-page scene presents the highly anticipated debut of Reepicheep, the swashbuckling mouse whose deceptively cute appearance masks a ferocious warrior. Like many of his fellow Narnians, Reepicheep will be completely constructed from CGI.

Upon walking into this dense forest, one begins to feel a bit like Little Red Riding Hood. The columns of trees are so thick the sun barely filters through the leaves some sixty feet up the thin trunks. The ground is covered with ferns as high as your hip—some seventeen thousand of them, actually, each in a pot, courtesy of Kiwi greens foreman Robbie Penny and supervising art director Frank Walsh. The company's horticulturalists, responsible for all plant life on the set, grabbed every fern they could find, searching as far as Belgium to find their leafy props.

POLAND

Among the score of countries James Crowley scouted in 2006, he spent the most time in Poland, searching for a location in which the production was scheduled to shoot for just six days. That shoot time ultimately increased to a total of ten days, spread over two separate visits to different national parks on the country's southwestern border with the Czech Republic.

"Poland is a big country, bigger than you would think," Crowley marvels. "It had a lot of possibilities, and our host there, Marianna Rowinska, would not rest until we had seen every square inch of it. She deserved a medal for 'love of country.'"

As the head of her own production company in Warsaw, Ozumi Films, Marianna first hosted Andrew and company when they scouted her homeland for the first Narnia movie a few years ago. This time, the ambassador to Poland's film world landed a big fish with *Prince Caspian* after guiding Crowley to every single one of the country's twenty-three national parks over three separate scouts in April, July, and November 2006.

During the second of these scouts, the filmmakers joined the trek, and saw seven of the parks (try to say them fast: Bialowieza, Pieninski, Bieszczady, Tatry, Ojcowski, Jura, and Stolowe) before settling on Stolowe for their prime location.

Stolowe

The European road show from Prague began in a sleepy, idyllic village nestled in the Góry Stolowe Mountains just one kilometer over the border from the Czech Republic. The pastoral town of Kudowa-Zdrój is a popular destination for tourists and outdoorsmen because of its proximity to the Table Mountains, which

comprise part of the range known as the Central Sude-
tans. The area is also renowned as one of the oldest spa
resorts in Poland ("Zdrój" is Polish for "spa"), if not the
entire continent.

The first visit to Poland (May 14–21) covered six days
of filming in Park Narodowy Gor Stolowych, which
began with the Pevensies and Trumpkin trekking amidst
Stolowe's otherworldly rock formations, the primary
reason for choosing the location. Known as the Table
Mountains, or "Lost Rocks," these massive sandstone
boulders look as if they were sculpted and positioned
into a maze of, curiously enough, stone tables.

A small, circular clearing framed by these boulders was
the setting for scene 43, where, according to the schedule,
"Peter leads the gang through rocks, insisting he's not lost."
The actual area chosen for the scene was so idyllic that,
even out in the woods, surrounded entirely by natural
landmarks, producer Philip Steuer felt that this could
have been a set, specifically designed for this scene.

Its labyrinthine layout presented quite a challenge to
the crew, who had to deduce how to get their tons of
gear (cameras, lights, monitors, sandbags) through the
very narrow rock passageways, some barely three feet
wide, into the area where the cameras would roll. Just
ask cameraman Greg Irwin about lugging his seventy-
pound Steadicam rig through these crevasses!

For the two other sequences on this leg of our Polish
visit, the company retreated deep into a wooded grove
outside a village called Pasterka, another six miles
beyond the Lost Rocks maze in Stolowe National Park.
This remote village was almost prehistoric in its isola-
tion. The turnoff from the main road wound through
luxuriously green and lush rolling hillsides blanketed

Lost Rocks, Stolowe National Park, Poland.

with trees and ferns (naturally occurring, not placed by our art department).

The trek from base camp into the set was close to a third of a mile, meaning another rigorous workout for those hauling equipment. The mud, several inches deep, sucked at shoes and boots like a leech drawing blood. The slight incline, through mud, tree roots, and rocks caused more than a few slips and falls.

For our weeklong stay in Poland, the company retained a dozen or so locals to assist with lugging all the equipment into the Stolowe forest. Like Sherpas carrying gear up Mt. Everest, these savvy porters worked in pairs with crew members, carrying the gear on military stretchers through the stone mazes and mud.

It was worth the trouble, as the site for scene 54 ("Caspian encounters Pevensies; swordplay and realizations") was a stunning and wonderful backdrop for the moment in the film where Caspian discovers the Pevensies in the forest and introduces himself as the one who called them back to Narnia. It's the first time in the story that the Prince meets the high kings and queens of Narnia, hoping their presence will help his quest to overthrow Miraz.

The filmmakers returned to Poland for a second, brief visit in mid-July for three more scenes that featured the Pevensies and Trumpkin, their Narnian guide, atop a cliff rising about 150 feet above a river gorge. These scenes depict the first time Lucy sees Aslan, while her companions do not—thus testing the faith of all.

This gorge location had been a thorn in the side of the production for quite some time. When films kick off principal photography, producers prefer to have locations scouted and selected well in advance. This location had eluded Andrew and the scouts for months, and was still being debated well into the filming schedule. Credit goes to the untiring Polish production manager, Marianna Rowinska, for finding this dramatic spot near the town of Szklarska Poreba, a mere two-hour drive from Prague.

Lucy and Aslan's "stand-in," Stolowe National Park, Poland.

CRAZY CAMERA WORK

The sequences featured yet another intriguing camera rig from photographer Lindenlaub's cinematic toy chest—a Cablecam. The remote-controlled camera suspended on a cable rigged to a hydraulic motor (under the supervision of the grip department's Brian Bouma) requires two operators—cameraman Lundsgaard at the wheels to guide the movement of the camera itself, and a second guy who programs the computer that controls its movement (for this scene, a vertical drop) on the cable. Such inventions allow the filmmakers to dazzle the audience with camera moves that elicit those wondrous "how did they do that?" reactions after seeing such scenes on the big screen. Lundsgaard believes that this was one of the most inventive camera setups devised for the film and a shot that *will* evoke such amazement from moviegoers.

So, when you see the Pevensies and Trumpkin walk to the edge of a cliff, and the camera dives rapidly downward to reveal the sheer depth of the gorge over which the characters stand in awe, you get an idea of the marvel of moviemaking—to say nothing of the logistics of rigging a device like this in the middle of a remote national park in rural western Poland.

SLOVENIA

Slovenia was the fourth and final country chosen to portray Narnia for this second story in the series. No geography scholar, I admit that before filming began on *Prince Caspian*, I could not have located the country on an atlas.

This is likely because Slovenia is a relatively young republic, having celebrated its independence from the former Yugoslavia on June 25, 1991, thus making it a mere sixteen years old when filming commenced there in early July. (This is, of course, arguable; the country actually dates back to the sixth century under various rulers).

Slovenia is a hidden gem in a region that sparkles. The company settled in for two weeks in and around yet another idyllic European village, Boveč, ringed by jagged peaks not far from the borders of Italy and Austria, in Slovenia's northwest corner. The surrounding mountain-sides are dotted with the remnants of aging fortresses and pillboxes, reminders of some of World War I's deadliest battles, which turned the emerald green waters of the River Soča red as Italian and Austro-Hungarian forces fought ferociously, with over a million casualties recorded.

Our task, thankfully, was a more picturesque affair. "The River Soča and surrounding valley in Slovenia was some of the most incredible country I've seen, and was a pretty good match for New Zealand," says scout Crowley. Many of the Kiwi crew embraced and marveled at its beauty and seeming familiarity. "Pavel Mrkous, our Czech locations manager, showed us a couple of sample photos, and that was all it took. I was on the next plane. It just immediately felt right."

July 3 marked the company's first day of filming (out of nine total scheduled) in this spectacular river valley bookended by the towering peaks of the Julian Alps.

Once again, the production (assisted by Diego Zanco's Propeler Films, one of the country's premier TV commercial producers) overcame demanding logistics to move a company of 1,100 people (cast, crew, *and* extras accommodated in 102 hotels in 28 villages throughout Slovenia and nearby Italy), a caravan of 300 vehicles, and 70 horses from Prague to Bovec in one weekend to ready filming. We got a crash course in the downside to this spectacular region when the company's location headquarters, known as base camp, was hit with a flash flood the night before shooting. Thanks to the quick thinking of our location managers and the Bovec fire department, thousands of gallons of water were pumped out of the tents and stables, and the two-week shoot kicked off without a hitch, on an overcast morning that quickly gave way to clear blue skies.

As it had in Usti, Prague, and Poland, the weather proved fickle in this mountainous region. As our first day of filming drew to a close around 5:00 P.M., assistant director K. C. Hodenfield, surrounded by weather reports warning of ominous forecasts, called a weather day, meaning that July 4 would be an unexpected day off.

The forecasts held their water. The crew spent America's Independence Day cooped up indoors, weathering violent rainstorms.

Upon arriving back at set the next day, the crew found snow blanketing the limestone peaks of the Julian Alps. That day off came at a heavy price, however. With the heavy downpours drenching the Bovec area and running off the mountains, concerns turned to whether the River Soča would overflow its banks, thus washing away the Telmarine tent village dressed by set decorator Kerrie Brown and her crew, which perched precariously on the opposite shoreline across the amazing bridge that spanned the river. Luck was barely on our side, however, and the rising waters came within a mere four inches of washing away not only the village but the entire bridge as well.

Constructing the bridge was a feat unto itself. The massive log structure, designed for the story's climactic showdown between Aslan, the Telmarine army, and the River God, was erected by the Primorje Group, Slovenia's leading civil engineering firm, which specializes in constructing highways, viaducts, and, yes, bridges. The magnificent set piece took a crew of twenty men a full month to erect, requiring the river to be rerouted in order to sink the structure into dry rockbed.

Scene 159 depicts the Narnian army, led by Caspian, Peter, Edmund, and Susan, chasing the Telmarine soldiers out from the woods over the Beruna Bridge (built by King Miraz in the story) and into the chilly river waters. The action proved somewhat treacherous after the heavy rains, which upsurged the river's current so much that it became risky to send the extras, both on foot and on horseback, into the swelling waters for fear that they might be swept away.

As the week progressed, the weather improved, and Andrew continued guiding the spectacular sequence in which Aslan calls forth the River God (a CGI creation) to decisively wipe out the Telmarine troops charging at Lucy. As hundreds of crew watched the 294 extras (playing both Narnian creatures and Telmarine soldiers), Andrew manned a bullhorn to call the action.

After each take, the filmmaker seemed extremely pleased not only with his key cast, but also the stunt riders and extras, who weathered the blast of a wall of water courtesy of Gerd Feuchter's mechanical effects crew, which had rigged a water cannon in the river to create the effect of the River God rising from the depths. Operated by pneumatics with an electronic control, the cannon blasted a huge, forceful spray of water from mortars onto the actors and horses charging across the bridge.

Before the company departed Slovenia, Andrew arranged a little something special for the crew. The grips rigged a makeshift movie screen in the massive catering tent, and the editors, with help from local impresario Diego Zanco, set up a projector. This would be a thank-you for the Czech extras, who labored day after day for long hours under grueling conditions. Working in battle gear that weighed almost thirty pounds, sometimes in extreme heat, sometimes in chilly cold, these men, mostly novices, never complained as they strived to add magnificent color and character to the scenes.

Their unexpected reward on this July afternoon was that they would be the first ever audience to see any footage at all from the movie they were filming. Andrew, working with the editors, had put together a four-minute clip of cut scenes from the movie, including some of the Beruna Bridge shots filmed just a day earlier.

As the footage began to unspool, a hush fell over the huge crowd of several hundred, munching on their daily wrap meal. About two and a half minutes into the clip, the Beruna Bridge came into view from a helicopter shot. The moment drew a roar from the extras, recognizing themselves on screen.

A second clip showed the soldiers marching in perfect unison, parading over the incredible bridge with pride and precision, and another outburst greeted the footage. When the final title credit came on screen, the crowd leapt to its feet and burst into deafening applause, giving the film, and its creator, standing off to the side, a resounding reception.

The moment was mesmerizing. Everyone gathered, cast, crew, and extras side by side, and marveled at the fruits of each other's hard labor on a big screen for the very first time during production.

As we departed Europe in early September, back to our homes scattered around the globe, we kept these images in mind, knowing, like the Pevensies, that Narnia was indeed a real place.

TOP: *Aerial filming at Slovenia's Beruna Bridge location.*
MIDDLE: *Ben Barnes and Andrew Adamson.*
BOTTOM: *Charlotte Hayes helps record VFX reference for the River God sequence.*

THE CAST

Family Reunion

Making a full-scale motion picture like *Prince Caspian* is a journey unto itself—not only a physical one that took hundreds of filmmakers thousands of miles across two hemispheres, but also a spiritual and emotional voyage for the film's family members.

With mothers and fathers, sisters and brothers, sons and daughters, and husbands and wives away from home for close to a full year, the film company's 600-plus members bonded closely, sharing in both work and play, to create not only a friendly on-set environment over the lengthy seven-month shoot, but hopefully something greater than the sum of its parts—something all can hail proudly when the lights go down, the projector flickers, the film unspools, and their collective movie magic enchants audiences the world over.

As production began over a year ago on that mid-February morning in Auckland, there stood Andrew, the lanky director, alongside his Pevensie clan like a

The Pevensies explore their ruined palace, Cair Paravel.

proud father with his children, home for the holidays. Even though it had been barely two years since the completion of *The Lion, the Witch and the Wardrobe*, his film family had, indeed, matured, both physically and emotionally. Their patriarch grinned with pride at their progress.

There they were, anticipating their forthcoming experience and joyously reliving the last one—Peter, Susan, Edmund, and Lucy, in the guises of actors William Moseley (now a dashing 20-year-old), Anna Popplewell (a newly minted Oxford freshman), Skandar Keynes (with vocal octaves much deeper at age 15), and Georgie Henley (approaching teenhood, a good six inches taller than we last saw her).

"They've all grown up really well," Andrew beams about his young English cast. "It was nice to see them go back to a really normal life. They were excited about doing this again, and treated it like another adventure. There's change in very positive ways about growing up, but I'd like to say the movie hadn't changed who they

A Day in the Life
February 19–20 (Days 6–7)
Coromandel Peninsula, New Zealand

Today, a storm is brewing over the Narnia shoot (both literally and figuratively).

Back after a sun-filled weekend of fun on the Coromandel, we return to work Monday morning to gray skies over Mercury Bay.

It is not what Andrew pictured for the key sequences where the four children find their way to the castle ruins set designed by Roger Ford.

While there are no teardrops falling from the heavens, you'd have suspected some moist eyes (especially from the accountants) as the cloudy skies cast a gloomy pall over the production, forcing Andrew to wait out the overcast morning for sunnier weather.

Three hours pass excruciatingly slowly. Andrew and company anxiously wait like passengers on a plane on the tarmac anticipating its takeoff. Finally, just before 11:00 A.M., the clouds dissipate, cinematographer Walter Lindenlaub gives the OK, and Andrew rolls cameras on his first take on the Cair Paravel ruins set.

The following morning, the last of two on this set and location, sunshine bathes the set in a glorious golden light, welcoming the crew to an 8:30 A.M. call. By our 1:30 P.M. lunch break, the sunlight quickly disappears behind storm clouds. It doesn't show its bright face again until sometime after four—more waiting on the tarmac for Andrew and his fellow passengers.

TOP: *Anna Popplewell and William Moseley.*
BOTTOM: *The Pevensies with producer Mark Johnson.*

are, which I'm really happy about. A lot of that's attributed to their parents. They've all got great parents."

"We're a really tight unit . . . a formidable four, you could say," quips Will, the eldest of the quartet. Adds Anna, "The dynamic among the four of us has pretty much remained constant, which is great. I know we'll all still be friends after the movie finishes."

"Do I feel like the leader of the group?" the handsome, fair-haired Moseley wonders when asked about the professional and personal dynamics of the four Pevensie actors. He responds proudly and without hesitation: "I definitely do!

A *prince among kings and queens: Ben, Skandar, Anna, Will, and Georgie.*

"Like I said before, I'm the oldest in my family," he continues. "Anna is the oldest in hers, so she is also kind of the leader. Skandar is the youngest, but wants to be the elder as well. Georgie is the youngest as well. We form a very tight unit. The parallels to our characters are simple—we're all playing ourselves, drawing on our own lives, to show how similar we are to these characters."

While reflecting back to the beginning of the lengthy shoot, Anna was not surprised at the changes the cast experienced since they last worked together, over two years ago. Except, maybe about herself.

"What's nice is everyone has grown up a little bit and changed a little bit," she observes. "But, I've probably grown up the least, I'd say. Maybe that's just because I haven't noticed the change in myself." To which Andrew

smiles and replies, "Anna's right. When I first met her, she was 13 going on 40. Now she's 18 going on 40."

Perry Moore's wonderfully evocative book took us behind the scenes of *The Lion, the Witch and the Wardrobe*, where we first met these four relative unknowns, memorably through Perry's vivid and poetic portraits in each actor's chapter. Let's take a further peek at the lives of the four Pevensies, now older and (one hopes) wiser, as they venture from their own private worlds in England back to a magical landscape that has changed drastically since the first movie—much like the actors themselves!

WILLIAM MOSELEY
A Boy and His Horse

Looking back to almost five years ago, Andrew remembers when he cast then-15-year-old William Moseley as Peter Pevensie. "He had never done anything like this before," the director recalls. "I don't think he'd even been on a movie set before. He was just this really great kid and handsome young man whom you wanted to be your big brother."

What impressed Andrew the most during the filming of *The Lion, the Witch and the Wardrobe*? "I saw Will grow from this 17-year-old boy to this young man who becomes a warrior, a kid who absolutely loved the action stuff. I mean, you would not have believed in the beginning that by the end of filming, he would be riding a horse bareback to the point where I actually used Will instead of the stunt riders because he actually rode better than they did. You just saw him come to life as a young hero and young man in the film."

Not much has changed, except maybe for the "young" part!

One of the most thrilling moments of the action-packed castle raid sequence, about halfway into the film, spotlights our hero Peter running at full throttle while trying to mount his horse as he battles assorted Telmarines during a daring escape from the failed assault.

"I chase a running horse, grab the saddle horn, kick a bad guy while still running, then jump on back of this horse galloping at full speed in this castle courtyard at four in the morning in the rain," Moseley enthuses.

After practicing the daring and tricky move for two weeks under the watchful eye of the veteran Spanish horse master Ricardo Cruz, the dashing 20-year-old actor heroically executed the stunt himself (with a little help from his stallion, Thibilon) on the drizzly night of May 2. Says Will, "You don't realize at the time while you're doing this again and again how dangerous it is. When we reached take seven, I should have taken a break. And, I was allowed only seven takes. I wanted to do another, but two were perfect and for the other five, I was holding on for dear life."

Will would be the first to attest that it really was an intense stunt, though he admits, "It actually looks a lot harder than it is." He trained under the direction of the handsome Spaniard Cruz, one of Hollywood's premier equestrian experts and a second-generation movie horse trainer who followed in the footsteps (or hoofprints?) of his legendary father, who brought his young son to the sets of some of the most well known spaghetti Westerns shot in his homeland.

Cruz's troops, which comprised some of the most amazing horse-riding instructors in the world, taught Will the special technique to help him overcome his early struggles with the perilous stunt.

"Once you have the technique down, it became easy and good fun," Will recalls. "It involved digging your feet in, then flying up onto the horse as it cantered. Now, I remind you that there were no safety wires involved. Andrew and Allan must have had a lot of faith in me."

The Allan that Moseley refers to is the film's wiry, inventive stunt coordinator and action choreographer, Allan Poppleton, who reprised his role from the first film (on which he also served as the company's sword master). Allan's faith in this neophyte action hero wasn't unfounded, however. The low-key stuntman gives all the credit to his enthusiastic and attentive pupil.

"If, for some reason, Will decided not to pursue acting, he could potentially go into the stunt field," the Kiwi native raves about his gutsy student. Allan recalls that whenever Will had any spare time, he would always track down the stunties to rehearse one of the film's fight sequences—such as the epic swordfight with Miraz,

one of the film's climactic scenes, which required much more time than Will anticipated to learn the 115-beat swordplay.

"It was amazing what he could actually do," Poppleton hails. "Sometimes filmmakers hope to get a lot more out of some actors who maybe aren't so physical. I think Will's an exception to the rule there. Which you'll see from the film. Some of the stuff he's done is just amazing!"

His feats of daring were not limited to the movie sets.

During weekends and assorted days off from filming, Will and fellow cast member Skandar Keynes always found time for some extracurricular activities, especially during the New Zealand portion of the shoot. These were the sorts of daredevil workouts they wouldn't necessarily tell the producers about.

How about diving off the world's third-highest bungee jump at the Nevis Highwire near Queenstown? "It was 440 feet, or 130 meters for you metric people," Moseley brags—not to mention an 8.5 second freefall. "It was huge and it was amazing. I thought I might die. But I did survive.

How about falling 600 feet from Auckland's Sky Tower (attached to a wire, of course), swinging 400 feet over a canyon, or rafting down rapids in Slovenia?

While Will may have DVD footage and photos of those high-octane thrills, what will endure most for this kind and considerate young country Englishman are the

Peter comforts Lucy.

recollections and overall experience of working on both movies.

"I hope I'm not taking this experience and privilege for granted," he says, knowing this is his last stand in Narnia (Peter does not return in the upcoming films). "Because when it's done, I'll be wishing I were right back here in Narnia. Ironically enough, you can't really appreciate it until you take a step back. You can't really reflect properly until you're out of the loop."

Will gets a bit philosophic about the two years between the completion of the first movie and the start of *Prince Caspian* in early 2007. The anticipation, the anxiety, echoed all too well what his character Peter endured in the time between his fifteen-year reign as king in *The Lion, the Witch and the Wardrobe* and his desire to rule that kingdom again in *Prince Caspian*.

Just like Peter, Will returned to secondary school, a year older than everyone else, "like that kid that was a bit thick and got kicked behind," he reflects. "Finishing the first film was an amazing experience. Then it was all taken away and I had to go back to school. Even though I don't react the same way Peter does, I can really understand how he feels."

The handsome and committed young man, who dedicated himself to the study of acting in New York in the hiatus between films, also yearned to reunite with his director and co-stars, and play the big brother to his comrades, especially the youngest, Georgie Henley,

ABOVE: *William Moseley's daring nighttime horse stunt.*
RIGHT: *Andrew gives direction to Will.*

whom you'd always find in the comfort of Will's arms between takes.

"Will has grown into a man," Georgie affirms with delight. "He's 20 years old and I've known him since he was 15, when we first met during the casting of the last film. He's grown before everybody's eyes and has just made that transformation from boy to man. I still look to him as the big brother I never had. But, he's still got those boyish instincts. Like, he forgets things. But we still love him."

Anna chimes in, "Although Will is 20, he's playing a 16- or 17-year-old. But he's an adult now. I had my first audition with him when I was 13. And we really have sort of grown up together. We go back a long way.

"I just felt really fortunate to be back for the second Narnia," the young Moseley admits as filming draws to a close in late August. "Just because the first one, my

very first film, was an amazing, eye-opening adventure for me."

All this is quite a long journey for the country lad from England's Cotswolds, but as he gallops toward his future in Los Angeles (an idea he acknowledges is "scary"), there's little doubt he'll make his way forward with the same grace, dignity, and humility he brought to the role of Peter Pevensie.

ANNA POPPLEWELL
A Fairy-Tale Story

In the movie's final scene in Narnia, just before the Pevensie children magically return to the tube stop in London, Prince Caspian bids good-bye to Peter, Susan, Edmund, and Lucy.

The dashing prince saves his final farewell for the brave and beautiful Susan, who gallantly fought alongside her siblings, the Narnian army, and the prince himself to restore majesty to the land—her land. They exchange a heartfelt glance, both well-knowing Caspian will not see her again.

This ending scene was fraught with meaning. We, the audience, will not see her character again in Narnia for quite some time.

More personally, we the cast and crew who make up this close-knit Narnian film family also bid a bittersweet farewell to the lovely actress who brought pathos and courage to the role of the elder Pevensie daughter, first as the logical and precocious big sister in *The Lion, the Witch and the Wardrobe*, and now as the empowered warrior in *Prince Caspian*.

We say good-bye to Anna Popplewell.

"Queen Susan *is* in *The Horse and His Boy*," the 19-year-old actress retorts, emphatically reminding us that she can still return to Narnia. "However, with this story, the teenage Susan is done. Which is really sad. Filming the scene where the Pevensies leave Narnia was quite hard. Especially for Will and me, knowing we won't be returning."

There was a small silver lining to scene 166 on Barrandov's backlot in late June, one that may have helped her through the moment's emotions—the luxurious gown created for her by costume designer Isis Mussenden.

"Without a doubt, it was my favorite costume!" Anna exclaims. The dress that I wore at the end of the movie was just stunning and made me feel like Cinderella. I think any girl who's ever played dress-up would want to be in that costume. I felt really special being in it."

As the company completed the colorful, jubilant sequence over a six-day span, Anna's own midnight bell was about to toll, turning an elegant actress who had starred in one of the most successful movies of all time back into a school girl with a fairy-tale story of her own to tell.

While she did not aspire to perform as a young girl growing up in London's Highbury neighborhood (by sheer coincidence, just a few blocks away from co-star Skandar Keynes), summer courses in drama led to what Anna calls "a very happy accident" on the road to acting at age six. One audition led to the next, and her parents (mom Debra, a physician, and dad Andrew, a barrister) supported her new hobby that eventually brought her to Narnia's wardrobe door in 2004. Coincidentally, Anna is the eldest of three children—her siblings, 16-year-old Lulu and 13-year-old Freddie, are also talented actors.

When production began on the first movie almost four years ago, Anna had the most accomplished acting resume of the four Pevensies, having appeared in about a dozen movie and TV projects (most notably *The Girl With a Pearl Earring*), mostly in small roles.

She did not pursue an acting job after *The Lion, the Witch and the Wardrobe*, instead setting her sights on secondary school studies with the aim of landing a coveted spot at Oxford's Magdalen College, the same bastion of higher learning where author C. S. Lewis spent a three-decade tenure from 1925 to 1954.

"When I picked that college, I didn't know that," Anna admits. "I read a biography of C. S. Lewis and learned about his involvement with Magdalen. And that was, in a way, a bit spooky, but also really nice. Even though I won't be a part of [the next few] movies, I feel as though C. S. Lewis will still be a big part of my life in the next three years."

During the filming of *Prince Caspian*, you could usually find the charming, blue-eyed beauty studying

for her exams, engaged in archery practice under Allan Poppleton's watchful eye, or taking riding lessons with equestrian master Ricardo Cruz.

"Working for my exams on *Prince Caspian* was a big challenge," Anna confesses, "but, I think it was something separate from 'Susan.' I reckon she would have studied more than I did! That said, I think all experiences provide you with a potential bank to draw from when acting, but I don't think there was anything in particular about my A levels that I channeled into Narnia!"

A word on those exams—Anna explains that secondary school in the U.K. requires a series of exams, termed A levels (much like the SAT exams in the States), in order to earn a spot in the incoming class at one's chosen university.

Susan says good-bye to Caspian, and to Narnia.

"I've always really wanted to go to university. So that was something that was really important to me."

On the first film, as a 15-year-old, she had a mandatory three hours of school a day, but now, at age 18, "I didn't have that protective time to do tutoring and study that I would have had if I were a child, a minor," she explains. "So, for most of this movie, I worked twelve hour days, just like an adult, then went home and did three hours of school. *That* was difficult and a real challenge."

Production scheduled Anna's scenes to allow her a seventeen-day window to return to London to take her A levels in the first half of June. Upon returning to the set and reuniting with her fellow Narnia family members, she let out a deep sigh of relief: "I'm glad they're finally over.

"I had such a great time on the first movie and really wanted to be involved again, but the only drawback for

me was the fact that I had these end-of-school exams. I needed three weeks' time off in the middle of shooting, which was really difficult to organize. They had to move a lot of stuff around in order to accommodate that, so I'm really grateful that they could do that to help me out. That meant I could do the movie."

But there was still another two-month wait for her grades after she completed the June exams, about which she wouldn't hear back until August. While her film family offered encouragement to the apprehensive student during what must have felt like an eternity, we all knew she had nothing to fear. We know well enough that Anna, who truly possesses the poise and wisdom of a queen of Narnia, will someday rule her own kingdom.

For now, however, there is more to learn, and for this newly anointed literature major at Oxford, there are many stories to explore.

"To me, the power of storytelling is all about people and transformation," she confides. As an actor, your power of storytelling comes through transformation. The fact that Ben can put on an accent and become someone completely different, or that Will can jump onto the side of a horse and suddenly become this action hero. That Georgie or I can put on a dress and be transported into a fairy-tale world. In such instances, you're presented visually with something that doesn't really exist. That idea of complete transformation, either through the power of C. S. Lewis's words or through Howard's creatures, defines the power and importance of storytelling."

Anna's own story is far from over. While she turns the page and begins a new chapter of that fable, it's inevitable that we all must say good-bye.

"On the one hand, I feel incredibly lucky to have had this experience, and I've had a fantastic time," she exclaims. "I'd so much rather have been here than not been here. But at the same time, it's really sad that I won't be coming back. And I will feel sad that the others are doing the next movie and I'm not. But, it's time for me to carry on and do other things in my life."

SKANDAR KEYNES
Daredevil in Disguise

With a nod to Elvis Presley, we bring you Skandar Keynes.

Like Elvis, he carries around a guitar that he taught himself to play (though he tends to prefer Dylan and Hendrix to Presley).

And, like the King of Rock 'n' Roll, this young king of Narnia will be a heartthrob, per director Andrew Adamson.

"Will has turned out to be a handsome young man, shedding that baby face he had on the first film," he offers. "However, I think Skandar is the one who will need to worry about female fans this time. His face has thinned out and become angular, giving him a matinee idol look and appeal."

And, if that doesn't do it, his daredevil antics during production will certainly have girls swooning over the 16-year-old London native.

"There's been lots of cool stuff we did, especially in New Zealand," raves Skandar, who has spent, by his own calculations, a fifth of his life in Narnia. "We had lots of time off in Queenstown, which is the adventure capital of the world. We did the third-highest bungee jump in the world. Did a canyon swing, also the largest in the world. Jumped off the Sky Tower, the tallest building in the Southern Hemisphere. It was all really good fun."

The "we" he refers to usually includes his onscreen big brother, Will Moseley, or "Wizzle," Skandar's nickname for his British mate. Not surprisingly, they carried on like inseparable brothers offscreen as well.

"It was all really cool," Skandar continues with gusto, though he finally admits that one of their grand schemes turned out to seem "not so cool" on the day. What might sound like a good idea at the time becomes all too real when one stands precariously on the tiny platform affixed to the top of Auckland's Sky Tower, some 630 feet above the pavement.

"We'll be fine, we'll be fine," he chanted as his harness was secured to the free-fall wire attached to the city's iconic spire. Once hooked into the wire, he then stepped off the small 2x4 they call a platform, and hung completely suspended in midair, before spiraling downward over 600 feet in under fifteen seconds at a speed of over 50mph, slowly decelerating before landing on the street.

"I think they've actually got some footage of that," the mischievous teen remarks. "The DVD guys came along and filmed it. OK, I admit it. Beforehand, I was really nervous about it and I was like, 'This is so high and so scary.' But Will was like, 'Oh, it's fine, it's fine.'"

When the pair arrived, on the company's next-to-last day in New Zealand before leaving for Prague, Skandar recalls that all of a sudden "it was Will who began freaking out, nervously echoing 'It's so high . . . it's so high. . . .' That was a good role reversal."

As for role reversals in the story, it's fascinating to watch how the character of Edmund has changed from the first film. Though he was the catalyst for the Pevensies' problems in Lewis's first story, Edmund has now matured (like the young man who plays him), and become much more pragmatic than his older brother, Peter, who still lets his emotions get the better of him. For those unfamiliar with the second Narnia tale, there are moments when Edmund actually comes to the rescue in *Prince Caspian*, unlike the first story, where the naïve and impulsive boy had to be rescued after falling under the spell of the wicked White Witch.

In one such instance, scene 115, set in the cavernous Aslan's How, the teenage hero must battle the forces of evil to bail Caspian out of a potentially catastrophic situation.

"That was the day on the call sheet where the scene description was 'Edmund saves the day,'" Skandar boasts. "I didn't let anyone forget it. I walked around with a call sheet in my hands all day. 'Edmund saves the day.' That was really cool."

While his friend and co-star Will executed his thrilling and perilous castle raid horse-riding stunt sans safety wires, the daredevil Skandar, no stranger to safety

admit). Like many his age, he spent his perfect afternoon watching *Dodgeball* (Ben Stiller is one of his idols) and eating pizza.

A little over a year later, I was privileged and honored to visit the Keynes' home in London, and surprised to find that Skandar now sported the first sprouts of facial hair, the unruly locks of a rock guitarist, and spoke with a deep voice more suited to Elvis than to Edmund. Over

*T*hat was the day on the call sheet where the scene description was "Edmund saves the day," I didn't let anyone forget it.

the course of a scrumptious Middle Eastern banquet prepared by his mom, Zelfa Hourani, we talked the evening away about what to expect when Skandar began his first international marketing blitz to promote *The Lion, the Witch and the Wardrobe*—a tour that would include stops in Orlando, New York, and Japan.

TOP: *Skandar tries to keep a straight face during Edmund's challenge to Miraz.*
BOTTOM: *Will spars with Skandar near the dueling arena.*

rigs, donned a harness for a complicated stunt devised by Andrew and Allan Poppleton to fling Edmund 20 feet in the air to avoid being sliced to death. Another "cool" moment for the lively teenager.

In spite of his fearlessness and his mischievous streak, Skandar is remarkably modest and down-to-earth—ironic for someone who spends so much time suspended above it!

I first met Skandar when he was just 12 years old, when I came on board the first film as unit publicist. He immediately understood what my job was, even assigning me a nickname—"Mr. EM, PR!"

He marveled at my bowling ability at his thirteenth birthday party at an alley near Henderson Studios outside Auckland (I did have the day's high game, I

In our various chats, Skandar admits he is not married to an acting career. He has always expressed interest in behind-the-scenes crafts, such as cinematography, and on both films, he could frequently be spotted hanging around the various artists and technicians, constantly grilling them about their work and careers with the fervor of a journalist. On this production, he became something of an artist himself, jamming on his guitar in his trailer, entertaining his co-stars, the crew, or whomever happened to be passing by.

In fact, Skandar's love of music became a part of daily life on set, when Andrew introduced the custom of playing songs on a hefty speaker system normally used for the assistant directors to address the crew and extras. If you happened to be anywhere near the Soča River Valley in Slovenia in mid-July, and heard the familiar strains of "All Along the Watchtower" (Skandar prefers

Bob Dylan's acoustic version to Jimi Hendrix's electric workout) echoing among the jagged peaks, you have young Mr. Keynes to thank for the song selection.

When I reconnected with Skandar on *Prince Caspian* at our Auckland production offices in February 2007, a week before filming commenced, he had grown at least another half-foot (he and Georgie were always arguing who had grown the most). The coif still needed some grooming (hairstylist Kevin Alexander took immediate care of that). And he approached me, hand extended, to say "hello" with the most complicated handshake I have ever encountered, requiring a contortionist's skill to execute.

I constantly ribbed him when autograph-seekers wanted a signed picture on this project, and all we had available was a group shot from the first film that depicted the now-adolescent Skandar as a baby-faced preteen who had not yet learned to sign his name in script.

Recalling Andrew's comment about what this handsome young man is about to experience from his fan base, watch out! He'll definitely need to sign more autographs and shake some hands, but he'll no doubt have some cheeks to peck as well when the film opens.

Not that fame comes immediately. When Skandar and Will reunited at the production office in February, they immediately regaled us with anecdotes about being recognized in public after the tremendous success of *The Lion, the Witch and the Wardrobe.*

If you've ever been to London, you've probably set foot on the bustling Oxford Street, which runs right through the city's popular Soho neighborhood. The two boys were at a Gap store when Will was spotted by some teenage girls, who boldly approached the pair. Will coyly admitted to being the star of the film, but tried to divert the girls' attention to Skandar. There was some faint recognition of the young boy Edmund from the film, to be sure, but their focus was on Peter. Not that Skandar minded—for him, this was a narrow escape!

This time around, the roles will reverse. No longer will Skandar be able to dodge recognition, and no longer will fans be able to overlook this dark-haired, freckle-faced rising star. As he continues to grow up, and carry his role forward, maturity and adulthood will only deepen his character.

And if Andrew's right (which is most of the time), this fun-loving daredevil, who relished every thrilling stunt on set and off, may find himself on a new thrill ride, enjoying the spotlight of celebrity.

In the meantime, young Skandar, like his co-star Anna Popplewell and teenagers everywhere, is concentrating on school exams, with his sights set on university, as we all wait for *Prince Caspian* to hit movie screens in spring 2008. Not long after, he will return as Edmund in the next Narnian adventure, the seaborne *Voyage of the Dawn Treader,* continuing to rack up a few more years spent in Lewis's enchanted world. And, quite probably, taking his daredevil act offshore.

This Elvis has not yet left the building.

GEORGIE HENLEY
A Flower Blossoms

On *The Lion, the Witch and the Wardrobe*, our four youngsters, Will Moseley, Anna Popplewell, Skandar Keynes, and Georgie Henley, were virtual unknowns when brought to Andrew Adamson's attention in preproduction by London casting agent Pippa Hall, who specializes in bringing young actors to the screen. Anna and Skandar had each shot several projects, mostly in the UK, but Will and the precocious 8-year-old Georgie were complete newcomers.

"I hadn't done anything like that before," Georgie attests. She had never been on a movie set, let alone one of the biggest productions ever! "It was a big hurdle for me and I did feel like I wasn't going to do very well at it. I didn't realize it was going to be such a big film. However, once I'd had a little taste of it, I felt fine with it. Coming back to this, the second film, felt completely different. Like coming back to see old friends again."

Georgie and her soft-spoken mom, Helen, her companion through both films, arrived in Auckland on February 5, 2007, a week before filming, for a packed schedule of hair and makeup tests, scene rehearsals, riding lessons, stunt practice, and more. As she walked into the production office, we immediately noticed a striking change in this beautiful young girl. Taller, wiser, and more self-assured, she greeted familiar faces on that warm February morning with unending bearhugs, like a child reuniting with long-lost relatives.

Andrew also noticed her preteen maturity. "She is growing into an absolute beauty," he notes, alluding not only to her physical growth but her emotional spirit as well. Which, in itself, is hard to believe, as we all thought the precocious Georgie from *The Lion, the Witch and the Wardrobe* possessed the wisdom of someone twice her age. Fortunately, she's no less inquisitive for being older—just ask Andrew about her quizzing him about camera angles and lenses, always curious how the director was framing her in the shot.

"I think the character's grown along, as I have," the budding adolescent affirms. "Now that I'm older, Lucy seems to have grown. And I just love that, because I wouldn't have liked it as much if I was still playing the innocent sweet with no action side to her. But now that I'm older, I feel like that just totally suits me and I've kind of grown with it. So that was a happy part of filming for me."

After the first film, Georgie's face adorned posters everywhere, from theater lobbies to bus kiosks, from subway stations to giant billboards. She won critical praise for her performance in her movie debut, along with assorted critics' awards. When the acclaim quieted down and the movie's theatrical run ran its course, Georgie returned to her northern England home, almost as if nothing had happened.

"The movie didn't really change my life," she admits, modestly. "Well, I should say that I have this quite glamorous life in London when I go down there for press and stuff. It's like having the best of both worlds, and I love that."

"Quite glamorous" might be an understatement for a girl whose Narnian odyssey has taken her to Japan ("Kyoto, just lovely with its massive temples," she recalls), New York ("amazing and cosmopolitan"), New Zealand ("Queenstown on the South Island is just so beautiful!"), and Prague ("I think the architecture is amazing"), not to mention such out of the way locales as Bovec, Slovenia, where the cast and many of the crew of *Prince Caspian* gathered in a cozy ballroom during a spectacular thunderstorm to wish Georgie a happy twelfth birthday in July.

But, true to her onscreen character, she doesn't get carried away. "When I go back to Ilkley, I'm just Georgie and I really like that. I don't really get recognized a lot

and I like it that way. I just like being at school and, you know, being a normal person, just doing normal things and not being caught up in this world."

Once life returned to normal for the youngest of the three Henley sisters (you may recall the eldest, Rachael, playing the grown-up Lucy in the final moments of *The Lion, the Witch and the Wardrobe*), Georgie returned to

> *I write my own stories. I think the good thing about stories is they carry you to another place that you've never been.*

another movie set—in fact, she was the only one of the Pevensie quartet to do so between the Narnia films. She appeared briefly as the young Jane Eyre in the BBC's 2006 adaptation of Charlotte Brontë's classic novel, which, by coincidence, was broadcast on New Zealand television during the early days of production on *Prince Caspian*.

Now that she's completed her third movie role, it's curious to note that her resume consists exclusively of classic literature adaptations—a fact of which this youngster is well aware.

English is one of her favorite subjects in school, and Georgie is a budding writer herself. The bright and studious girl, now 12, has penned two stories of her own: "The Snow Stag" and "A Pillar of Secrets," both of which she's quite proud. "I write my own stories. I like telling stories to little children. I think the good thing about stories is they carry you to another place which you've never been. And you feel like you're just enveloped by the book and the characters."

Of course, the Narnia books occupy a special place in her heart. "They're just brilliant because of the way C. S. Lewis wrote them. Just the way he didn't put too much description in. So Narnia is almost our complete imagination. We can interpret it however we like. I do think that most people have their own interpretation of these books and these characters."

As for her own character, Lucy Pevensie, Georgie notes two major changes in *Prince Caspian*. "Lucy got to do some more action stuff!" she gushes. She dares not give too much away about the plot, but not for nothing did Georgie learn to ride a horse and wield a dagger! "In the last film, I was sweet little Lucy, and now I'm a bit more actiony, which was quite fun!"

The second is a deeper, more serious change to her character: "Lucy stands for what she believes in more than in the last film—her faith in Aslan. She sees Aslan before her siblings do, which I think shows Lucy's trust in Aslan more than the others. She seems to be more brave and she seems to have her own view about what she thinks is right."

So, taking into account all the changes and experiences that young Georgie Henley has undergone in her first twelve years, you have to step back in wonder at the exploits of this adventurous and creative child.

Producer Mark Johnson may have said it best when he described his then 8-year-old star during production on the first movie—"She seemed really curious, like the kind of little girl who would really go into the wardrobe."

"Well, although I love where I live and all that, I probably *would* go in, just for the sake of having an adventure," she confesses, and we're reminded why she was the perfect choice to play Lucy Pevensie. "Although, maybe I wouldn't find Narnia. In *The Magician's Nephew*, there are all kinds of worlds. Which one would I go to?"

Life offers any number of doors to be opened. As Georgie herself said, what lies beyond the wardrobe door is up to our own imagination. As for which door Georgie chooses next . . . whatever she finds is bound to enrich an already wonderful life.

Georgie with producer Philip Steuer.

The New Cast

Heroes and Villains

One thing that distinguishes the Chronicles of Narnia from other popular children's series is how author C. S. Lewis did not use the same characters in all seven books. From Peter to Caspian, from Eustace to Digory, Lewis stepson and co-producer Doug Gresham felt that "in Jack's development of new characters in Narnia, he was dealing, as always, with the two elements of good and evil. As the Chronicles of Narnia progress, we meet more and more fascinating new characters, some of whom represent evil as an outgrowth of human, or humanoid, frailty."

While the four Pevensie siblings return in *Prince Caspian*, the story introduces several brand-new characters, all colorful and memorable not only for their depiction by the British writer, but also through the portraits created by the actors who embodied them. Their personal adventures in Narnia follow in these profiles.

OPPOSITE: *Ben Barnes as Caspian.*
RIGHT: *Sergio Castellitto as the battle weary Miraz.*

BEN BARNES
Prince Caspian

"I f you're sitting on a horse holding a sword inside a castle courtyard, it's not too hard to feel like a prince."

Spoken by an unassuming young Londoner, this may help explain why it wasn't too much of a stretch for him to transform himself into the heir to the Narnian throne.

His name is Ben Barnes. He *is* Prince Caspian. And he is about to begin his reign over the Disney kingdom in the title role of the second adventure in Narnia.

The year 2007 seemed to be one of great destiny for the twenty-six-year-old British stage actor.

He landed the coveted role of C. S. Lewis's dashing prince just as he was conquering London's prestigious West End theater empire with his role of Dakin in Alan Bennett's award-winning play *The History Boys*. The role of Caspian was only his third motion picture assignment and his first Hollywood starring role.

That's like hitting a grand slam home run out of the park after only three times at the plate!

With all that—the triumph in London's celebrated West End theater world, and the title character of not only a major motion picture, but the eagerly anticipated second chapter in what could be one of Hollywood's most successful franchises ever—still, Barnes was dragged kicking and screaming into his very first shot in the movie!

"It was extraordinary and good fun at the same time," Ben recalls of his very first camera shot back on March 5 on New Zealand's South Island. "I was literally dragged, kicking and screaming, into this film." The day's work began with scene 16 ("EXT. Woods, Caspian hits head, takes out horn and blows"), which depicts the young prince taken prisoner by Trumpkin and Nikabrik before he blows Susan's horn, summoning the Pevensies back to Narnia.

To dramatically portray the moment when Caspian, escaping on horseback from Miraz's castle, slams into a tree branch and falls from his horse with his leg caught in one of the stirrups, stunt coordinator Allan Poppleton actually dragged the actor into the shot to effect the illusion that Ben was being pulled through the underbrush by his runaway horse.

The two Narnian dwarfs threaten to kill Caspian. "Luckily, I don't die," the actor says, breathing a sigh of relief. "It's only about five minutes into a movie called *Prince Caspian* when this happens. Guess they would have had to call it something else if that were the case!"

It took the filmmakers, director Andrew Adamson and producer Mark Johnson, much more than five minutes to choose the actor to play their title hero in the much-anticipated follow-up to *The Lion, the Witch and the Wardrobe*. More like five months!

Once the filmmakers had created a history for the Telmarines (Spanish pirates, according to Andrew and production designer Roger Ford), they began their search for Caspian by looking at Spanish-speaking actors "because of the challenge of giving Caspian a slight Mediterranean accent," producer Johnson explains.

Their initial pursuit focused on actors with a pure Spanish or Hispanic background, including candidates from Argentina, Mexico, and Spain. Casting director Gail Stevens confirms that the filmmakers also cast their net to France, Italy, Israel, Scandinavia, Holland, Germany, and Morocco. While the search produced a viable list of aspirants who were also the right age (Caspian is supposed to be in his late teens), Andrew and Mark agreed that if they could not find the right actor from those regions, a dialect coach could be one solution for a non-Spanish-speaking actor.

That turned out to be the answer once Ben entered the picture. A native Londoner, the stage veteran ("can one be called that at my age?" Ben asks) had previously auditioned for producer Johnson for one of his other recent projects, *The Hunting Party*, a part that was ultimately awarded to someone else. During his pursuit of that role,

the actor never met the longtime producer in person. They met at last during a screen test for *Prince Caspian*.

"We took a long time to find Ben and saw many actors for this role," Mark admits. The search, led by casting directors Gail Stevens and Pippa Hall, who respectively handle adult and child casting, eventually brought the filmmakers to the dark-haired talent.

"The role of Prince Caspian was obviously an important one in a film called *Prince Caspian*," Mark muses with a smile. "We needed a young man who could be heroic but who also had something in his personality that reflected what the character accrues through the journey in this film."

Stevens had an assistant who had seen Ben in *The History Boys*. When she contacted his agent and passed word along of the filmmakers' interest, Ben taped an audition reading, which was sent to director Adamson. "We put several young British actors on tape, including Ben, someone we admired and whose work we knew by

repute," Stevens explains. "Everyone, including Andrew, Mark, Disney, and Walden, unanimously reacted warmly to his reading."

Andrew, in particular, admired Ben's work ethic. "He put himself on tape," the director remembers fondly. Ben's boundless enthusiasm and intense effort left no question how much he wanted the role, and his insight was apparent to all. "What interested me about his reading was he did something with the scene, an inflection, that nobody else got. A certain ironic meaning to a line that he understood and brought through in his reading. He was very relaxed, comfortable, and realistic on that taped audition."

That video introduction led to a personal audition with Andrew in which the director finally met his new prince and crowned him the star of his new movie. "When we finally met Ben in person, we again found him charming and fun and comfortable. He won us over."

Ben had resumed his stage role for the National Theatre, one he would be reluctant to leave if he got the part. He found out he won the starring role "at three o'clock in the morning, 'cause it was on American time when I got the call to say I'd had the job. My reaction—screaming around the house! It was just one of those life-changing moments. For me, a new adventure was about to begin."

Not long after the good news, Ben found himself sitting on a field enveloped by New Zealand's majestic Southern Alps, where the charming actor shared his very first thoughts about his upcoming experience: "Caspian goes on this journey in the story, one that I think will parallel my own journey as we make the movie over the next six months. It will be exciting and daunting at the same time."

Before his whirlwind adventure began with costume fittings, horseback-riding practice, dialect lessons, and fencing and dueling rehearsals, Ben scoured the bookcase at his London flat to find his worn copy of Lewis's book.

"I was a massive Narnia fan as a kid," he exclaims, his enthusiasm not unlike that of an eight-year-old boy reading the novel for the very first time. "I definitely remember the books being a big part of my childhood. When I found out I got the part, I looked through my bookshelves and found this copy of *Prince Caspian* that was published in 1989, when I was eight. And it had a little sticker in the front where I'd written 'Benjamin Barnes' in my eight-year-old's handwriting. That was the copy I went back and re-read when I found out I got the part."

At London's Kingston College, where he graduated in 2001, "I studied children's literature as one of my special topics," he says, "so I came back and studied the chronicles from a completely fresh angle. And I thought that was about as far as my relationship with these books would go. But then this came along."

Just days after the *London Times* broke the news of his casting (and subsequent departure from *The History Boys*),

Ben arrived in New Zealand and immediately began his transformation from an English schoolboy circa 1981, in Bennett's play, into a sword-wielding prince on a quest to avenge his father's murder.

But first, there was a matter of his hair.

Unlike castmates Will Moseley and Skandar Keynes, whose locks needed severe pruning from hairstylist Kevin Alexander, Ben needed more hair to make his appearance more princely, more regal, says director Adamson.

"He auditioned with short hair," the filmmaker remembers. Following that screen test, Andrew found Ben's headshot, the eight-by-ten photo that every actor on the planet has on file with his/her agency, sort of an actor's calling card. "I found that photo online, the one with the longer hair, and that's what we modeled Caspian's look on . . . the very, very dark eyes and dark hair. That's the look we were after."

Hairstylist Alexander, a fellow Brit whose résumé includes the latest James Bond opus, *Casino Royale*, arranged for Barnes to undergo the addition of hair extensions to simulate the coif in his photo headshot. While giving Barnes a princely (and dare we say "sexy") appearance, these extensions required constant maintenance, a somewhat uncomfortable process that the new prince valiantly endured every six weeks or so. Alexander's hair design was so authentic, you could never tell Barnes had hair extensions.

Add to that the olive shading to his complexion that ace makeup artist Paul Engelen says "gave him a more Mediterranean look," Isis Mussenden's regal wardrobe ("boots, a royal shirt, and brigandine combining a Turkish, Spanish, and European flair," Ben says), and Weta's authentic weaponry (sword and dagger), and Barnes took on what he calls "this 'princely' energy."

Even though the story takes place in a fantasy world, "you have to play every moment as truth," Ben notes. "And I hope that those moments translate into something that the audience can really become involved with. If so, they will then get behind Caspian and see him through from the beginning to the end of his journey. If you play each moment as something that's real, which was easy to do on those huge sets, with great people around you, then hopefully the audience will be with you."

In addition to immersing himself in the role, he also had to accommodate himself into a tight-knit film family.

Most important was bonding with his four co-stars, whom he knew only from viewing the first film. What helped break the ice, so to speak, was "Andrew's keen objective to film things as chronologically as possible," actor Barnes observes. "In the same way that my relationship with the Pevensies grows on-screen, that mirrored how it also blossomed in real life."

"They were all very welcoming, as I would have expected them to be," Ben says about meeting his new castmates. "They were all-embracing, kind of prepared for this new character. But on my very first day on set, K. C. Hodenfield, our assistant director, said, 'This is Ben Barnes. He's going to be playing Prince Caspian. Please don't come within two meters of him or look him directly in the eye.' So on the first day, everyone was a little shifty around me until they realized he was joking."

The four returning cast members called Ben "the fifth Pevensie," jokes Skandar. "He's kind of like an honorary Pevensie. Not a true Pevensie. The fact that he was twenty-five when we made the movie made everyone else act a bit more mature. We had a lot of fun. He's a cool dude."

All four were anxious to meet Barnes when he first arrived in New Zealand not long after they had. The quartet was interested in how he would fit into their family, says actress Popplewell. Her character, Susan, develops a slight crush on Narnia's rightful heir. "Not a deep, romantic, passionate thing, however," she explains.

"When you're going to spend a significant amount of time with someone, on a project that you really value, that person becomes really important to the entire enterprise," she notes philosophically. "Especially for Will and me, because we knew that we were not in the next story. It was important that we would be, in a cast sense, kind of passing on the films to someone whom

we really liked. So Ben had a lot to live up to before we'd even met him. He managed to establish individual relationships with all of us. He had that something that we very much connected with."

Even the youngest, twelve-year-old Georgie Henley, had now found another big brother, one who would fill Will's shoes on those days when the young Moseley was not on the day's shooting schedule—certainly one who

Within an hour of arriving in New Zealand, I was thrown on a horse. I loved every second of it!

would do just that on the next film, in which Moseley does not appear.

"I remember being mad that Ben almost stepped into my role of Georgie's big brother," actor Moseley relates about the first time he witnessed his new co-star comforting the cast's youngest member between takes. Georgie seemed to treat Ben as an older sibling she had not seen in a long time and with whom she wanted to reestablish a long-lost bond. "I thought, 'This isn't right. This is my place.' Then I got used to that and used those feelings in my character's arguments with Caspian. But, as expected, Ben and I have got on really well. It was like having a good mate on the set."

There was one other requirement for the role that Ben wasn't quite ready for, however. "I don't think even Andrew had contemplated how much horse riding there would be for Caspian," he notes. Ben's instinct was to keep his mouth shut on the matter, but clearly, the stunt folks and producers would start asking him soon.

"I rang my mum afterward and asked her if I had ever been horse riding," he recalls. "She couldn't remember. Turned out I had once, when I was eight." Which, incidentally, is the same age he first read the book. Coincidence?

"I'd never really ridden a horse before," he finally confesses. "Within an hour of arriving in New Zealand, I was driven straight from the airport and thrown on a horse. I loved every second of it!"

A few weeks after filming had concluded, Disney released the first poster marketing images for the movie—the "one-sheet," the primary movie theater placard that adorns cinemas throughout the world. There stood our star, Ben Barnes, looking every inch an action hero and movie star. The poster was created for the film by Disney's key print marketing executive, John Sabel, who had spent a day in April with the cast, capturing such moments in still photos used for such purposes.

We all have indelible memories of this warm, funny, gracious and friendly young Londoner: his happy-go-lucky lip-synching to Travis's *Why Does It Always Rain on Me*, a song Andrew blasted over the set's PA system when an unexpected deluge shut down filming one late Saturday in June; the joyous relationship he shared with his younger brother, Jack, who visited our Prague shoot in July (not to mention his parents, Tom and Patricia, also set visitors in early May); and that million-dollar smile, which sparkled, hypnotized, and beckoned your friendship when flashed in your direction.

Now that Ben has concluded the journey of (and with) Caspian, we felt it appropriate to invite the new Hollywood actor to relate his experiences, which marked his first Hollywood starring role, in his own words later in this book.

As for my own closing words about this actor, this colleague, and this friend, I give him the last word here as well, which echoes those that opened this chapter: "It's every boy's dream to be swinging a sword on a horse in a castle."

Some dreams do come true.

SERGIO CASTELLITTO
Miraz

Our beloved Caspian was abducted by *Narnians!*" With spit flying from his mouth like the venom of an asp about to strike its victim, actor Sergio Castellitto bursts into the Great Hall of Miraz's castle, addressing his council of lords, who have gathered to discuss Caspian's "kidnapping" and how it might affect the future of Narnia. (The young prince is the rightful heir to the Telmarine throne.)

If he were a fire-breathing dragon, you'd be able to feel the heat as he sets the scene ablaze. His enunciation of the word *Narnians* is blistering in its delivery. The sequence (scene 28) marks the actor as the absolute best choice for the role. Castellitto is one of Italy's great cinema stars but little known outside Europe.

"The council scene was one of my favorites," says co-star Pierfrancesco Favino, who plays Gen. Glozelle opposite Castellitto's Miraz and sat opposite his fellow Italian during the three-day shoot. "It's this scene when you see who Miraz is, how clever he is, how he manipulates people, and how violent and determined he can be. It's going to come out as the most threatening scene of the movie."

Not only does the moment reveal Miraz for what he truly is, but it's also a sequence that illustrates the commanding presence that Castellitto has before the movie cameras. This kind, gentle, and generous man and father of four plays the essence of evil.

Others in this book have noted the Shakespearean tinge of some of Prince Caspian's darker moments. Miraz's diabolical actions (killing his brother to usurp the throne, then plotting the murder of his nephew) put him in a league with Richard III and *Hamlet*'s Claudius.

So what better performer to portray this Shakespearean villain than one who began his acting career starring in an Italian public theater staging of the Bard's

Sergio Castellitto has been called "one of the most popular Italian actors for international audiences since the heady days of [Marcello] Mastroianni and [Vittorio)] Gassman" by film scholar Richard Pena. His impressive acting career, encompassing work in films, on television, and on the Italian stage, is encyclopedic in length and contains some of Italy's best films over the last quarter century. Castellitto is also a noted writer-director (2004's *Don't Move* with Penelope Cruz, which he adapted from his wife Margaret Mazzantini's award-winning novel), a fact that did not escape filmmaker Adamson in his collaboration with the gentlemanly talent.

"He would sometimes ask me questions about character and motivation," Adamson remembers, adding, "like it was coming from the director's side of his artistic personality. After we wrapped the film, I received an e-mail from Sergio thanking me for everything he learned during the shoot. I, of course, reciprocated with my own thanks, as I also learned a lot about directing from him."

Fellow Italian and co-star Pierfrancesco Favino also considers his good friend and mentor to be "the best director we have in Italy. Working with him has always been a pleasure because he's one of those actors you always learn from. This movie, for me, our third together, has been a gift for many reasons. One of the most precious of them is the privilege of this friendship with Sergio."

"Sergio is one of the most accomplished and highly regarded European actors around today," hails producer Mark Johnson about his screen villain. "And as soon as we saw his audition tape, we immediately said, 'Who is that guy?' I then recognized him from other movies, particularly a film that he had done with Penelope Cruz, and said, 'You know, let's explore this further.' Sure enough, he was our Miraz."

The character of Miraz, like many characters, was open to interpretation, one that actor Castellitto and director Adamson discussed at length.

"Sergio wanted to get deep inside the character,"

Sergio Castellitto as Miraz, Pierfrancesco Favino as Glozelle.

those reasons for doing what he does. It's his right to be king. He is a soldier who worked all his life. He is also a murderer who killed his brother. He is not a coward. The first reference I had of Miraz was from *Hamlet*. He's a usurper who wants this kingdom for his son."

Castellitto never imagined starring in such an epic Hollywood production, for several reasons. First, C. S. Lewis's books, while available in Italy, are not well known there. In fact, Castellitto was not familiar with the series when auditioning for the role. Second, he says, "Our Italian cinema has forgotten how to tell epic tales. But at the same time, we are children of Federico Fellini, so we know very well what is fantasy and imagination."

He did, however, watch Andrew's first Narnia movie with his three older children (ages six to sixteen), who were "so enthusiastic when they knew I would be in the movie. They showed for the first time in their life a lot of esteem and admiration for me," he notes. (Co-star Favino mentions he had a similar experience with his eight-year-old niece, who wanted to know all about Anna Popplewell from her uncle.)

Once actor and director had conceived of Miraz's psychological profile, they next turned to another aspect of the character: physicality. "Acting is both athletic, or physical, and psychological," the Italian native says.

While Castellitto would use no prosthetic makeup appliances to create Miraz, he worked closely with key makeup artist Paul Engelen for the villain's distinctive Mediterranean look. While Howard Berger and his team of forty-plus artists gave birth to the Narnians in the story, the look of the human cast in the film (notably, the stylized Mediterranean characters of Miraz, Caspian, Glozelle, and the Telmarine society) fell to a whole separate team of makeup magicians led by two-time Academy Award® nominee Engelen and hairstylist Kevin Alexander.

The native Brit, a forty-year industry veteran (who sports one of his craft's best professional résumés), confirms that the filmmakers wanted to have an "El

Miraz is a villain (same thing I had with Tilda [Swinton] as the White Witch), such characters often become clichés. It is the challenge of the actor to avoid that cliché and find the reality of what drives the person. It's not enough to say they're crazy or evil. There has to be a humanity to them. We talked a lot about that — that the Telmarine culture shaped Miraz with the idea that it was perfectly acceptable for a Telmarine to kill his brother to become king. It was expected."

"Andrew had a very clear idea about my character," Castellitto adds. Amazingly, Miraz is the very first villain he has played in his thirty-year acting career. In his attempts to embody the character in the proper light, he recalls talking with Adamson about motivation.

"The first work for an actor is to defend his character's position and motivation," the actor says. "I am the ruler of my character. It is important to understand

Greco"/Hispanic feel for our Telmarine civilization. "With Sergio, although of Italian heritage, I had a good 'tone' with which to work," Engelen states.

The longtime makeup artist knew immediately that Miraz should have some degree of beard growth ("the Devil's beard," Castellitto laughs). "Andrew, and indeed the character of Miraz, demanded he should be very forceful and intimidating for the part to succeed, so I worked on some shapes for possibilities, and very soon arrived at the triangular design we decided to use," Engelen recounts.

While Engelen initially wanted to incorporate actor Castellitto's natural gray beard for depth, he decided against that idea. "It not only aged Sergio too much, it also diluted his intensity. So I decided to use his own natural growth as a base, but colored to a very dark brown-black. I enlarged the chin area with an extended piece that I would apply each day. With the addition of extended eyebrows, some darker color in and around the eyes, a little darker complexion on his skin tone—oh, and not forgetting the earring!—I think we ended up with a good 'character' look for Sergio to portray."

Add to this portrait Isis Mussenden's regal wardrobe, which carried a Sardinian influence, and Weta's magnificent armor and weapons, and Miraz came to life, not only in his castle environment, but also on the battlefield.

Just before the climactic war between the Telmarine army and the Narnians takes place toward the end of the film, Andrew recreated Lewis's epic sword fight from the book's Chapter 15.

It turned out to be an epic scene for the filmmakers and actor Castellitto, who called the week-long shoot "one of the hardest things I've ever done in my career. We learned many things in this film, one being to duel. I'll remember that for the rest of my life, the science of dueling. It was a unique experience in my life. For

ten days it was like going to war every morning. On the set, there were three women who dressed me in warrior clothes, gave me a sword, a shield, a helmet, a face guard, and I went to war every day. It was an extraordinary experience full of unique emotions."

The sequence also proved overwhelming at times. "There were a couple of mornings where I was afraid to go on the set. Not like I was afraid physically to face the scene, but it was a very strange, very particular, and very rare tentativeness that took much motivation to go in to another duel, to go and do another battle. I was really afraid. I was afraid I would hurt myself. I was afraid I would hurt other people."

Stunt coordinator Allan Poppleton, who choreographed the thrilling sequence, also stood in for the actor during the more physical and rigorous moments in the scene due to his physical resemblance to Castellitto. The eight-day shoot, notes Poppleton, carried 115 moves, or "beats" as he calls them, a sequence he began plotting out months before, and one that required both Castellitto and William Moseley several days of rehearsal to perfect.

Sergio concluded his role in the film in late July, a full month before production wrapped on August 31. One of the wonderful rituals on a movie set comes when an actor completes his last take, signaling the end of the journey on a film. The assistant director announces his or her final curtain call to cast and crew. A hearty and heartfelt round of good-byes ushers the actor offstage.

While the crew began rigging the next shot, it allowed ample time for everyone on the set to say good-bye to this marvelous actor and gentleman whose participation in *Prince Caspian* lifted the project to another level of artistry and achievement and inspired those of us lucky enough to share the stage with this talented artist.

Miraz (seated) about to begin the epic swordfight with Peter (and surrounded by his Lords — Pierfrancesco Favino as Glozelle, Damián Alcázar as Sopespian, David Bowles as Gregoire).

PETER DINKLAGE
Trumpkin the Red Dwarf

"My favorite Narnians are the dwarfs," creature effects expert Howard Berger exclaims. "I really, really love the dwarfs, and we have two fantastic dwarf characters in this film—Trumpkin, played by Peter Dinklage, and Nikabrik, played by Warwick Davis—two great actors."

Howard notes that the fraternity of such experienced actors is not huge. And one of the names at the top of the filmmakers' list was Peter Dinklage (the only American in the film's international cast), the New Jersey native whose two-decade acting career reached a professional pinnacle in the endearing 2003 comedy-drama *The Station Agent.*

His performance won rave reviews (as did the film), earning Dinklage nominations for the Independent Spirit Award, two Screen Actors Guild Awards (as Best Actor and as part of the film's Best Ensemble Cast), and the Online Film Critics Association Award.

Since *The Station Agent* hit screens, Dinklage's other projects include the popular holiday classic *Elf*, the courtroom drama *Find Me Guilty*, the acclaimed F/X series *Nip/Tuck*, *Lassie* opposite Peter O'Toole, *Tiptoes* with Gary Oldman, and the recently completed features *Penelope* with Reese Witherspoon and James McAvoy, *Death at a Funeral* (directed by Frank Oz), *3/5 of a Man*, and *Underdog* (in which his Dr. Barsinister is the only other character he has played under a heavy makeup application).

When his name came up for the role of Trumpkin, the filmmakers contacted his manager and asked if the quiet, introspective actor would be interested in flying to Los Angeles for a meeting with director Andrew Adamson. The meeting took place sometime during the summer of 2006, he recalls.

"We talked for about an hour," Dinklage recalls—at first, not even discussing the movie. "I like to talk to the writer or director or producer, whomever I'm meeting with, just to see if we get along, really."

During the conversation, the filmmakers began showing Dinklage some of the previsualization materials, "some computer animation on what appeared to be these big battle sequences," the actor remembers. "So I sat there in this room filled with computers and watched as my likeness came up on these computer images. I had never seen anything like that before. So I was looking at some computerized I don't know what. It kind of looked like me. It still haunts me." Laughing, he adds, "It was weird, really, but I felt like I couldn't say no at that point."

While Andrew explains they used Peter's face for reference, Dinklage jokingly states he thinks Andrew was putting pressure on him. "But I loved meeting Andrew. Soon after that, I agreed to do it."

When Trumpkin was being conceived in the script, the director knew all along that Dinklage would be his first (and only) choice to play the role. "I knew when I saw *Station Agent* that I wanted to cast him. On the first film, I had thought about casting Peter as Ginnarbrik. I don't recall if it was an availability issue or what. When we met for *Caspian*, he was mildly upset with me because I hadn't contacted him about the last movie. I'm glad that did not work out, because then he would not have been able to play this role."

Once signed on, Dinklage turned to the books, which he did not read as a youth, for research. ("I was more of a *Lord of the Rings* fan," he confesses.) He found the source materials a bit thin in providing a backstory or description of the character.

As depicted by author Lewis, Trumpkin is first described in Chapter 3 ("The Dwarf") and finally identified by name in Chapter 5 ("Caspian's Adventures in the Mountains") as follows: "Like most dwarfs, he was very stocky and deep-chested. He would have been about three feet high if he had been standing up, and immense beard and whiskers of coarse red hair left little of his face to be seen except a bear-like nose and twinkling

TOP: *KNB EFX's concept sketch of Trumpkin.*
BOTTOM: *Tami Lane touches up Trumpkin's makeup.*

black eyes." Later Lewis writes, "The other dwarf was a Red Dwarf with red hair rather like a Fox's and he was called Trumpkin."

"I don't really do that backstory thing anyway," he admits. "I actually like that C. S. Lewis doesn't do it either. He sort of leaves it up to the imagination of the viewer or the actor playing the role, I suppose."

Asked to describe Trumpkin in three words, Peter says with a wink and a smile, "Playing the role, I think he's very heroic and handsome and dashing." He then turns a bit more serious, offering that "Trumpkin is curmudgeonly, but too much of that and you're not going to want to spend time with him on the journey. Let's just say that the Pevensies annoy him, and he'd rather have a glass of wine back in his tree."

"Even though it is a fantasy film, you have to base it in reality," he continues. "You are a character, a creature. Yes, I live in a tree, but I also recognize that the same emotions apply as they do to people and reality. The same human traits apply. Even though Trumpkin is not human, I have to approach him as such. It doesn't matter what sort of film you're doing. Fantasy films like this one are rooted in the reality of our day-to-day existence."

Dinklage develops his characters by turning to the story and surroundings for inspiration on how to play a role. "I just come in and see my environment and the people I'm working with and create it from there. I think if you get too bogged down in backstory with something like this, it could taint it a little bit. Gives you preconceived notions, which I don't like."

Before filming started, Dinklage had no preconceived notions as to what to expect from Howard Berger and his team on what type of makeup application would be used to transform the blue-eyed actor into this vivid Narnian creature. Howard and Tami Lane, who both earned Oscars® for the first movie, rendered him totally unrecognizable, except for those piercing eyes, "a dead giveaway," as one website reporter stated after seeing the actor on location walking his canine companion, Kevin, during a visit last August.

Beyond Lewis's scant descriptive prose, the physicalized birth of Trumpkin began when the actor visited Howard's creature warehouse in Van Nuys, California, about a month or so before filming commenced in February 2007. As with many prosthetic makeup designs, the process of bringing Trumpkin to life began with a full mold of the actor's face, which allowed Howard's artists to fabricate duplicate latex pieces that Peter wore every day he worked on the film.

It's a unique and somewhat uncomfortable process to undergo, as most actors will confess. "You're breathing through a little straw while you get wrapped in all sorts of different products," Dinklage relates. "You have your eyes closed, so you don't know what they're doing to you. It's also a bit claustrophobic, I have to say. If you have severe claustrophobia, I wouldn't advise it."

Once the design was approved by Andrew, the actor and makeup artists formed a bond closer than the latex face pieces glued to Peter's skin. They spent hours together on any given day, first at call, when Dinklage reported for work, usually three hours before much of the crew (meaning 4:30 A.M.). The makeup application process took two and a half hours.

"I've grown so close to Howard and Tami because I spent so much time with them," he says. "They're such amazing people who really love what they do. I just can't sing their praises enough. Especially Tami, who did the first movie, working with James McAvoy as Tumnus."

"Peter was a dream to work with," Tami enthuses. "He always had complete respect for what I did for him. Always said it looked great. And thanked me at the end of each day. I did everything you could do with prosthetics makeup that is totally uncomfortable in one single makeup process. Peter never complained about any of it!"

Working from a concept painting of what Howard envisioned the character to look like that hung on her trailer mirror next to her makeup chair, Tami began her daily routine by shaving Peter's head completely bald. Then she painted his head and dyed his eyebrows. She then followed by gluing the latex face pieces before tackling the more intricate hair work that turned an ordinary-looking guy into a fantastical, otherworldly creature. This process took place a total of 93 days during the 136-day shoot!

And what was Peter's reaction the first time he opened his eyes and looked into the mirror after Tami's amazing metamorphosis?

TOP: *Oksana Nedavniaya's early costume concept sketch of Trumpkin with fabric samples.*
BOTTOM: *Peter and Warwick cool off after a shot in Usti.*

"Incredible!" Peter exclaims. "You start to lose yourself. And it's really neat. A really cool experience to just be transformed like that. And Howard and Tami are just the best at what they do. I've been spoiled by them."

The actor recalls that Howard's artists at KNB EFX group made a hundred nose pieces ("which tended to

melt sometimes") and about fifty fake ears, which Tami could reuse. Once the facial appliances were completed ("very little for Trumpkin, as it's mostly hair," says Howard), "the last thing was a really long red beard and wig made of yak hair," Peter explains. He then jokingly adds, "Somewhere there's a yak on top of a mountain who's very cold. And I'm sorry. However, this being summer in Prague, it was not the coolest of makeups for me. Everyone did look out for my comfort, though."

The success of any extensive and intricate makeup application not only changes the physical appearance of the actor underneath, but, more important, "allows the actor to come forth through the makeup," Dinklage points out. "With a lot of makeups, you can lose the actor underneath them. Howard and Tami really managed to make me look completely different. But, as Trumpkin, it still allowed my expressions, my emotions, to come through. If I did my job right, working with the makeup they provided, it all works well."

"Peter brought so much life to the character," Howard chimes in. "I always say that a makeup is half successful if we do our jobs right. But the other 50 percent is the actor really pulling it off. Combined with our makeups, we achieved this. Both of these actors pulled it off 100 percent. Great makeup. Beautiful costumes by Isis. That plus the performance makes Trumpkin truly alive and believable. I've said it before. We gave Trumpkin his look. Peter gave him his heart."

In the end, after a grueling 136-day shoot, Dinklage waxes poetic and philosophic about the experience. "It was pretty incredible," he asserts. "Having that makeup on, and coming into a world like this, really helps you. It really clicks your imagination. It was pretty impressive, I have to say, what these people have done. Actually amazing."

Just like Peter's performance.

WARWICK DAVIS
Nikabrik the Black Dwarf

Warwick Davis is a funny little guy.

The operative word there for the three feet six talent is *funny!*

We'll explain in a moment.

You may recognize Davis from his lengthy list of genre projects and roles, which have taken the veteran actor from his roots in Surrey, England, to galaxies far, far away; to the magical world of J. K. Rowling's Hogwarts; even (before this film) to C. S. Lewis's fantastical land of Narnia in a career spanning over two decades.

His film credits read like a greatest-hits list of Hollywood's finest genre efforts for the current generation of moviegoers. They include *Star Wars — Episode VI: Return of the Jedi* (he played the key Ewok of Wicket) and *Star Wars — Episode I: The Phantom Menace*; all five of the *Harry Potter* movies (in which he has portrayed a gallery of diverse characters); *Leprechaun* (the villainous title role in all five of this cult-classic horror franchise); the BBC's 1989 Narnian adventure *Prince Caspian and the Voyage of the Dawn Treader* (as the swashbuckling mouse, Reepicheep, a character he now shares screen time with here); and the title role (written especially for him) of the Ron Howard — George Lucas fantasy adventure, *Willow*.

You may also *not* recognize Davis from the very same list of big-screen achievements. Why? Simply because he rarely appears as himself but is usually hidden beneath layers of special prosthetic makeup to create everything from a leprechaun to a rodent; from a genie to an Ewok. You *can* see the talented actor as himself, sans makeup, in the supporting role of the dapper jazz club impresario in Taylor Hackford's Oscar®-winning *Ray*.

For those familiar with his career (and his actual look), you'll see not a recognizable feature of his face (save for those expressive baby blues) as the aged dwarf who may or may not be an ally to Caspian and the Narnians in *Prince Caspian*, thanks again to the masterful designs of Howard Berger and the careful, attentive makeup application performed more than fifty times during the shoot by Berger's tireless colleague, Sarah Rubano. A three-hour process (begun many days as early as 4 A.M.) that called for laughs to not only ease the monotonous rigors of the session, but also help awaken Sarah and Howard at such an ungodly hour!

Anticipating Warwick's predawn arrival, Howard always had a gag planned, many of which poked fun at the characters Warwick played in past films. "I always had something happening," Howard explains. "One time, I put the Ewok music on because Warwick played Wicket the Ewok in *Return of the Jedi*. He came in, we blasted the music loud, and he started laughing and laughing."

"Howard Berger constantly reminded me that he was an Oscar®-winning makeup artist," a yawning Davis counters. "I was under the hands of an Oscar®-winner. Blah blah blah. He has a great, great sense of humor. Very caring and kind. Seriously, he made my experience on the movie greater, lifted it 100 percent. Brilliant at his job. But how many times do I need to hear about the Oscar®?" Unfortunately, we cannot print Howard's reaction.

Andrew also liked Warwick's self-deprecating sense of humor, which constantly poked fun at his own size — sometimes at the expense of the person the actor addressed. "Warwick was very funny about his height, which always made people laugh . . . and maybe cringe a bit as well," the grinning director observes. "The one thing I found absolutely hilarious was when people leaned down to talk to him. He would stoop lower himself. In a way, he made people laugh *and* uncomfortable about his situation at the same time."

Davis says he wouldn't argue with people about the fact that he's been short since the day he was born. "I suppose human nature adapts to its situations," he says. He chooses humor to face all the challenges life offers, especially to someone his size. He also confirms he is the first to see the humorous side of a situation in light of his physical stature.

ABOVE: *KNB EFX's concept sketch of Nikabrik.* RIGHT: *Oksana Nedavniaya's early costume concept sketch of Nikabrik with fabric samples.*

"For instance, automatic doors, those with the infrared sensors above them that never seem to sense me," he notes with both a serious and humorous twinkle in his eye. "I can actually walk up to a bank or hospital, and the doors won't open. While you step back and do this ridiculous 'door dance' to get the doors to open, you've now attracted the attention of people inside the building, who stare and wonder what reaction *they* should have to all this. That makes me laugh, and I hope they would also see the funny side of the situation and laugh along with it."

Ben Barnes was among the cast and crew endeared to Davis and his upbeat personality. "Ben Barnes and I supposedly had this relationship where I made fun of

him," Davis says about their highjinks on-set. "I just felt it was my job to initiate him into the world of film." If there was a magnanimous reason to poke fun at the big screen rookie, Davis says, "it was to make sure that Ben's head did not get too big. That he did not get too big for his boots. And he wore huge boots!"

"Yes, I constantly reminded Warwick that the film was called *Prince Caspian*," Barnes chimes in. "It was not called *Nikabrik*." Davis counters, "And I constantly reminded him that he needed my character's image on the poster to give it some weight. The poster needed established actors like myself. Otherwise, audiences would stare at someone they didn't recognize and not see the movie."

All kidding aside, Warwick is also a complete and dedicated professional who took his role very seriously. At only thirty-eight years old, his spirit is that of a precocious youngster. Yet because of his successful longevity in the business (some twenty-five years and counting), many are surprised he's as young as he is.

He approached the role of Nikabrik, one he acutely coveted playing, by turning to the source material, Lewis's book, with which he was familiar from his childhood in England.

"I was familiar with the books as a child," Davis recounts, "but had an extra familiarity with the material because I worked on the BBC production of *Prince Caspian and the Voyage of the Dawn Treader*, in which I played Reepicheep the Mouse. I then went on to play Glimfeather the Owl in *The Silver Chair*. Being familiar with the written word and the TV series, I had a good background in Narnia."

In describing the character of Nikabrik, the key phrase for Davis is found in the book: "Nikabrik goes sour inside," the actor paraphrases from Chapter 5 ("Caspian's Adventure in the Mountains"). "That was perfect for me to help pivot the character on. Just that one expression."

Davis then fleshed out the role by using all of the physical traits provided by several collaborators who contributed so much to give birth to the character. "Of course, Howard's makeup helped loads. Then you find the character's voice. Then Isis's costume, which was such an immaculate piece of workmanship. While the detail may not come across for audiences, subliminally, it's all there. As an actor, it makes you feel so at home in the character. I lived, worked, and fought in those clothes. You are then placed in the surroundings, the sets, and magically, you are in Narnia."

Warwick's first test makeup application lasted somewhere between three and four hours on the very first day of production in Auckland back on February 12, 2007. The veteran, who had undergone similar time-consuming applications on many other projects, was still excited by the process because "you see it before your very eyes."

He was particularly fascinated by a clever illustration of the character done by one of Howard's associates at KNB, John Wheaton. "It was brilliant because it was me, but as an old man. It was my photograph over which he painted the character concept. It captured Nikabrik perfectly."

When Warwick looked in the mirror after the marathon session, "what I saw was the character in three dimensions that Howard's artist had portrayed in two dimensions," the actor notes. "An astounding thing to do. I was also thrilled that I was able to perform through the makeup."

Just like co-star Peter Dinklage, who played another prosthetically enhanced character, Trumpkin, Davis recognized the significance of bringing forth the character expressively through layers of artificial skin and hair.

"The true brilliance of a makeup artist is to create a makeup that allows the actor to perform underneath it," Davis notes, echoing co-star Dinklage's thoughts. "And to give a realistic performance at that."

While Howard may have been the architect of Nikabrik's design, colleague Rubano served as its builder. "She was responsible for applying and maintaining my makeup every day on this film," Davis says. He has high acclaim for the artist, who did her very first professional makeup applications on *The Lion, the Witch and the Wardrobe* under Berger's tutelage. "I spent over 150 hours in the chair with Sarah painting, gluing, creating my look for the film."

Rubano began the lengthy, four-stage, three-hour application by "glueing down the gelatin face and gelatin ears, then blending the edges into Warwick's own skin, which consumed the first hour." Next came the painting of the gelatin pieces to match his skin tone, which took another forty-five minutes. The next thirty minutes brought facial scars, scrapes, and dirt to the face and fingers. Sarah also coated his lips with a product called Gafquat for a chapped effect. The time-consuming process ended with the hair work—wig, eyebrows, mustache, and beard application. "I'd also lay human hair over the lace to soften and break up the beard line," she adds.

"When I work like this on a film, where I have a makeup application, it is a team effort," Davis says. "It's about the makeup department and me. A fifty-fifty team effort. And so when I walk on a set and perform, I'm holding the banner for them. I'm their canvas, basically."

When Warwick finally wrapped on the film in early August, some six months after first giving birth to one of the film's most memorable characters, he sang the praises once again for both his collaborators.

"Without people like Sarah and Howard, and there are few particularly gifted makeup artists in this world, I wouldn't be able to do what I do," he affirms. "Because I look like me, I am only suitable for a certain number of roles. But with Howard's genius, I can look like an old man, with a beard and long hair, and play a character like Nikabrik. So, my thanks to him and Sarah as well. And the audience should also be grateful to them because they get to watch me play someone I'm not due to the talents of people like Howard and Sarah."

There was one rare occasion to catch up with Warwick, out of his Nikabrik guise, on New Zealand's South Island. (You *could* always catch him as himself if you cared to visit the makeup trailer at 4:00 A.M.!) It was at a place called Paradise (appropriately named) where, twenty years ago, as a tender seventeen-year-old, he created another memorable screen character called Willow in the film of the same name. It was in the very same spot we were now working in mid-March.

Warwick came out to the location from his Queenstown hotel to revisit a special place—not only in his career, but in his heart as well. Surrounded by some of the planet's most spectacular scenery, he bathed in the memories of a teenage actor who traveled thousands of miles from Surrey, England, to this majestic landscape, working alongside his mentor at the time, filmmaker George Lucas, who crafted the character especially for Davis.

But the memory was not enough for the performer, whose talent might be bigger than all outdoors. Memories sometimes require a tangible memento. He asked the company's still photographer, Phil Bray, to snap a photo of him on the exact spot where he stood as the valiant movie hero some two decades before (which you can see on this page).

No makeup. No costume. Just a lovely guy who made us laugh behind the scenes while thrilling us with his performance in front of the cameras.

Thanks, Warwick.

THE EXTRAS

In January 2007, a month before filming would commence, a casting call was issued in the Usti area for locals interested in working as "extras," those nameless, uncredited roles that populate movie backgrounds. The production needed two to three hundred men to play the Telmarine army under King Miraz's command as well as assorted Narnian creatures such as centaurs, Minotaurs, satyrs, and fauns, most of whom would appear in the epic battle sequence filmed in Usti.

The filmmakers called veteran military adviser Billy Budd (*Kingdom of Heaven*, *Alexander*, HBO's *Rome*) to duty to train the hundreds of Czech locals, many of whom were unemployed and none of whom had ever appeared in a movie before, an unthinkable idea for sure. The salty-tongued, sandy-haired Brit, who spent fifteen years in the English marines, proudly claims that this group of Ustians, if you will, acquitted themselves before the cameras beyond compare under his rigorous command.

THE SUPPORTING CHARACTERS

Damián Alcázar as Lord Sopespian.

Pierfrancesco Favino as General Glozelle.

We would be remiss in not mentioning some of the other new characters (all appear in Lewis's novel) that were portrayed in the film, along with the actors who masterfully brought them to life.

As Andrew observes, "By choosing an international cast, we got to pick some of the top actors from all these different countries. Like Sergio [Castellitto], who's huge in Italy. Also, Pierfrancesco Favino, whom we called 'Little Sergio,' an astounding actor who went very deep into his role. And, Damián Alcázar as well."

"Some of my favorite scenes to shoot were these tiny moments with all three of these guys," the filmmaker continues, his tone tinged with pure fascination and awe. "There were moments when their characters would not say anything, and in the 'not saying anything,' you saw how lethal they were. Really remarkable . . . Vincent Grass as well. So phenomenal and believable in his role."

In addition to the aforementioned Castellitto, Italy delivered another talented, contemporary actor to the cast in Pierfrancesco Favino, who played the key role of General Glozelle, the leader of Miraz's army. Favino, hugely popular in his native country, recently expanded his profile internationally when he played Christopher Columbus in the hit comedy *Night at the Museum*.

Fluent in four languages (his native tongue, plus French, English, and Spanish), Favino has a soulfulness and stillness about him. Not to mention rugged good looks that define the stately Italian as a movie star. Pure and simple.

He calls his character "a professional soldier. In the book, more than in the movie, he's a bad guy. What Andrew and I tried to do was to give Glozelle a conscience, which makes him richer and more interesting." They also had to give the character a look, something lacking in the book because Glozelle is not developed much, if at all, in Lewis's prose (he pops up for the very first time in Chapter 14, "How All Were Very Busy," in the heroic pose of "picking (his) teeth after breakfast").

After learning that Andrew chose Mediterranean pirates as his influence for the Telmarine culture, "I started to think about Spanish painters as inspiration for Glozelle's look," Favino chimes in. "Like Velasquez and El Greco, a great one that worked in Spain in the sixteenth century. I know he also influenced the costumes and the sets. So we had the curled mustache, like in paintings from the era. I also thought of a gothic look that could be threatening, as well as references to the gypsy culture."

We should also mention that Favino and fellow Italian actor Castellitto have acted together in three film projects notable for one curious coincidence—Sergio slaps Pierfrancesco across the face in each movie!

"Yes, it's true," he confirms with a smile about the man he calls a mentor. "This is our third movie together and in all of them, the character he was playing happens to slap me. When we read the screenplay for this, we couldn't believe it would happen again. If there's an arc in my career, there will be a time when I slap him. That would mean that I've grown up."

Veteran actor Vincent Grass grew up in Belgium, but now considers himself a Frenchman, having resided in Paris for almost thirty of his fifty-nine years. While he maintains a busy profile in front of the movie and TV cameras in his adopted homeland (most recognize him, he says, by his baggy, expressive eyes), he is also well known in the French entertainment industry for his voiceover work in films.

In finding the inspiration to portray the wise sage and tutor, Doctor Cornelius, the stout Grass, of course turned to the book.

He calls Cornelius "a second father to Caspian. I think Cornelius is more Caspian's father than Miraz, who sort of pretends to be. So he treats him like a son. Teaches him everything. He's a tutor, but also a little bit of a magician. And he knows what Caspian's destiny is. And when he sends him to the woods, he knows that he's going to come back as a king."

Vincent Grass as Doctor Cornelius.

Cornell S. John as Glenstorm.

Alicia Borrachero as Queen Pruniprismia.

Shane Rangi (right) with Skandar Keynes.

The English musical theater star Cornell S. John once played a king—King Mufasa—in the *Lion King* in the show's debut in London's West End in 1999. In *Prince Caspian*, Andrew cast this commanding talent as Glenstorm, the powerful Afro-Narnian centaur who aides the Telmarine prince and the Pevensies in their fight against Miraz.

Like actors Dinklage and Davis, John also endured a lengthy seventy-five-minute makeup process that transformed the actor into one of mythology's quintessential creatures, the centaur—half-man/half-horse. Latex face appliances combined with the new fashion rage—green screen tights (over which VFX magician Dean Wright will superimpose the body and legs of a horse)—turned the soft-spoken but confident actor into one of the film's most imposing creations.

"I'm 160 percent Mike Fields, the guy who did my makeup," John states, praising his colleague. "His dedication was just amazing. Every day he did something different and tweaked it, inspiring me and making me earn the right to wear the face. In the beginning, I had no idea what I should look like, but after talking with the designers (my contribution was the hair), the look finally came together. I was hoping for something that expressed honor, pride, and tradition. Because centaurs can live for hundreds of years, there's no age limit on this. I put myself at 170 Earth years. Like I said earlier, I had to earn the right. This face is Glenstorm. It's a face of time. A face of honor. A face of dignity."

As for what the English native (by way of Birmingham) expects when he sees that face on-screen for the first time, John candidly states, "I haven't got a clue what's going to happen when I see it for the first time. And I like that. I never watched any of the video playbacks during filming. I just lived the character. So when I sit down in the cinema house for the first time, I could be shocked. I could be surprised. I could be sad. I could be happy. I don't know. Anyway, it will be an event."

Andrew rounded out his multilingual cast with several Spanish-speaking talents—most notably, the great Mexican star Damián Alcázar, who, the director notes, gave a "powerful breakout performance" as the conniving Lord Sopespian. Also filling the screen are the popular Madrid-born star Alicia Borrachero as Miraz's protective wife, Queen Prunaprismia, and another Spanish native, Simon Andreu, who plays one of Miraz's council members, Lord Scythely.

And let's not forget one of the hardest-working men in show business, the muscular, versatile Kiwi Shane Rangi, who convincingly played a bear, a Wer-wolf, and the courageous Minotaur Asterius beneath Howard Berger's lifelike suits.

Add in the actors who represent the United Kingdom (Ben Barnes, Warwick Davis) and the United States (Peter Dinklage), and the *Prince Caspian* cast truly spans the entire globe.

A Day in the Life
March 14 (Day 22)
Queenstown, New Zealand

Paradise becomes a wonderland—a winter wonderland (in late summer, I remind you)—as a morning snowfall dusts base camp. The company's second unit (the crew charged with completing unfinished scenes or staging stunt-oriented action) is scheduled to begin the first of eight shooting days while the main unit heads to Queenstown Airport to board a charter flight back to Auckland. From there, it's back to Henderson, where filming will end in a few days on two new sets designed by Roger Ford: Trufflehunter's Den and the Treasure Chamber.

While the second unit, under the direction of Kiwi veteran John Mahaffie, who will mount scenes with key cast Ben Barnes as Caspian and Pierfrancesco Favino as Glozelle, waits out the snowfall, the first-unit crew finds out early this Wednesday morning that the Queenstown airport is closed, not because snow is now falling at sea level, but because precipitation has cast a dense fog over most of this popular resort village, grounding all outgoing and incoming flights.

Like the young heroes in the story, Kiwi production manager Tim Coddington rides in to rescue the potentially stranded crew, which is expected back in Auckland around 1:30 P.M. to begin filming by late afternoon (a scenario quickly terminated).

The veteran moviemaker quickly contacts the airline, which reroutes the jet to Dunedin on the South Island's

UPM Tim Coddington.

east coast, south of Christchurch and some 186 miles from Queenstown. Now Coddington must figure out how to get his crew (some 150-plus folks, including Andrew, the producers, and cast members Georgie Henley and Anna Popplewell) across the South Island to Dunedin, a village steeped in Scottish lore. The airline company tries to arrange three buses, but it is Kay Taylor, one of Reg Gibson's transportation coordinators, who quickly locates a pair of 44-seaters that can race across Motorway 8A to Dunedin to make the charter, now scheduled to depart at 3:00 P.M.

Location moves such as this are like school field trips. Everyone is told where and what time to report, and a master log of names (prepared by the production office coordinators) is checked by the company chaperone, here second assistant director Jeff "O" Okabayashi, ensuring no one misses the bus and flight. The itinerary includes a fifteen-minute potty break in a rustic village called Roxburgh (about halfway to Dunedin), where the crew visits the public restrooms and loads up on snacks at the local dairy café, a Kiwi version of 7-Eleven.

Once in Henderson, the company dines on a catered meal originally prepared for the scheduled shoot day. They also attend to their own luggage outside the soundstages like immigrants trying to locate their bags upon arriving at Ellis Island at the turn of the twentieth century.

"As company moves go, this one was something else," Coddington admits as he chows down on his well-earned roast lamb dinner.

THE VISUALISTS

Creating the Look of Narnia

ROGER FORD
Production Designer

Roger Ford is an unlikely empire builder. The soft-spoken Aussie production designer probably wouldn't even yell if he hit his thumb with a hammer, and yet he created from scratch an entire culture—cities, castles, bridges, villages, and caves.

Mild-mannered as he may be, however, he does not take his responsibility lightly. And as complex and imposing as some of his designs may be, his starting point, both for *Prince Caspian* and *The Lion, the Witch and the Wardrobe*, is a familiar one.

"The imagery in these books is provided by the child's imagination, which is part of the magic of the book. I've said this before. With a children's film, the child's imagination will take them much further

Roger Ford with Narnians on the castle set.

than the book illustrations. Even Andrew said he remembers Narnia as being a certain way in his mind from having read the books as a child."

For *Prince Caspian*, how did Roger approach the sobering responsibility that prospective audiences for the books now had yet another visual reference of Narnia before tackling the texts?

"We now have the films, a visual starting point for these young readers," he said as he began his second journey through that make-believe world. "It's not imagination anymore. You're sitting looking at pictures. And it's my responsibility to take the film further than a child's imagination, so that the element of wonder and surprise is still there for them when they watch the movie. It's a big responsibility because a child's imagination is a wonderful thing. We had to try to do better the second time around, so that when the children who've read the book and seen the illustrations go see this movie, they'll be reinspired — so that it's even better than they thought possible. Time will tell if we succeeded."

Ford calls the first project, which consumed over two years of his life, a dream job for a movie production designer. With that film, Ford's realization of Lewis's words mesmerized and inspired.

Roger is what you might call a quiet genius. The forty-year industry veteran began his career with the BBC back in the 1960s as an art director on the cult series *Dr. Who*, and his designs on the first Narnia film established the look and iconography of the world.

After completing his work on the first movie in early 2005, he purposely took a well-deserved ten-month hiatus before journeying back to Lewis's imaginary world in October of that same year. His first order of business was defining the origins of the film's antagonists, the Telmarines. His inspiration was the Bard himself—and maybe a bit of Robert Louis Stevenson.

"This is a much darker film, more Shakespearean in many ways," Ford suggests. "Miraz, the uncle, kills his own brother, the father of Prince Caspian. He then wants to kill Caspian so his own son can ascend to the throne. It could be Shakespeare."

As he began to ruminate about the look of *Prince Caspian* in the early stages of the project, Roger assembled the beginnings of what would become his art department. He began with a half dozen concept artists who envisioned the look of the film through sketches and illustrations, all of which ultimately adorned the walls of Roger's office like a makeshift art gallery. "The

Production designer Roger Ford.

story of the entire film could be seen around that room at Barrandov [Studio]," he notes.

Once director Adamson endorsed the direction Roger's team wanted to take, he then recruited his entire team, "which began work on construction drawings, set design, bringing the film to life. A huge team of construction people—carpenters and painters. So it grows from a small group of concept people into a very big art department and construction workshop."

As Roger began preparations for what became another labor of love (he calls his four years in Narnia "brilliant . . . a career highlight"), he and Andrew charted a history for "these pirates that were shipwrecked on an island and found themselves in a cave that turned out to be a portal into Telmar, a different part of Narnia than the first story."

As the motif of a pirate culture began to take shape, the longtime film designer next looked at what ancestry to accord such an oppressive society. He sought a distinct contrast to the four Pevensies. "We wanted Prince Caspian, who is a Telmarine, to somehow be different than these English children," he notes.

"I said to Andrew, 'Why don't we make them French?'" he adds, alluding to the historic rivalry that's existed between these two European societies. "There's always been stuff between the English and the French. But Andrew wanted to go further, imagining the Telmarines as Spaniards from the Iberian Peninsula, which kind of fit better with the pirate theme."

The best way to illustrate Roger's unparalleled work in the second film is to go back to the book, like he himself does when he begins his architectural blueprints, citing the scant descriptive phrases from Lewis's prose alongside concept art and photos of the final set designs. The art is described by Roger and his key colleagues, as they recall the inspiration that guided these amazing designs, which represent a vastly different Narnia.

THE LONDON SUBWAY STATION

And now all four of them were sitting at a railway station. . . . They were, in fact, on their way back to school. They had traveled together as far as this station, which was a junction . . . an empty, sleepy country station. (Chapter 1, "The Island")

In the first movie, the story begins with the Pevensie quartet being whisked out of London on a train at Paddington Station to avoid the blitzkrieg unleashed on the city by the Germans. While the second book begins at another rural rail station, as noted in Lewis's text, Ford relocated the introduction of the Pevensies, now

a year older, to a London tube station in the heart of that world-class city because, he says, "The underground station seemed to be visually more interesting. We'd already been on a station platform in the first film, and it was Andrew's idea to situate the opening of this film with a completely different look."

Built on Stage 4 at Henderson Studios in Auckland, the authentic set that hosted the crew for the first three days of filming included a subway platform and two hundred feet of wooden track on which sat fabricated train cars. The cars actually moved along the rails with the aid of hydraulic motors added by special effects coordinator Jason Durey.

Aided by a talented art department (headed by Kiwi senior art director Jules Cook) and construction crew, the tube station may not have smelled like the real thing (no bouquet of damp overcoats), but it sure looked like a central London subway stop. The signs indicated that this was the Strand, near Trafalgar Square.

The subway platform setting turned out to be an inspired choice based on the location Andrew found on the Coromandel Peninsula, which brings the children from this tube stop in World War II London back to Narnia, albeit to a different part of the fantastical world that they do not immediately recognize.

"In New Zealand, we found this beautiful beach called Cathedral Cove where the children emerge in Narnia," Ford notes. "It has an arched cave through a cliff and goes from one beach to another beach through this tunnel. It made for this great transition where they're in the underground tunnel, and gradually they go through this rock tunnel on the beach in New Zealand. It had the same sort of scale as a tube station tunnel. So the idea that the transition took place from one tunnel to another tunnel was quite easy to realize. And it worked really well."

THE ANCIENT RUINS OF CAIR PARAVEL

"This wasn't a garden," said Susan presently. "It was a castle and this must have been the courtyard." While they were talking they had crossed the courtyard and gone through the other doorway into what had once been the hall. We could pretend we were in Cair Paravel now. (Chapter 2, "The Ancient Treasure House")

Roger notes that the ruins of Cair Paravel are one of two sets in the new story adapted from designs he created for *The Lion, the Witch and the Wardrobe*. "It is the same set, but we don't know it is when we first see it. The children make their way up this bluff and eventually

discover that it is, in fact, Cair Paravel, the castle of the Narnians in the first film. So we had to exactly recreate the Great Hall of Cair Paravel as a ruin on a location on the headland. We made it a subtle ruin. The kids don't quite figure it out until they stand where the thrones used to be. They look down and see the columns. So that carried on through from the last movie."

Consisting of huge blocks of carved Styrofoam and adorned by Russell Hoffman's greens crew with vines, roses, tall grass, and apple trees, the place looks and feels like an otherworldly ruin, completely convincing until one spies the wooden supports propping it up!

The set required two months' work for a mere two days of filming. That may seem excessive, but Ford notes that "it was important to portray this set piece properly, as it served as the bridge from the first film to this one."

THE TREASURE CHAMBER

The castle ruins also included the door that leads the Pevensies down to the hidden Treasure Chamber (a set also built at Henderson Studios), which was inspired by the following passage from Lewis's second chapter, "The Ancient Treasure Chamber":

For all they knew it was indeed the ancient treasure chamber of Cair Paravel, where they had once reigned as Kings and Queens of Narnia. There was a kind of path up the middle (as it might be in a greenhouse), and along each side at intervals stood rich suits of armor, like knights guarding the treasures. In between the suits of armor, on each side of the path, were shelves covered with precious things—necklaces and arm rings and finger rings and golden bowls and dishes and long tusks of ivory, brooches and coronets and chains of gold, and heaps of unset stones lying piled anyhow as if they were marbles or potatoes—diamonds, rubies, carbuncles, emeralds, topazes, and amethysts.

While Ford's set, a two-story decaying subterranean cavern, was indeed spectacular, it came to sparkling life through his collaboration with longtime set decorator Kerrie Brown, the Aussie native and industry veteran with whom Roger has worked for over fifteen years now. The pair have a shorthand in their ongoing association. As Brown muses, "We're a bit like yin and yang. The two of us are a good balance together. Our association is telepathic. We almost don't even have to talk to each other anymore."

While Brown admits to reading the books for her inspiration, she did copious amounts of research to decorate Ford's magnificent set designs. She visited several different museums in London and Paris and took lots of photographs of treasures that had been presented to the nobility of various countries and cultures. "We wanted to make the room feel like that," she says, "to show that Peter and Susan and Lucy, when they were kings and queens in Narnia, had been presented with gifts from people from different lands."

She next scoured prop stores in Australia and New Zealand to see whether such items like chalices, urns, armor, and such could be rented, "but there wasn't enough to fill up this huge room." She supplemented what she could rent with over two thousand props that were designed, molded, and sculpted by her prop department. Roland Stevenson, its supervisor, notes that his busy department, thirty-five strong working around the clock, manufactured between seven and eight thousand prop pieces for the entire film.

Brown says, "We made everything in Prague, at Barrandov, then shipped it to New Zealand because we simply couldn't get the volume out of prop stores and couldn't get the look that I wanted as well. We also had a very competent prop-making department in the Czech Republic."

The finished set, which glistened before the cameras for just one day's filming, radiated from the bevy of gold treasures strewn throughout.

TRUFFLEHUNTER'S DEN

The other key set erected in Henderson's tin-shed studios was that of Trufflehunter's Den, the haven for the loyal badger who accompanies Caspian, the four children, and Trumpkin on their journey to liberate Narnia from Miraz's tyrannical hold.

Lewis's very brief description of the setting in the fifth chapter, entitled "Caspian's Adventure in the Mountains" (*"on a bed of heather in a cave"*), inspired Andrew to take a still photo camera, mount it on a pole, and photograph an actual badger's den inside the hollow of an oak tree.

What he found, says designer Ford, was that "families of badgers can live in the same setting for hundreds of years." Those photos influenced Ford's set design, which structurally simulated that of the Beaver's Lodge in the first movie and Brown's set dressing, which added a touch of verisimilitude to Lewis's imaginary world.

Like the Beaver's Lodge (an octagonal structure built on wheels so pieces of the set could be dismantled to allow intricate camera angles), everything in Trufflehunter's Den was designed for the scale of the badger and manufactured by Brown's crafty props department. "We decided that Trufflehunter's furniture would have belonged to his great, great, great grandparents—really nice carved pieces in their day," explains Brown.

"Once the Narnians fell on hard times, the pieces had crumbled and fallen to bits," she continues. "They then found bits of sticks and logs and whatnot from the forest and cobbled them together. I think his bed was a great image of that. It had a branch on one end, and then it's got this lovely kind of Spanish-looking carved headboard at the other half. Our designs sort of developed from there, using bits from the forest but also his old family furniture."

"This set was great fun to dress," Brown adds. Andrew spent a single day filming the adorable set piece.

DOCTOR CORNELIUS'S STUDY

Cosmography . . . History . . . Physics . . . Alchemy . . . Astronomy . . . Navigation (Chapter 5, "Caspian's Adventure in the Mountains")

Those six descriptive nouns (and the brilliant touches brought to the chamber by dresser Kerrie Brown) helped Roger shape the look of Doctor Cornelius's castle room, which he admits was his favorite set of the thirty-odd designs he created for the film. He fondly calls it "a delightful space."

Cornelius's study may have had its roots in a twelfth-century Romanesque crypt outside Prague, which Ford says "could be Cornelius's room. It had all these lovely columns and arches. It felt right for him. It felt mysterious, with spaces there that went off into darkness. Absolutely right for that character."

The crypt's design proved unwieldy for a film shoot, so Roger borrowed its look, especially its distinctive columns, to fashion the room onstage at Modrany Studios in Prague. His architectural pattern was then embellished by set decorator Brown and her team, who added props and furniture (all rented) to make the set look, as Roger notes, "a bit like Professor Kirke's study in the first film."

For Brown, Cornelius's room "was quite different from the other rooms in the Telmarine castle. We looked at him as kind of a Leonardo da Vinci–type character in that he studied astronomy. He was an alchemist and a teacher for Caspian."

Audiences may not be aware of the detail for a set piece that required just a half-day of filming, but if you had the chance to walk around such a set, Roger notes that "you would be amazed at how relevant the stuff is to that character, to fleshing out the character. You get the right sense of this person. It's not just another room full of astronomical equipment, books, and so on. It's something that, as in all design for film, tells you much about the character."

The Dancing Lawn

The place where they had met the Fauns was, of course, Dancing Lawn itself, and here Caspian and his friends remained till the night of the Great Council. (Chapter 7, "Old Danger in Narnia")

Once again, Roger Ford had the opportunity to create a forest inside a soundstage!

While much smaller than Lantern Waste from *The Lion, the Witch and the Wardrobe*, the Dancing Lawn setting mesmerized those who visited the idyllic woodsy thicket built inside Barrandov's Max Studio 8.

Dancing Lawn is a place deep in the forest, "so deep

that the Telmarines have never found it," designer Ford explains. "In the book, it's a place where the Fauns and other Narnian creatures go to dance in the night. In the film, Andrew changed its purpose to something more dramatic—a place where the Narnians gather for the meeting about how to aid Caspian in his plight against the evil rule of Miraz."

Director Adamson and scout James Crowley note that many of the sites chosen for the film were dictated by the motif of ancient, old-growth forests, be it the unspoiled, uncultivated landscape of New Zealand or the rock-strewn sites found in Poland and the Czech Republic.

Yet the filmmakers elected to grow their own forest inside a building in Prague. Roger Ford explains. "We seriously looked at locations for this set, especially a place in Poland surrounded by rocks called Green Gorge," the designer recalls. "Upon finding that, we understood the look that Andrew wanted. Unfortunately, there were one too many trees in the wrong place. In situations like that, you then have to adapt the scene to the location, rather than the set to the scene."

The Polish location was in a national park (just like the settings finally chosen for filming) where permission would have been denied to actually fell any trees that would have spoiled the look of the set. Roger had the perfect solution—filling a studio soundstage with rocks and a little waterfall amidst seven giant oak trees hand-carved by his art department from Styrofoam and wood and dozens of real fir trees. It was like a greenhouse, complete with an artificial watering system to keep the foliage alive until Andrew filmed the set in mid-June.

Set decorator Brown added her own touch of magic and whimsy to the setting. She explains, "We imagined that the Narnians had brought little lanterns and put them around in the trees. So the whole place started to take on a sort of magic that it should have. That was something that we might not have been able to achieve on location. It all added a bit of atmosphere in a studio environment that's completely controllable. In the end, we got exactly what we wanted. It looked magical."

ASLAN'S HOW

*But in the secret and magical chamber at the heart
of the How, King Caspian, with Cornelius and the
Badger and Nikabrik and Trumpkin, were at council.
Thick pillars of ancient workmanship supported the
roof. In the center was the Stone itself—a stone table,
split right down the center, and covered with what
had once been writing of some kind: but ages of wind
and rain and snow had almost worn them away in
old times when the Stone Table had stood at the
hilltop, and the Mound had not yet been built above
it . . . This . . . is the most ancient and deeply magical
of all. (Chapter 7, "Old Danger in Narnia")*

Aslan's How is the cryptic name for a huge earth
mound that the Narnians have built to cover up
the original Stone Table where the lion king was slain in
The Lion, the Witch and the Wardrobe. The Narnians have
enshrined the Stone Table, considered a sacred site, now
split in two, to protect and keep it secret.

When recreating this set from the first movie (originally built in a helicopter hangar at the Hobsonville
Airbase in West Auckland), Ford and his set designers
"reproduced it from the same drawings," he says. "The
Stone Table itself is the same one. We brought it all the
way over from New Zealand to Prague after retrieving it
out of Disney's warehouse. Then we drew up plans for
this cavelike interior of the How to see where the action
in this set would occur in the film."

Circular in design, the How also contained a series
of detailed plaster carvings (done by a staff of four
plasterers under the supervision of a young and gifted
English artist named Jonathan Moore) that illustrate the
history of the Narnians over the past thirteen hundred
years. Ford likens these carvings to "a guardian watching
over the Stone Table. They consume the entire circumference of the room and came from ideas we discussed
with Andrew."

"The How was such an important storytelling piece

because of the Stone Table," echoes supervising art
director Frank Walsh. "It was a reflection from the
last film. But we had to develop and tell the story of
what happened in between the two films, those missing
hundreds of years. These carved stone panels were all
very important images."

Once the concepts were approved by Andrew, each
individual part of the eight panels was hand-cast in
plaster, affixed into the walls, then painted to look like
stone. The central carving features Aslan and dominates
the How as it hangs over a stone proscenium that Roger
calls "the Great Arch."

To enhance the drama and majesty of the set, Andrew
came up with the fantastic idea, Roger recalls, "that
there's a channel or trough around the How directly
beneath the wall carvings. It is a well of oil that Caspian
lights with a torch. Flames then travel around the room,
lighting up the panels."

"You cannot use real oil or burning liquid because
it's hard to control," mechanical effects supervisor and
designer Gerd Feuchter notes about the challenge of
creating the desired fire effect for the underground How
set. "So we had to create a special propane burner, which
we then placed underneath a level of colored water."

Feuchter, whose company, Die Nefzers GmbH, is
based near Stuttgart, Germany, took three weeks to
design and build the fiery trough that covered virtually
the entire circumference of this set.

On catwalks high above the actual set, one of Gerd's
technicians operated the control panel that ignited all
or some of the twenty-nine valves that allowed the flow
of propane into the set. The infrastructure was a series
of hoses "like those garden hoses that emit a mist in
tiny holes punctured into the length of the hose," he
explains.

The hoses sat underwater in the circular trough,
which baffled set visitors who had no idea that propane
could burn underwater. When any or all of the length
of the submerged hose had to be ignited for a scene,
Gerd radioed the instructions to a colleague high above

FILMING THE FIGHT

The eight-day sequence featured an array of different camera toys chosen by Andrew, cinematographer Lindenlaub, and camera operator Lundsgaard to shoot the mortal fight. These included the ubiquitous Techno-cranes (two different machines, one with a thirty-foot reach, the other with a fifty-foot arm) that key grip Brian Bouma's crew assembled almost daily; Lundsgaard's nifty Steadicam, one of the industry's finest inventions; and a Chapman dolly sitting on a 360-degree circular track that added wonderful effect to the entire sequence.

The execution of the 360-degree dolly shots required the entire crew to either leave the location or burrow themselves into the surrounding grass below the level of the battle ring set, where infectious ticks make their home (and burrowed into the legs of several crew members during the month-long stay, sometimes requiring medical attention).

During the extended sword fight sequence, Lindenlaub and his crew were inspired and inventive in their use of an Arriflex 235 camera, the smallest of Arri's line of film equipment. When stunt coordinator Allan Poppleton doubled for actor Sergio Castellitto during the grueling shoot, the wiry daredevil donned cameraman Lundsgaard's Steadicam arm on which they attached the little Arri camera.

That, in turn, was mounted to a faux wooden shield with a Plexiglas™ window that Poppleton held while standing in for the Italian star. As Poppleton swung his saber at Peter stunt double Sean Button, Button continually smashed his sword forcefully down onto the shield, a move that will simulate a unique perspective to heighten the thrills of this action-packed duel.

the action. When the valves were opened, Gerd's crew then ignited the specific areas with a portable propane torch, and flames spewed from out of the water (which looked black to the eye, but was actually potable water dyed with food coloring).

The cavernous interior of this crucial set design took shape inside the colossal Stage 6 at Barrandov Studios and represented one of four different pieces of Aslan's How erected for filming. Once Andrew completed scene 115 over several shooting days in mid-April (the key sequence in this set), supervising art director Walsh began to modify the structure as another area of the How for the weapons-forging scenes in the story (filmed months later). Ford always felt that these scenes would be spectacular.

"Imagine a colony of dwarfs manufacturing weapons in an underground cavern," he says. "The fire. The heat. The noise of the blacksmithing. Just a fantastic image in the film. Quite spectacular, I think. But as the script took shape, there wasn't a setting specified for this moment in the story. Andrew liked this set so much, he looked for a reason to go back to it somehow. So we redesigned it to be this huge weapons chamber."

Walsh also oversaw the construction of the entrance of the How out in the rural Czech Republic area of Usti nad Labem, about 90 miles from Prague. There, on a verdant prairie the size of a dozen American football fields, his builders fashioned a six-story-high stone structure ("the look of temple ruins," says Ford) leading from the subterranean How out to what would become the battlefield for the film's climactic war between the Narnians and the Telmarine army. Ford expects the final look, enhanced by computer generated imagery, to be "three times bigger than what appeared on location."

The last piece of this elaborate and extraordinary setting was dubbed a "cistern" ("because we couldn't think of anything better to call it," muses Ford), another chamber that extends underground for what appears to be infinity. It's where the Narnians are able to overcome the first wave of attack from the Telmarines.

This fourth part of the How found its home at the Modrany Studios and featured rows of stone columns that support the battlefield above this subterranean hideaway.

Beruna Bridge/ The Fords of Beruna

The river gorge had just made a bend and the whole view spread out beneath them. They could see open country stretching before them to the horizon and, between it and them, the broad silver ribbon of the Great River. They could see the specially broad and shallow place which had once been the Fords of Beruna but was now spanned by a long, many-arched bridge. (Chapter 10, "The Return of the Lion")

The Beruna Bridge was yet another spectacular set build set against one of the planet's most stunning, picturesque landscapes: the Julian Alps in Boveĉ, Slovenia.

"This mountainous location looks very much like New Zealand," Roger notes about the stunning European backdrop chosen for the climactic sequence. It was indeed a good match to the Southern Alps region of the Kiwi's South Island. "So it tied into our New Zealand footage very nicely. And with its stony riverbed, it was very typical of New Zealand. The beautiful color of the water, an aquamarine shade, also resembled New Zealand."

"In the book, the bridge at Beruna is a stone bridge that has been there for some time, a few hundred years," Roger says. "When the Narnians are finally victorious, Aslan calls on the River God to destroy the bridge, which has been built by the Telmarines, to free the river."

Ford explains that his design was also influenced by a documentary on Julius Caesar attacking the Germans and crossing the Rhine, "where he literally built a bridge, much bigger than our bridge, spanning the Rhine in ten days."

When watching this documentary, Ford transposed such an idea into his bridge design. "We surmised that the Telmarines built a bridge to cross the river to attack the Narnians. In that sense, the bridge is an insult to the river because it's been built for purposes of war. This causes Aslan to summon the River God to appear and destroy the bridge."

The massive log structure, designed for the story's climactic Beruna Bridge/River God sequence (scene 159 in the script, parts of which took a week to film), was erected by the Primorje Group, the country's top civil engineering firm. The magnificent set piece, built under the watchful eyes of supervising art director Frank Walsh and his Slovenian art director, Katja Soltes, took a crew of twenty men a full month to erect.

Ford's team constructed the bridge out of big pine logs lashed together with thick, massive ropes. It also had to be a practical bridge that could hold two hundred soldiers charging across it. Adds Walsh, "I can remember going there on the [scout] with Andrew, who asked if we could build a bridge on this roaring mountain river. And I'm thinking, 'Okay, we'll give it a go.' Basically, it required a real piece of civil engineering. We were introduced to the biggest bridge builder in Slovenia, Primorje, and they didn't even bat an eye. They adapted their operation and approach to what we wanted, came on board, and were fantastic!"

Bunyanesque in style and magnitude, the span reached sixty meters across the crystal clear, aquamarine waters of the Soča, a sacred site known as the country's "Emerald River" because of the water's greenish hue.

The monumental construction also required the builders to reroute the river in order to sink the support structure into dry rockbed, a feat supervised by Ford's senior art director, Dave Allday.

"In order to facilitate building the bridge, we temporarily rerouted the river, a very wide, stony flood plan," Roger says. About sixty permits issued by the Slovenian government allowed Ford's team to alter the flow of the River Soča, erect the bridge on dry land, then reroute the flow back underneath the bridge set.

"It's not the sort of thing you attempt to do lightly," Ford notes. "But we were assured by the engineers and the local authorities that it was not a big deal because it's not like we were shifting soil or doing any ecological damage to the water. This region of Slovenia is a tourist-development area. The local community wanted to change the flow of the river and, in fact, may finish up with a river better suited to their dream to make it a place where people can come for such recreational activities as swimming and trout and salmon fishing."

MIRAZ'S CASTLE

Prince Caspian lived in a great castle in the center of Narnia with his uncle, Miraz, the King of Narnia, and his aunt, who had red hair and was called Queen Pruniprismia. (Chapter 4, "The Dwarf Tells of Prince Caspian")

Roger notes that, unlike the first movie's wardrobe or the lamppost where Lucy first ventures into Narnia and meets Mr. Tumnus, there were no iconic set pieces in the *Prince Caspian* book.

However, the talented designer created one in the towering and incomparable edifice called Miraz's castle, the largest film set he has ever designed and constructed during his four-decade career. He calls the set "a character" in a story that began with "Prince Caspian lived in a great castle . . ."

Illustrator Pauline Baynes's simple sketches that adorn the books portray the castle as medieval and gothic in stature, something Ford claims "we've all seen repeatedly in fairy-tale books and illustrations. We went in a slightly different direction with this one."

When audiences see the film, nobody will believe Andrew and company did not film in a real castle! And that was the initial intention.

"When exploring a backstory for the Telmarine society, we were thinking French," Ford explains. "My set decorator, Kerrie Brown, came across an illustration of a castle in France called Pierrefonds. Andrew was very interested in its look, so we decided to visit this castle."

The Castle of Pierrefonds, next to Compiègne, was built in the fifteenth century by Philippe d' Orléans and later demolished on order of Louis XIII. Napoleon III made Viollet-le-Duc rebuild the castle into an imperial house in the nineteenth century.

The castle, located about 50 miles outside Paris sports a huge courtyard "which had appealed to us as a place to stage the castle raid sequence," Roger says.

"Now, most castles don't have huge courtyards. When you get inside them, the courtyards are quite small. So this was an exception, and it was very impressive. And Andrew started to think about the possibility of filming there."

However, filming in France proved to be difficult and costly. Andrew comments that "we needed to own the structure for several weeks of night work, which would have proved unwieldy." So the filmmakers thought

about building a castle set, which prompted Ford to study several styles of architecture: Spanish, Italian, and Mediterranean. "And that's how this set started to take shape," he says.

Once Roger had found the right look, one with a Mediterranean flair, Malcolm Roberts, the production's veteran construction coordinator, took his architectural plans, assembled a team of two hundred carpenters, plasterers, and painters, and achieved what many thought impossible—erecting the estimated twenty-thousand-square-foot, six-story-high edifice in just fifteen weeks. On-screen, the castle will appear three times as high, towering over a thousand-foot chasm, through the magic of visual effects. According to the shooting calendar, Miraz's castle had to be camera-ready by April 23, the night the castle raid sequence was scheduled to begin.

Once he completed the castle's basic floor plan, Roger next looked to give his inanimate set piece some life, some character. "As a designer, you look for motifs, because they add strength and give meaning to the culture," Ford explains. For "this culture that came from

pirates maybe a thousand years ago, we needed a symbol to represent this society."

Ford chose the powerful bird of prey, the eagle, as a symbol for a people he calls "thugs and fascists. They're not nice people at all." While the eagle is a prominent

With the castle, we looked for an identity for it. A moodiness, to make it a character of its own.

figure on the American landscape, Roger points out that the image was also used by Hitler. "So we thought, why not try to get it in? Our eagle motif has much more of a fascist architectural look."

Ford's soaring design adorned the sides of the castle balconies and were also prominently featured on torch fixtures scattered throughout the Telmarine village town square set adjacent to the castle. This image not only embellished the castle courtyard on the backlot, but also

the crossbows used by the Telmarine soldiers and the thrones of Miraz's lords in the castle's Great Hall set.

Noting the Telmarines' origins in a pirate culture, Roger added yet another strong symbol: the compass. "It crops up on the soldiers' shields and in the architecture of the Great Hall." (Note the marble floor in this magnificent set.) Ford and Brown also used the compass motif in the banners fabricated for each of the twenty-one lords under Miraz's rule.

"With the castle, we looked for an identity for it. A moodiness, to make it a character of its own. It's impressive and oppressive at the same time. Spanish architecture with a fascist flair. So that, combined with its size and scope, will I hope give it a life of its own and [make it] a memorable building—and hopefully a character, reflecting Miraz and his Telmarine culture."

Those unfamiliar with the art and craft of filmmaking and production design may not realize that such an exterior setting does not contain the various interior chambers, halls, rooms, and such that add character to the overall set design.

Indeed, the assorted sets representing Miraz's Great Hall, Caspian's bedroom, Cornelius's library-study, the castle stables, the wheelhouse that controls the gate leading out to the drawbridge, and the tyrant's own chamber, were erected, separately, on various soundstages at both Barrandov and Modrany Studios. The integration of interior and exterior sets into a whole represents another intriguing challenge for a production designer.

Miraz's Great Hall, a stunning piece of movie architecture in this gallery of incredible set pieces, was another memorable accomplishment of the film's relaxed designer. Built on Barrandov's Stage 7, which would later be transformed into the castle stables, the Great Hall boasted pageantry and majesty, two qualities that also defined the character of Miraz.

The Spanish architecture housed three massive arched doorways. The fascist-like eagle head appeared prominently throughout—on the arms of the twenty-one thrones (all designed in shades of black and silver) scattered throughout the huge hall, and over the mantel of the magnificent fireplace. A giant chandelier said to weigh over a ton bathes the set in an imperial glow.

"Roger always saw the Great Hall as having a giant, heavy chandelier," set decorator Brown notes. "We ended up making it 1.8 tons, I think." She had the gargantuan wood-and-metal light made in the Czech Republic, a country she claims has "many great carvers and craftsmen. It's been a real advantage working there. I think it's made this film a lot richer."

VFX art director Christian Huband sheds light on another aspect of Miraz's castle—two separate miniature versions of the castle. Both versions (one at 1/24 scale; the other at 1/100 scale) were constructed at Weta Workshop in New Zealand.

"I would say it's a huge miniatures movie," Huband exclaims. "Andrew's a particular fan of using miniatures. With some movies, you can do a castle shot using a digital castle. But in this film, there's a particularly involved sequence, so complex, that happens in the castle. You see parts of the castle in such closeup that, really, to try to do them as pure digital elements would really not hold up."

Miraz's castle (and the adjacent Telmarine village), on which Roger collaborated with art director Matt Grey, stands as a monument to the craftsmanship of those who contributed to its artistry and majesty. Ford's international crew featured Brits, Aussies, Kiwis, and, most notably, the local Czechs, a group he calls "a fantastic team, the best I've worked with."

Its design, and that of the entire world of Narnia in these two epic motion pictures, distinguishes Ford as not only a talented artist, but a unique visionary. He took the concise descriptions of a literary giant and conceived an original world that existed previously only in the imaginations of the book's readers.

THE DESIGN, CREATION, AND ADVENTURE OF THE NARNIAN INHABITANTS

by Howard Berger, KNB EFX Group Creature Supervisor

To get the chance to walk through the wardrobe once for *The Lion, the Witch and the Wardrobe* was an amazing adventure and opportunity in itself. But to have the chance for all of us at KNB EFX Group to do it again was even more astounding.

When Greg Nicotero and I received the call from Andrew Adamson, Mark Johnson, and Philip Steuer in September 2006 that we were finally going to embark on the next Narnia film, we were all set to go. It had been two years since the last film had wrapped, and we were chomping at the bit to go back and get a chance to revisit all the Narnian inhabitants we helped create for the first film. Not unlike William Moseley's character of Peter, once a king, and now relegated to an ordinary

Howard Berger on the castle set.

schoolboy who so yearned to return to Narnia, we were ready to get back to Narnia.

The first thing Greg and I spoke about doing differently from a design phase was to expand the age groups and genders of the Narnians. We knew the fauns, Minotaurs, dwarfs, satyrs, and centaurs would be back in this film, and unlike the first film, where all the creatures seemed to be in their thirties, we wanted to have faun

children, female dwarfs, old centaurs. We wanted to have a more organic variety of Narnians, creatures that encompassed the history and life cycle of Narnia.

We had our team of concept artists at KNB (including Jaremy Aiello, Andy Schoenberg, Aaron Simms, John Wheaton, Eddie Yang, and Aki Ikeda) start working on artwork that would help illustrate our ideas for Andrew. We utilized a combination of Photoshop illustrations, three-dimensional sculpture, and makeup tests to depict our concepts. We had Andrew come to our shop in Van Nuys, California, to have a look (similar to what we did with our weekly reviews on the first film), so he could see up close the work being conceptualized. This allowed the artists to hear Andrew's comments and suggestions firsthand. He liked what he saw, saying my favorite things, like "I think this is heading down the right path" and "This is looking very promising." I let a little smirk appear on my face as I knew what those comments meant—a good thing. This was our first leaping-off point so we could begin to travel down that long road to Narnia in a much shorter preproduction period then we had on the first

All photos show a diverse mix of the assorted makeup applications created by Oscar®-winner Howard Berger (N.B. middle right photo shows two key crew members playing Narnians—Mark Ceryak, Marketa Tom).

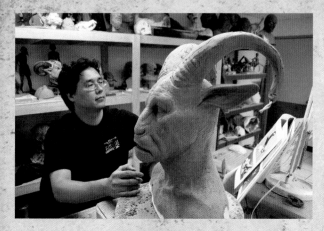

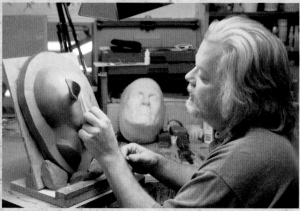

film. We had gone from six months to now *four* months and the clock was ticking, but we were all ready to meet the challenge head-on as we had done before.

The first order of business was to gather our core team to help us oversee the task at hand. Greg and I conferred with our shop supervisors, Michael Deak and Shannon Shea, and we chose Alex Diaz to be the art director on the show. Alex has worked with us for many years—but nothing this big before—and we knew he would do an excellent job coordinating the creative team. Beth Hathaway, who supervised all the fabrication and suit creation on the first film, came back to handle these same tasks, while another returning veteran, Dawn Dininger (who worked under Beth on the first film), would supervise the new satyr design and bring these Narnians to life. Mark Boley headed the hair department, as he had done before. Ben Rittenhouse, Derek Krout, and their crew were responsible for all the thousands of foam latex and gelatin prosthetic pieces that needed to be fabricated for the film. We estimated close to three-thousand-plus makeups (what we call an extensive makeup application, which often includes facial prosthetics, hair, and more) on the film, a tremendous amount of work for the foam department, which operated almost around the clock for the next nine months. We ended up applying four thousand six hundred makeups by the end of the shoot, which is, I believe, a world record. James Leonard oversaw the mold and lab department, making sure each mold for the makeups and creatures was 100 percent. He assembled a fantastic team—the best of the best. Rob Derry, under mechanical supervisor Dave Wogh, oversaw the

Top to bottom: (1) *KNB Designer John Wheaton works on one of many new satyr concepts. (2) KNB's Steve Katz readies molds for foam running in the foam department. (3) KNB's Beth Hathaway's fabrication department, where all the satyr and Minotaur suits are created. (4) KNB head sculptor Andy Schoenberg, works on a centaur makeup.*

construction of the radio control heads we require on top of all the other fun things that seem to fall under that department, like armatures for sculptures, under-structure skulls for all the background Minotaur and satyr heads, and so forth.

THE NARNIAN CREATURES . . . OLD AND NEW

It is rare that you get a chance to revisit things you did before and have an opportunity to improve upon them. On the first film, we created the twenty satyrs in the eleventh hour, eight weeks before filming began, as they were originally going to be created in the CGI realm. This time, we had Aaron Simms work on their design, and he came up with a fantastic look. Andrew wanted the satyrs to be more animalistic than humanoid,

RIGHT: *The musculature undersuit of one of KNB's Narnian creatures.* BELOW: *Prosthetic makeup artist Tracey Reebey tends to a satyr character.*

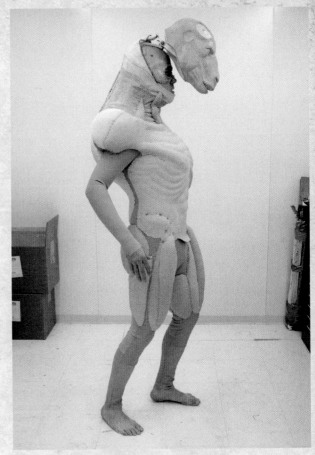

so we had to break the human form the best we could, still mindful that these are suits inhabited by actors. We altered the position of the head, "stovepiping" them out, as we call it, to create a more goatlike appearance. The artwork was approved, allowing Jaremy Aiello to bring the heads to life with his sculpting talents, followed by the construction of the twenty suits under Dawn Dininger's supervision.

We had a new hero Minotaur, Asterius, a new main character in the film, played by New Zealand actor and suit performer Shane Rangi. (Coincidentally, Rangi played General Otmin, the evil Minotaur, in the first film.) We wanted Asterius to be very old and war-torn, so Jaremy readied his sculpting tool, and produced the perfect aged Minotaur. Beth Hathaway and crew began redesigning the Minotaur suits to make them more functional than what we had on the first film. Originally, we had a lot of cast parts that made up the suits, but this time around we ended up fabricating each muscle out of different density foams. From there, everything was sewn together onto a black spandex bodysuit, then covered with skin-painted spandex that had been all hand-tied with hair by Mark Boley's department. We knew that we would have scenes where our previously armor-clad creatures would appear without armor, almost rendering these creatures "naked," something we needed to take into account. The fabrication team brainstormed and came up with some great ideas to

make things more prominent beneath the skin of the creatures. We wanted to add fluidity to certain muscles and fatty areas. Mark Ballou, who would become our on-set coordinator, researched and found a company that made the bladders for breast implants and was able to get a slew of these to use for the Minotaur chests. This saved us tons of work and ended up looking great.

Aslan was on the move again, but this time he needed to be bigger in size, as he grows in each book. Andrew wanted him to be 15 percent larger, so Jeff Himmel was brought back to oversee all the Aslan suit work as he did on the first movie. We were able to utilize the digital scanning information from the first film and have Cyber FX mill out a new sculpture at 15 percent larger than the first. You would not think that 15 percent would make a difference, but it does, and we had a very large lion ready in the shop on which Jeff could do his magic.

Wanting to make the Narnians as real as possible, we brought in Val Crawford, the best in the world at

OPPOSITE PAGE — †OP LEFT: *Shane Rangi as Asterius the Minotaur with Warwick Davis as Nikabrik.* TOP RIGHT: *A KNB artist sculpting the head of one of the Minotaur masks.* RIGHT MIDDLE: *A display of the assorted creature masks created by KNB.* BOTTOM: *A Minotaur gets the Hollywood treatment on-set in Usti, Czech Republic.*
THIS PAGE — TOP: *(left to right) Makeup artist Tami Lane, Howard Berger, Sarah Rubano, and Aslan supervisor Jeff Himmel at KNB's warehouse in California.*
BOTTOM: *Two of the Aslan designs at KNB's Southern California headquarters.*

Top: *Warwick Davis as Nikabrik, with his makeup artist, Sarah Rubano.* Bottom: *Tami Lane applies a finishing touch to the character of Trumpkin, played by Peter Dinklage.*

head skins from Alex, applied an adhesive to that skin, loaded the flocking gun (which looks like a strange alien device) with the fur shaved from the pelts, and carefully applyied the hair to the skin. At first, all the fur was standing on end due to the static electricity, but this is where the magic comes in—she was then able to control the fur direction with very soft brushes and compressed air. The fur lays down and looks just like the real fur on an animal's muzzle would look. Amazing!

We had two new hero makeups to design for a pair of dwarf characters—Trumpkin the Red Dwarf and Nikabrik the Black Dwarf. The first order of business was to find the perfect actors to play these parts. To tell the truth, there are very few great short actors out there. In my mind, the only two candidates were Peter Dinklage, who was amazing in the film *The Station Agent,* and Warwick Davis of *Willow* fame, on top of about four hundred other films. I knew Andrew had these two actors in mind as well, but now the task was to see if they were available and willing to commit to the lengthy shoot and to days and days of sitting in the makeup chairs. Luckily, they were available, and both actors were locked in and we were ready to start designing their looks to bring them to life.

We had John Wheaton do some Photoshop designs, and he captured their looks perfectly. When Andrew saw the designs, he loved them. We wanted to make sure that we did not disguise Peter, who has this amazingly expressive face capable of showing a wide range of emotions. So I spoke to Tami Lane, who was back as my key makeup artist on the show, and we decided to give Peter only a new nose, ears, and hairpieces. I wanted his hair color not to be a stark red, but really more in the blondes, which would subtly graduate into a shade of red. I think Mark Boley ended up using at least a dozen different colors of human hair to create his lace pieces. Peter, who has thick dark hair, agreed to let us shave his head each day, which cut down the application process by at least an hour. It allowed us to avoid applying a bald cap on him each day, an immense time-saver. On the first test day, Peter truly brought Trumpkin to life, and

"flocking," in my opinion, to handle all the facial hair work on the satyrs. Flocking is an interesting technique, one that uses static electricity to work. Val got tons of cow and goat pelts and carefully shaved all the fur off into containers, all labeled so she would know what and where everything was. Then she got the painted

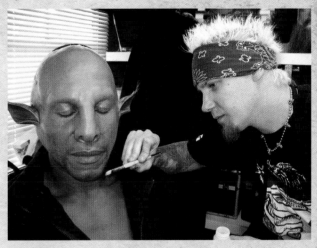

TOP LEFT: *Lejla Abbasova as Glenstorm's wife, Windmane.* TOP RIGHT: *Mike Fields readies actor Cornell S. John as Glenstorm the centaur.* BOTTOM LEFT: *Elka Wardega seeing to Suncloud.* BOTTOM RIGHT: *Makeup artist Katherine Brown finishes touch-up on Yammy (Ironhoof).*

as I always said, he has these incredible dreamy blue eyes and eyebrows that tell you everything he is feeling. I felt that Trumpkin would be our Tumnus on this show, and I truly believe I was right. We all fell in love with the character, not to mention the fact that we really liked Peter to no end, as well.

As for Nikabrik, we wanted to do the opposite for Warwick. He has a very recognizable face, and we wanted Nikabrik to not resemble any other character Warwick had played in the past. Once again, John Wheaton came up with a series of designs, making him old, craggy, and mean. Warwick's face would be entirely covered with gelatin prosthetics, a salt-and-pepper gray wig, and facial pieces, to give him the final look. It took several makeup

tests to nail his look, as his makeup artist, Sarah Rubano, and I tried different designs to make him older, more scarred, and so on. Finally, we hit the right look on test number four. We finished the makeup, stood back, and watched Warwick bring Nikabrik to life. The appliances were so thin that once glued down to his own face, it all molded perfectly, allowing Warwick great facial flexibility. We now had our dwarf characters, and they were great!

The centaurs are very prominent in this film, and we had a family of them, the Glenstorm family. Cornell John, a great stage actor out of London, was cast to play Glenstorm, the leader of the centaurs. His presence alone is so powerful, but in the makeup applied by Canadian artist Michael Fields, Cornell became

a commanding centaur. Next came his three sons, Rainstone, Ironhoof, and Suncloud. Local Czech actors were hired, and they were perfect. They had similarities to Cornell, but they needed to have their own looks and be their own characters to stand out. This was mostly created by the hair team, as Mark Boley had designed some beautiful wigs. They were all in full facial prosthetics, including foreheads, noses, cheeks, and ears. Three artists brought these creatures to life in the makeup chair: Kevin Wasner applied Rainstone; Katherine Brown handled Ironhoof; and Elka Wardega saw to Suncloud each day. And let's not forget that Glenstorm had a wife. I called her Gladys, but her character name was Windmane, and Kerrin Jackson handled her day-to-day application. The whole family looked great, our first African-Narnian centaur family.

Now that our preproduction period had ended in Los Angeles, it was time for us to pack up thousands of boxes and crates and head to New Zealand for two months, and then to the Czech Republic for six months.

Greg and the KNB team in California would continue building for months more following our departure for overseas. For now, it was time to let the games begin!

THROUGH THE WARDROBE . . . AGAIN

When you approach New Zealand, as the plane flies over the beautiful countryside, your heart remembers how wonderful and magical a place it is. I sat on the plane, my face pressed against the window. I took a deep breath and whispered, "I'm home." That is the feeling that overtakes you there. It is amazingly calming and peaceful, even though we were at the beginning of this very lengthy adventure.

We did not have a huge amount of Narnians filming during the New Zealand leg of the shoot. It was primarily Trumpkin, Nikabrik, and the Aslan suit, but these were our most important characters, so they had to be great. Similar to the first film, where we had James McAvoy as Mr. Tumnus kicking off our duties in Narnia, we needed to hit a home run during our first at bat. It was a great way to start the film. K. C. Hodenfield, our first assistant director on both films, scheduled everything just right. It was the perfect way to be welcomed back to Narnia.

Trumpkin was up first, and we filmed on South Island in a place called the Haast River Valley. It was a beautiful beachfront community where the sights were breathtaking and the beach we were filming on was just unbelievable. The only drawback was these horrible sand flies. They were the worst creatures on earth, as these things would not leave you alone and just kept eating you alive. There was no escape from them, even when we applied 80 percent DDT to ourselves. These guys were relentless. Poor Peter was eaten up. Each night when Tami would clean him up, his now bald head was covered in tons of bites, and they were miserable. How could such a gorgeous place be infested with the worst insect invasion anywhere? Go figure. But the consolation prize was that this beach was so remote that we all had to be helicoptered to the location. Once we finished Peter's makeup, Tami, Sarah, and I would climb into a chopper, fly over the ocean, and land right there on the beach. It was so cool. From time to time I would say I left something behind and have to be coptered back to base camp to get it. (I just really loved riding back and forth, as it was an amazing experience.) At times like that, you sit there and say, "What a great life and job I have!"

When it was time for Warwick to work, at first both Sarah and I applied his makeup. But Sarah did such a great job and had such a command of the makeup that I ultimately backed off and let her see it through solo for the rest of the show. She began working for KNB on the first Narnia film, collaborating with Beth Hathaway in fabrication. While filming *The Lion, the Witch and the Wardrobe*, she expressed interest in wanting to apply makeup, so Tami and I gave her the chance and she did a faun here and there. We watched her get better and better through the course of the shoot, and by the end, I felt she really had a strong grasp of what it took. She is a shining star in my eyes and has brought so much to the

Top: *The helicopter on location on South Island.*
Bottom: *Makeup artist Sarah Rubano, Warwick Davis as Nikabrik, and Howard Berger.*

table for KNB on this film. Nikabrik looked great every day. I am so proud of her and her work.

Once the shoot in New Zealand came (sadly) to an end, we packed up our gear once again and headed to Prague in the Czech Republic. Although Prague is a beautiful city, with great sights and experiences, it was very different than where we had just come from. Tami and I had filmed two weeks in Prague on the first film in the freezing cold of winter, with poor James McAvoy running around in the snow practically naked as Mr. Tumnus. I think even today, James is still half frozen from that shoot. This time, it was spring heading into summer, and it was gorgeous. Mark Ballou, who was our on-set coordinator, had arrived in Prague a few weeks earlier to start facilitating our needs there, like organizing our shop space, KNB CZ, which was located at

Barrandov Studios where we would be shooting all the stage and castle work. Mark met up with our CZ on-set coordinator, Eliska Malikova.

There were hundreds of appliances to get ready, all the finishing work on the hero and background Minotaur and satyr heads, fine-tuning the mechanical heads to get them up and running, and setting up all the makeup stations and trailers so we could accommodate the huge numbers of actors and extras whom we transformed each day into Narnian creatures.

The first big Narnian scene we tackled was the war council at the Stone Table. This would be the first time establishing the Glenstorm family, Asterius the Minotaur, Tyrus the satyr, Mentius the faun, and a slew of other Narnians, such as male and female dwarfs, fauns, centaurs, Minotaurs, and satyrs. The monumental task required at least eight hours to get everyone (about eighty-five creatures) ready for the first day of filming this scene. Working with Jeff "O" Okabayashi, our second assistant director, we were able to come up with a "firing list," as we call it, that would block out the artists and

the Narnians they would be responsible for creating. For the most part, all makeup artists were required to apply at least two makeups a day (one hero and a background makeup per artist), but some people were able to squeeze out three. This meant that Jeff and I were able to reduce the time to get everyone ready from eight hours to six. Still, to have everyone ready on set by 8:00 A.M., our team arose at the ungodly hour of 1:00 A.M. to catch the vans at 1:30 A.M., ready at our makeup stations for actors at 2:00 A.M. This was just day 1 of 100 like this. Like I said, let the games begin.

Once we finished the first portion of the Prague shoot, it was time to move to shoot in Usti (after a brief respite in Poland). This had to be one of the craziest places I had ever lived and filmed in. The scene was the final battle at Aslan's How, and we would be there off and on for eleven weeks. The set was amazing, and Peta Sinclair and his location team surpassed themselves with huge tents, similar to the ones he masterminded in New Zealand at Flock Hill on the first film. These had dressing rooms, wood floors, heaters, air conditioning, running hot and cold water—pretty much everything we needed. With our work space the size of a football field, supplemented by five makeup and fabrication stations outside the tent, it was a well-oiled machine.

Unfortunately, the weather conditions were against us for the most part. The foul weather would torture Walter Lindenlaub, our director of photography, and of course K. C. would be driven mad half the time by how bad the weather would get.

We had plenty of days where actors in full prosthetics just never made it to the set and sat in the lunch tent waiting. It was always interesting to see what Narnian species would sit with other Narnian species. The centaurs would all gather together. The fauns were their own group, too. Same with the dwarfs, but there were always two female dwarfs not included with the others. I never understood why, but that was just how it was. The satyrs and Minotaurs were all friendly with each other and shared their living space during the day between

The special makeup tent (or marquee) erected at Barrandov.

setups. This is how it was on the first film, and it was funny to see it all happen again. It was a great social experiment to see this start to form at the beginning of the shoot and then watch as it developed through the six months we filmed in the Czech Republic.

When Andrew filmed Caspian's coronation scene toward the end of the shoot, all of the king's subjects attend, with a huge party in the courtyard of the Telmarine village. I called this "family day," as Andrew decided that it would be great to have the crew's children in this scene. I had not seen my wife, Sandi, nor hugged my three children (Travis, Kelsey, and Jake), in six months! Travis and Kelsey were dressed and made up as Telmarine children, and Jake was to be a faun. I got to personally make him up, which entailed applying a foam faun nose glued to his own, with ears and a faun wig. He got to don the blue-screen leggings that would then be digitally

A DAY IN THE LIFE
July 28 (Day 110) Barrandov Studios, Ceska Televise, Prague

Today's schedule calls for a return to the backlot castle courtyard for a variety of scenes featuring Italian actors Sergio Castellitto and Pierfrancesco Favino and Spanish actress Alicia Borachero as Queen Pruniprismia. (Scenes 25 and 26 would mark her last on the schedule.) Once the morning scenes are complete, scene 164 (featuring Caspian, Peter, Susan, and Aslan) will comprise the afternoon shoot.

Once filming concludes around 7:00 P.M., Andrew's day is still not over. At 11:15 on this overcast Saturday night, the director and his star, Ben Barnes, are scheduled to trek over to Ceska Televise, the country's twenty-four-hour news channel, for a live satellite hookup to San Diego. (The nine-hour time difference puts the Southern California city at mid-afternoon.)

During the last weekend of July, just as it has every year since 1969, one of the country's biggest fan conventions, Comic-Con, takes place in San Diego. While originally conceived as an outlet for comic-book fans, it has evolved over the last decade as a venue for movie studios to unveil scenes from upcoming films whose appeal lies squarely with the genre enthusiasts who frequent this unique event.

Disney secured the prime mid-Saturday-afternoon slot to promote *Prince Caspian* to this eager crowd, which, amazingly, numbers around six thousand at the San Diego Convention Center. In addition to showing exclusive footage and previsualization animation from the film, the company sent costume designer Isis Mussenden, Oscar®-winning makeup artist Howard Berger, VFX supervisor Dean Wright, and producer

FROM LEFT: *VFX co-supervisor Dean Wright, costume designer Isis Mussenden, makeup artist Howard Berger, and Weta Workshop's Richard Taylor during their visit to the 2007 Comic-Con convention in San Diego, California.*

Mark Johnson from Prague to chair a panel discussion on their contributions. The panel was moderated by Weta's own Richard Taylor, attending to promote the special maquettes he manufactures from the designs Weta has made for many of their titles over the years.

Joining the panel discussion from Prague were Andrew and Ben. They were seated in front of two TV cameras at a tiny desk in a blue-screen stage over which the Miraz castle and title treatment for the film were superimposed. Talking straight into a video camera lens, especially with no visual reference of what's on the other end, can be awkward. Although Andrew's done it before, he prefers satellite feeds with a two-way transmission, thus allowing him to see his listeners.

Once again, that's where the company's IT wizards come to the rescue. Gareth Daley (the wily Brit, as I affectionately call him) jumps into a taxi and arrives at the Czech TV network barely ten minutes before the live feed begins. Much like a magician waving a wand over a top hat, Daley pulls out not a rabbit, but all the stops, as Andrew gets the audio feed from San Diego in his ear, confirming the panel discussion is about to commence.

On the other side of the world stands associate producer Tom Williams, positioned in front of the panel with his own laptop faced directly at the quintet. Through the magic of Skype, and who knows what else floating around cyberspace, Daley beams the panel up and over to the Czech Republic. While the computer-to-computer picture is somewhat crude, like one of those video phone hookups you see on CNN, it allows Andrew the convenience of seeing his audience while he takes several questions from the attentive convention crowd.

Afterward, I suggest to Andrew that Daley be named "employee of the week" for his Herculean efforts.

replaced with animated faun legs. All the other children were dressed as Telmarines, but Jake was going to be right there in front, leading the procession through the streets. He ate it up, and after each take he ran over to Andrew and sat in the director's chair next to him to watch a playback of the scene. I would watch Andrew, with his kind and gentle ways, have them play the take back just for Jake each time so he could see it. Andrew is truly the sweetest person I have ever met and I love him dearly. No other director would ever do this, but Andrew is one of a kind.

Though the shoot was the most difficult one I had ever been on (I know my team felt the same way), the big payoff was on the last night of the shoot, when we had blue-screen elements to film with all the Narnians so that Dean Wright and his VFX team could mix and match all our creatures

Howard's son, Jake Berger as a child faun.

in different shots and duplicate them to increase the numbers in certain shots. As we filmed this day, we all had the sense that reality was setting in and that this would be the last time we would be doing this for the film. That this was the last faun makeup, the final female centaur application, the last time we would dress our twenty satyr actors in their suits. It is almost like a child opening up presents on Christmas morning, only to realize he has just a few left to open and then it will all be done until next year. It is a feeling that sits heavy in my heart when I think about it. So the day went on and we filmed for hours, after which Dean (who directed that day) shouted out, "That's a wrap for all Narnians and KNB!" Our hearts sank as we knew

it was all over. Our journey had come to an end a year after we started the film at KNB. Soon, we would be saying farewell to our teammates whom we all loved so much. One by one, the actors came into the trailers for their final cleanup. The last faun was handed his hot towel for the final stage of his wrap, and that was it. I looked at my trailer mates, Andrea, Sarah, and Tracey, and said, "That was the last makeup for this show. We are done." Our eyes welled up and we hugged. We were sad, but relieved as well.

We finished packing up our gear and walked out of the trailers, and there stood all the actors and extras we had been making up for months. They all started applauding and cheering. In all our sadness, we had forgotten that these 130 actors were sad to see us all go, and this was the end for them as well. We walked through the crowd saying our good-byes, signing

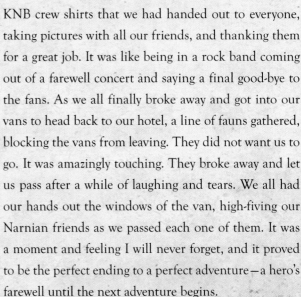

KNB crew shirts that we had handed out to everyone, taking pictures with all our friends, and thanking them for a great job. It was like being in a rock band coming out of a farewell concert and saying a final good-bye to the fans. As we all finally broke away and got into our vans to head back to our hotel, a line of fauns gathered, blocking the vans from leaving. They did not want us to go. It was amazingly touching. They broke away and let us pass after a while of laughing and tears. We all had our hands out the windows of the van, high-fiving our Narnian friends as we passed each one of them. It was a moment and feeling I will never forget, and it proved to be the perfect ending to a perfect adventure—a hero's farewell until the next adventure begins.

ISIS MUSSENDEN
Costume Designer

Along with composer Harry Gregson-Williams and film editor Sim Evan-Jones, costume designer Isis Mussenden has worked with director Andrew Adamson on all four of his movies, first collaborating with the film-maker on his Oscar®-winning animated feature, *Shrek*.

We know what you're thinking—a costume designer on a cartoon?

She remembers getting a call from the film's producer, a longtime friend named Aron Warner. He mentioned to Isis (with whom he had worked several times before) that he needed a designer to create patterns for some dresses for the character of Fiona (voiced by Cameron Diaz).

"I am no computer genius, believe me," Isis muses. "I don't know how they do that. But somehow, I gave them the patterns, the fabric, the color, the design, the textures, and they basically made the dress inside a computer."

While designing these various elements for the computer-animated hit, she met Andrew, and a bond and partnership developed. "I think the reason Andrew and I work together so well is that we share a design sensibility," she says. "We share a simplicity in design, a boldness that works for the two of us."

In joining her longtime colleague for their second journey through Narnia, Isis supervised a fresh crew in a whole new country, a team that doubled in size from the first movie, but included several dependable collaborators also back for another adventure in Narnia—associate costume designer Kimberly Adams, key supervisor Di Foothead, textile artist Sarah Shepard, costume prop maker Robin Forster, lead key costumer Andrea Hood, and key set costumer Samantha Morley.

Costume designer Isis Mussenden (right) with her longtime colleague and associate designer, Kimberly Adams and another staffer on the green-screen set adjacent to the Telmarine Village at Barrandov Studios.

All of these, along with about seventy-five other costume department dressers, tailors, seamstresses, dyers, cutters, and embroiderers, manufactured and worked on over six thousand costume pieces, many of which were fabricated in the designer's ten-thousand-square-foot workshop at Barrandov Studios.

There Isis, a vibrant and personable designer of Puerto Rican descent, sat down for a detailed chat about the biggest project of her lengthy and successful twenty-year career.

Tell us about working with Andrew again in the world of Narnia.
Andrew and I share a design sensibility that allows us to communicate in shorthand. Usually, I can guess what his comments will be when I show him a new design sketch. On the other hand, when I am stuck, he is always there for me. When something is bugging me, he is able to pinpoint the problem immediately. He possesses an incredibly keen eye, which I'm sure you've heard from many others who have worked with him.

Andrew is always the leader. He sets the pace and the mood for the entire production. He is very respectful of everybody who works on the film, from the crafts service person handing out snacks to the director of photography. Each individual receives a good morning greeting and equal courtesy.

As for my own relationship with Andrew, this is the fourth film that Andrew's made, and this is the fourth film I've designed for him. I make every effort to maintain his vision. He provides perceptive direction for the characters. He is a story master, and that is why I love working with him, because it is always about the story.

For the costume department, how does this film differ from _The Lion, the Witch and the Wardrobe_?
The scope of this film for us in the wardrobe department was ten times bigger than the first one. Massive. Not only in the actual count of how many characters and extras for whom we had to make costumes, but also the

Top: _Isis with Andrew Adamson._ Bottom: _The Czech extras adorned as Telmarine soldiers._

amount of multiple costumes we had to make to cover stunt doubles, photo doubles, growth, and just wear and tear of the costumes over six months of shooting.

I designed and manufactured an army, which I have never done before. While it was fascinating and interesting, it was also more work than I could have ever imagined, hundreds of hours of work. We built over two thousand pieces just for the extras. For soldiers, we made their boots, brigandines, greaves, pants, shirts, and gloves. Not to mention the helmets, gauntlets, masks, and gorgets. The only items that were personal were their underwear and socks. And we even provided that from time to time.

I could not do this project without my fabulous assistant, associate designer Kimberly Adams. In addition to overseeing the dwarfs, midwives, and Telmar villagers, she kept count of all the pieces we manufactured.

Total cast outfits built—262

Total number of items built for main cast—1,042

Individual items made for the Telmarine army (including Miraz and his lords)—3,722 (includes helmets, masks, brigandines, underbrigs, shirts, pants, boots, gloves, and greaves)

Number of metal rivets per brigandine—2,184 (totaling nearly one million for the entire army)

Telmarine villagers stock items manufactured—1,003

What's happened to the kids in terms of your work?
When the film starts, we find the four children heading off to school, still in wartime London. Peter has not quite adjusted. Susan has decided that this is where they should be and that their fifteen years spent in Narnia is in the past. Lucy is always looking for the door to get back in but is also quite happy where she is.

I hope our costuming portrays what's happened to these characters as well as who they are. They've come back to Narnia a year later with a sense of entitlement. They're a little older, a little brasher, and a little more mature. And you can see it all in their faces. They've grown up.

They're not adults yet, but they've definitely grown up. We had to adjust to that in the costumes. First, we started with their school uniforms. Nothing like a school uniform to make you look like a kid. Anna hated wearing her uniform. She said she does that every day at regular school. Making movies should be more fun than that! After a short period of time in those, we moved on to the first "Narnian" clothes that they find in the treasure chest of Cair Paravel. It was curious watching them throughout the first weeks of shooting, even the very first day that they entered Narnia, which was I guess the fourth day of shooting in New Zealand. They were where they belonged. They had been there before. They are the kings and queens of Narnia.

During filming, I also did my last fittings with William

TOP: *Armorer Joe Dunckley working on some of his weaponry.* BOTTOM: *Costume designer Isis Mussenden (left) and makeup artist Tami Lane (center), along with one of Mussenden's staff members, transform actor Peter Dinklage into Trumpkin in the Auckland production office.* OPPOSITE: *Georgie Henley as Lucy, discovering her gown in the Treasure Chamber.*

and Anna, and it was surprisingly emotional. They do not come back in the next movie. I mean, we couldn't believe it. It's been a wonderful three-and-a-half-year journey together.

How does wardrobe interface with visual effects?

The puzzle is always working out what's real and what's not and how much of it you see. I have done *Shrek* and *Shrek 2*, so I understand the whole CG interconnection. The experience of *The Lion, the Witch and the Wardrobe* was priceless. But each new film brings its own challenges. Not to mention technology is moving at the speed of light. There are always new programs and therefore new problems to solve in regard to CGI.

In the beginning of the project, we asked lots of questions. What's prosthetic? What's CG? What's motion-captured? What is green-screened? What is blue-screened? How many of them are there? How many are we going to scan so that we can get twenty-five hundred? Five thousand? When it is all said and done, no one should be able to tell the difference between

what was shot practically and what is a visual effect.

We also made a book, like an encyclopedia, of the Telmarines, which showed different patterns for the various soldiers. We knew that for the end battle, CG would enhance the number of extras by thousands, and we didn't want it to all look the same. About three hundred extras will look like five thousand! We handed that over to the VFX supervisors, Dean and Wendy, so when they had to create groups of soldiers, it won't look cookie-cutter. There will be variety.

Who is the villain in this film?

The "bad guys," so to speak, are human characters in *Prince Caspian*. The Telmarines are our villains, and we have Sergio Castellitto, who's the leader of Telmar. He's a fantastic villain, and his name is Miraz.

His first costume was the key to the civilian look of the Telmarines. I was inspired by the Sardinian cultural dress where the rugged menswear echoed another era. They were mean and dirty and yet "lord" like.

It was essential that Miraz be strong, Mediterranean, a

bit pirate, ruthless, barbaric in character, but more sophisticated in style. I was inspired initially by images from fifteenth-century Spanish soldiers. I came upon something I was not familiar with as an armor piece, and that was the brigandine. After my wonderful and productive visit to the Metropolitan Museum of Art in New York, I worked with Weta Workshop and their wonderful armorist, and the bronze armor was adopted and executed to complement and finish the military look.

I had already decided on my palette for the Telmarines, taken from a set of paintings by El Greco, who was considered a Spanish painter, although Greek (thus the name). These paintings hang in the Prado Museum in Madrid. Gruesome images, acidic and cool, perfect for our needs. The next piece of the puzzle was a book about the Sardinian cultural dress that I came upon on a shopping trip to Italy. From a notorious rough and tough island, it was just the new look I was after. The

mood was set. Skirts, vest, wide belts, gaiters, and jackets . . . no capes! My lord was going to be all Telmarine, and that was going to be a fresh and unique look.

On the first movie, you worked with an illustrator named Gypsy Taylor. Who was your illustrator this time?

As you might be able to see behind me, we have some beautiful, beautiful illustrations. About six weeks into this project, I had done enough concept and research work and was ready to lay some ideas down on paper. I began to look for an illustrator, as Gypsy lives in Sydney and I was in Los Angeles.

About this time I was asked to speak on a panel for the Costume Designer's Guild at Comic-Con in San Diego. That would have been in 2006. After the discussion, my colleagues and I stayed to answer questions, and a few people came by with portfolios. I wasn't expecting to see anybody's portfolio that day. Most of them were mediocre, but then this one beautiful young girl, Oksana Nedavniaya, walks up. She had just graduated from Long Beach State in California, and she opened up her book. She's an amazingly talented illustrator. I knew I was going to hire her right there. She is very disciplined. She's of Russian descent, had moved to Los Angeles when she was twelve, and just loves to draw. And you can see it. She uses traditional methods of drawing and illustrating, much to the envy of several of our concept artists.

Her work was very good. So after a couple of weeks, I offered her a full-time job, not knowing if we would bring her to Prague with us, but knowing that I needed her in Los Angeles. To this day, she calls me her fairy godmother. But you know, it wasn't me. It was her talent and hard work. She was with the project for ten months.

How did your collaboration with Weta Workshop in New Zealand differ on this film?
It was a long-distance collaboration, which was not easy. They were in New Zealand, and we were in Prague, Czech Republic. We started the project by working together on the designs of the armor and weapons. The Telmarine army was the closest collaboration, throwing ideas back and forth and inspiring each other to reach the final product. The Narnian armor on all the creatures

except the dwarfs was designed and manufactured by Richard and Weta under the supervision of Roger Ford and me. They have also designed and manufactured all the weapons for both the Telmarines and Narnians. These are truly beautiful pieces.

But when it came time to manufacture the Telmarine army, we ended up building it all in Europe. We made the boots in Italy at Pompeii, a famous shoe manufacturer in Rome. We made the helmets and all the hard armor at Argo, two hours south of Prague. It was made of very lightweight metal. Each piece was handmade and given a patina for individual character.

We had a local sculptor sculpt the masks for us.

Together with Andrew, I designed the generic soldier mask. The team at Weta originally designed the lords' masks. From there, we made our alterations to fit the faces of the actors cast. Honza, the sculptor, also made all the stunt armor for the cavalry, soldiers, and lords.

By keeping this all local, we were able to troubleshoot problems and also make additional orders without problems. I was able to make many sizes and build custom uniforms for any particular actor Andrew wanted to hire.

Lucky Horse, another local, made all the leather goods under the direction of Chenda. Hundreds of hides, rivets, and hours of back-breaking work later, Chenda delivered, over a four-month span, three-hundred-plus brigandines, leather greaves, cross belts for the weapons, and underbrigandines. Each of these pieces was also made one by one without a mold.

Distance in geography and time made it more difficult and at times downright frustrating. Meetings would take place via videoconference. We would be having our morning coffee and barely awake, and Richard and the gang were ready to go home and grab an after-work beer.

What have been the physical challenges to make this movie?
Stamina. By the time I finish on this, it'll have been about fourteen months. The hardest part was the winter there in Prague, where we prepped the film. Then the first six weeks of shooting, which took place in New Zealand, early in 2007.

Nobody was in the same place at the same time. We had four clocks on the wall in every room for quick recognition of the different zones. You were working all the time because no matter what, somebody in the world was working. And that's what was so hard.

When the company went to New Zealand to start shooting on the North Island on February 12, I would get up in the morning at 5:30, go to the set, deal with the set all day, collect the e-mails from the night before coming in from Europe, then get on my computer to Prague until midnight.

I would go through every department head I had in my workshop. They'd come on screen; we'd talk about the details of the day and how to proceed. And then I'd go to bed while they went to work, and I'd wake up at five the next morning and do exactly the same thing over again. I have to tell you, after six weeks of doing that, I said, "I need to get back to the Czech Republic

LEFT: *Hairstylist Roxie Hodenfield touches up son Cameron, who plays a Telmarine villager.*
BELOW: *Narnians and Telmarine extras.*

because I cannot do it another day." It was difficult. For me, physically, it was the most challenging.

What makes it worth it?

These are fantastic projects to work on. There are only a handful of projects every year where you get to make everything, where you get to create from the bottom up. It's fantasy.

It's not period, but we get to base ourselves in a period. If it works for the story, I can do whatever I want. I don't have to be anywhere. I don't have to be in the 1000s or the 1200s or the 1500s. I can use something from last week's *Vogue* magazine, cut it with a little bit of sixteenth century, put a medieval shoe on, slap something else in there, and if it works for the story and it works for Narnia, that's it.

I had my entire manufacturing workshop there in the Czech Republic. So in addition to the leather, metal, and sculpting crafts, I also had the embroiderers (including two from the Czech Republic who were phenomenal), the dyers, the agers, the costume props who make leather belts, jewelry, crowns, etc., right here in my workroom. We make each piece from sketch to finished product. It starts with the one who cuts the original patterns, moving on to the stitchers. The next person dyes it. The next person ages it. The next person takes it and puts on a little embroidery and gives it a little touch and then it gets to the set, they shoot it, and it lives on from there.

These crafts are slipping away because of the lack of opportunity to make a living doing them. It is very rewarding to work on films such as *Prince Caspian* that offer a place for these craftspeople. They're talented, and they love what they do. Rarely does one get the opportunity to sit there for ten months embroidering and get paid to do it. So it's been a very good experience.

These are just great projects to work on. Dream projects, believe me! I'm sure a lot of people at home would be happy to have this job. And I'm lucky enough to have hooked up with Andrew at a time when his career was just taking off.

RICHARD TAYLOR
Weta Workshop

In the long and illustrious history of the Academy Awards® dating back to 1927, only thirteen people (of thousands nominated in various categories for Hollywood's highest honor) can boast of having won five or more Oscar® statuettes.

New Zealander Richard Taylor, the co-founder and guiding light (along with his partner, Tanya Rodger) behind Weta Workshop and Weta Digital in the Kiwi capital of Wellington, is a member of that elite fraternity.

No stranger to the podium at the Kodak Theatre in Hollywood, Taylor has been nominated nine times for his visual magic on Peter Jackson's *The Lord of the Rings* trilogy and his 2005 epic retelling of *King Kong*. Weta's innovative collaborators have won four Academy Awards® for their contributions to *The Lord of the Rings*—Best Visual Effects and Best Makeup for the first movie, *Fellowship of the Ring*, and Best Costume Design and Best Makeup on the final installment, *Return of the King*. He collected his fifth honor for Best Visual Effects on *King Kong*.

Seemingly, the modest Kiwi is *not* one to boast of such achievements; his name does not even appear on the faceplate of the five gold statuettes that adorn the shelves in his executive conference room. Instead, the blank nameplates imply that these awards are not singular triumphs. Taylor *would* boast that everyone at Weta involved in all four films deserves equal credit for these unique and coveted honors. Upon his return from each of the Oscar® ceremonies, he encouraged his Weta employees to take the statuettes home to proudly share with their families.

While his triumphs in Middle Earth and on Skull Island have cemented his legend in Oscar® history and put Weta on the world stage, Taylor is also a distinguished member of the Narnia family for his creative contributions to the first film, *The Lion, the Witch and the Wardrobe*. On the first project, he and his associates were credited with the design and fabrication of all the weapons and armor featured in the story, along with an assortment of designs for such mythological creatures as Minotaurs, griffins, centaurs, and several other species never before seen on the movie screen.

Taylor's studio near Wellington's airport is a wonderland of models, weapons, creatures, and assorted movie props the company's artisans have manufactured for past projects. All are on display in Weta's warehouse to amaze visitors and remind employees of past achievements. Upon entering the firm's lobby, your eyes are immediately drawn to the stunning maquette (a three-dimensional sculpted model by Taylor) showing King Kong engaged in a fierce fight with three *Tyrannosaurus rexes*, a scene brilliantly staged by director Jackson (with the help of Weta's digital wizards) in his 2005 reimagining of the 1933 film classic.

Taylor's workshop is like a Hollywood museum or theme park attraction, filled with an array of ghouls, goblins, and Gollum (the computer generated creature amazingly brought to life in *The Lord of the Rings*

Designs for Miraz's shield and sword.

by Weta Digital and actor Andy Serkis). These mesmerizing creations loom in all corners of the subterranean factory where the firm's cunning tradespeople, experts in leather, paint, metal, miniatures, and other crafts, labor lovingly on an array of lifelike movie props, many of which, like Gollum, are now considered masterpieces.

But they are more than just physical props on display in a movie. Taylor and his artisans approached their work on the Tolkien and Lewis projects with a cerebral flair, using the films' source material, the books, as blueprints to their designs. Before entering the wardrobe on the first Narnia film, Taylor and Weta had just logged seven years on Jackson's landmark movie trilogy. As they began their design approach on the C. S. Lewis story, Taylor realized how different, and challenging, the new project would be. He began his journey on the first film by asking himself a question: "What were the fantastical elements that would come alive in front of you if you were a child entering a world through the back of a wardrobe?"

"C. S. Lewis is completely different than Tolkien," Taylor explains. "When you entered Middle Earth, you entered a real world. This was not a fanciful world on another planet. This was our own world at a different time and a different era. In the case of Narnia, you entered through the back of a wardrobe, potentially into a dream world, potentially into a child's dreams, a much more fanciful, enriched world. There wasn't the same architecture. There wasn't the same written brief for us to hang our design on. We realized that we were able to bridge out to a much greater extent into fantasy, drawing on the rich mythology that C. S. Lewis's writings took on. It gave us a broader and richer palette of design than maybe we had on *Lord of the Rings.*"

Faced with new challenges on the second Narnian tale, Taylor notes that "the look of the Narnians' armor and weapons had to evolve in a new direction since we last saw them. They had to be much more simplistic,

Top: *Weta leathersmith Mike Grealish.*
Bottom: *Armorsmith Stu Johnson.*

A   B   C

Top left: *Concept art of a Narnian warrior.*
Top right: *Designs for Trumpkin's knife.*
Bottom: *Peter Dinklage as Trumpkin.*

much more rugged, much more of a handmade look, and a lot less crafted than what we saw in the first film. Additionally, the Telmarine culture had to be conceived from scratch, and a great deal of work was done in the quest to find their unique design signature.

"The Telmarines were a very exciting race of people to design," he continues. "They are humans, pirates, who have journeyed into Narnia and have become almost feudal. They live under a royalty system that's since been set aside. Now Miraz rules his people through force and

fear. Their armor is resplendent and rich and beautiful, complemented by some very fine weaponry. They are a very fierce fighting force, so quite an adversary for the Narnian creatures."

As the Weta team (whose extensive and highly skilled staff included the company's senior designers, swordsmith Peter Lyon, costumer and armorsmith Matt Appleton, senior props makers John Harvey and Callum Lingard, and foreman Gareth McGhie) set out to reimagine Narnia in this new story, Taylor posed some questions to his associates: Where did the Telmarines come from? What influenced the design of their armor? What period of our own history are we trying to suggest they represent?

"The design of Miraz's ornate armor had its roots in the backstory of the Telmarine culture" that the team conjured up to inspire Weta's weaponry and armor designs. According to the backstory, "one of the pirates from ancient Earth who found their way into Narnia centuries ago . . . established a new civilization there," Taylor explains. "Despite now being a people estranged from the sea, elements of their nautical past are evident in the direction of the design their armory took, and in turn these same motifs were incorporated into Miraz's plate armor."

In creating the special weapons that helped define the Telmarine culture, Taylor was inspired by a look of "heraldry and ceremony that befits rulers of such a vast kingdom." He felt strongly that the sword defines and signifies such a society and culture. For Miraz and his fierce army of soldiers, he chose rapiers and falchions. The rapier is a sophisticated weapon with a very long blade and a basketed hilt "that is used in a much more refined and subtle motion than the hack-and-slash motion of some of the weapons in the first film," he says.

"There's a lot of ceremony in these various pieces," Taylor notes. "An ornamentation that illustrates the pomp and ceremony of Miraz and his people. And that's what we've tried to emulate in the look of the armor and weapons." His design team created individual swords, scabbards, and sculpted faceplate helmets for the featured lords including Glozelle, who also has a beautiful dagger. Miraz himself was given a special shield, sword, scabbard, full plate armor, and an ornate faceplate helmet.

"Miraz's helmet and facial mask represent the pomp under which he tries to command his forces," Taylor says about the mask designs that evolved through discussions with Andrew. "The idea [is] that it's a faceless army hidden behind these masks, not showing their emotions or their war faces because it's captured in these very stylistic Italian ceremonial masks that they wear." Weta's designs have strong features, a chiseled sculptural look that adds a sternness and a power to Miraz's poise and expression, which made for a rich texture and a stark contrast to the Narnian army.

Miraz's helmet was the first component of his armor to find a strong direction during the design phase. Taylor continues, "From the outset, Andrew suggested

---

Top: *Max Patte sculpts Miraz's faceplate.*
Middle and bottom: *Miraz's armor.*

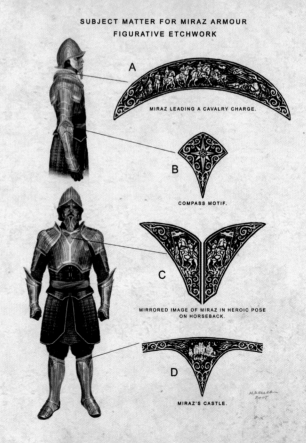

SUBJECT MATTER FOR MIRAZ ARMOUR
FIGURATIVE ETCHWORK

A

MIRAZ LEADING A CAVALRY CHARGE.

B

COMPASS MOTIF.

C

MIRRORED IMAGE OF MIRAZ IN HEROIC POSE
ON HORSEBACK.

D

MIRAZ'S CASTLE.

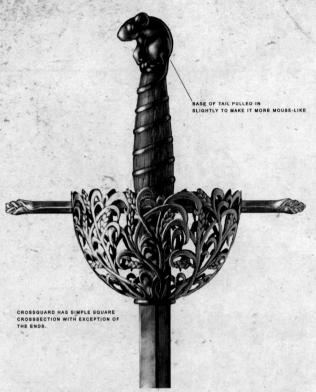

BASE OF TAIL PULLED IN
SLIGHTLY TO MAKE IT MORE MOUSE-LIKE

CROSSGUARD HAS SIMPLE SQUARE
CROSSSECTION WITH EXCEPTION OF
THE ENDS.

experimenting with this idea of masks." This eventually lead Weta's designers to create the stylized, bearded faceplate seen in the final helmet, crafted by Weta sculptor Max Patte.

"Designer Paul Tobin found inspiration for the shape of Miraz's helmet in the styles of the Spanish conquistador explorers, while the mask was influenced by the intimidating masks of samurai helmets," Taylor adds. "Paul reinterpreted them, using sculptural stylization derived from classical European statuary and the iconic representations of the marauding conquistador explorers to marry the helmet and mask together into something new and original."

"For the evil ruler's elaborate sword, designer Brad Goff gave a distinctive, deeply etched hilt. The rich engravings were a mixture of pictorial elements, illustrating the Telmarines' history, and swirling wave and ivy motifs. At the same time, Paul Tobin was honing the design of Miraz's shields, employing three motif themes—that of the compass (another hint to the Telmarines' seagoing past); stylized fish scales; and strong architectural shapes that would appear also in the design of Miraz's castle. The shields also established Miraz's color palette, one of deep sea blue-greens against burnished bronze."

Weta spent over two years creating the weaponry on the first film, but a shorter deadline and more complexity in the designs on *Prince Caspian* compelled the team to come up with new techniques this time out, notably a three-dimensional milling technology.

"We modeled a lot of our swords in 3-D, using high-pressure water jet cutting to cut the blades," he explains. This process involves 3-D digital data to engrave and shape the sword blades. To complete the blade fabrication, technology gives way to good old-fashioned

TOP: *Design for Reepicheep's sword.*
MIDDLE LEFT: *Dan Bennett works on Miraz's shield.*
MIDDLE RIGHT: *A Weta technician works on a Telmarine horse faceplate.* BOTTOM: *Cathy "Tree" Harris edges leather for the centaur armor.*

hand"techniques to put a finished polish on them. Even the hilts and crossbars in some cases have been printed in 3-D, waxed, then sent to bronze casters, who pour molten bronze to create the cast for the weapon using lost-wax casting.

"Reepicheep's sword is a great example of this process," Taylor says. "It is a tiny little weapon, maybe seven inches long. The basket of it is no bigger than the end of your thumb. For this special weapon, we employed three-dimensional dental printing technology, the very thing that prints the top of a crown for your broken tooth, because of the incredible delicacy needed and the fine silver of his sword." The prop was ultimately lost during filming in Usti, and never found again.

The Weta design and fabrication team included fourteen designers "working with me and with Andrew across video conferencing," Taylor says. This elaborate communication system connecting two continents was fashioned for the first movie. His manufacturing team numbered between fifty and sixty people, including swordsmiths, mold makers, and urethane casters.

By his own count for *Prince Caspian*, Taylor's talented staff manufactured over two thousand five hundred prop weapons, which included 200 polearms in two different styles; 200 rapiers of varying design; over a hundred falchions; 250 shields, and 55 crossbows, including the handsome and deadly weapon wielded by Miraz's queen, Prunaprismia. The Telmarine cavalry was equipped with soft shields and stunt gear for use with live horses, which included stunt-safe horse faceplates for the warhorses and unusual sculpted faceplate helmets for the soldiers.

Taylor remarks, "We've always had the attitude that if we are tasked to make a military prop such as a sword, a suit of armor, any form of weapon, then we want to try to create the originals as closely as the technology would have [allowed] in the period it was originally

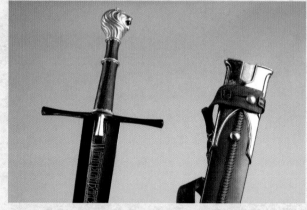

Top and middle: *Peter's shield and sword.*
Bottom: *Armorer Joe Dunckley working on actor Will Moseley.*

made, which means you have to draw on traditional hand skills. Over the years, we've looked for people who can bring that depth of traditional hand skills to our workshop. In some cases, we've got people who are third-generation artists using their family techniques that we benefit from here."

The hand-ground, spring steel sword made for the film's hero, High King Peter, was designed by conceptual artist John Howe for the first film and made by twelve-year Weta employee, master sword maker Peter Lyon. "It was inspired by medieval broadswords," Taylor says. "It carries continual reminders of Aslan's central role, vis-à-vis in the lion head pommel and inscriptions along the blade."

For Peter's shield, Taylor says, "we started with Lewis's rather brief description, from which Weta designer Paul Tobin began to add a greater visual depth to the design by looking for other appropriate references found within all the Narnian Chronicles. This meant incorporating imagery of the Tree of Protection—the Magic Apple Tree planted in the first book by Digory, which is a major icon of Narnia."

Weta not only created armor for the film's human characters, the Telmarines, but also for the assorted four-legged creatures, both real and mythological, that roam Narnia. "The horse faceplates for Miraz's army were great fun as well," Taylor relates. "A laminated plate armor that we've taken to a single casting using two different densities of urethane so that if the horses were to press up against each other, at least the spike on its forehead wouldn't pierce the skin. It is flexible enough to not cause injury."

The designer points out that because they add majesty to the character brandishing the armor and weaponry, these complex combinations of leather, fabric, steel, and chain mail "have to look very beautiful and metallic and rich. Not only must they appear real and majestic, they must also be practical, meaning stunt-friendly, comfortable, safe film prop armor. So in the case of our work, we mostly produce the masters out of steel, hand-beating

them, which Weta's Stu Johnson and his team do, beating them on an anvil. From there, once we've prototyped them, leather strapped them together, tested them, got them approved by the director, they may go through six to eight prototypes in steel before we finally lock down on the design," Taylor elaborates.

"Next, they go through to the molding shop. We've come up with a clever technique for molding our armor that allows us to pump it out at incredible speed, molded out of silicone with a two-part semiflexible urethane, CC-60, being the shore of the product—similar to the component used on skateboard wheels. We then hand lay the more complex components. They're trimmed, cleaned, and once again reassembled, painted, and embellished as is necessary with fine detail. Hopefully we produce an amazing array of visually stunning armor that is safe for the young actors to wear and doesn't look like it's made of some sort of plastic."

While Taylor enjoys the fabrication phase of his work on the southern tip of New Zealand's North Island, ulti-

mately he must ship the materials to the film location. Weta sends some of the core group of workshop technicians to location as on-set technicians and costumers who dress the key cast and the hundreds of extras.

"Where possible, we like the dressers to be the people that made the armor, because then they're responsible for it," Taylor remarks. "In a population of four million people in New Zealand, there's not that many who actually know how to do armor and weapons on a movie set. We have a core group of maybe twelve people, led by a couple of colleagues who returned from the first movie—Joe Dunckley and Rob Gillies."

Dunckley and Gillies, both 29, are lifelong friends from Dunedin, the Scottish-flavored college town on the eastern shore of New Zealand's South Island. Both began their careers with Weta back in early 2000, "fresh out of high school," comments the armorer Dunckley.

In addition to the local crew members from the Czech Republic and neighboring Slovakia who comprised much of the thirty-strong staff, the pair also worked with a small group of fellow New Zealanders that included five other Weta crew members—Tim Tozer, Simon Hall, Ben Price, and Laki Laban (all Dunedin natives and lifelong friends), and Tristan McCallum. Under the supervision of another Kiwi, the raven-haired Jenny Morgan, Dunckley and Gillies were responsible for equipping the main cast (on both film units) with their assorted weapons and armor, while a support staff worked behind the scenes around the clock to maintain the movie props' longevity and appearance.

"These weapons take a beating from scene to scene," the guys relate about the punishing wear and tear endured by the artificial swords and armor, especially in action-oriented scenes like the grueling sword fight between Peter and Miraz. "We always had multiple swords for each character. We'd switch them out from one take to the next so our painters could touch up the nicks and scratches for coming scenes—all to protect the integrity of the props and ensure their continuity in front of the cameras."

After a long day's filming, the weapons crew spent another hour collecting all the armor and such from the key cast and hundreds of extras. While they packed up for a restful evening, their "night repair crew" would begin their day at 7:00 P.M. inspecting the assorted weaponry for repairs before the next day's filming began.

Of the main cast members with whom the pair worked daily, no one expressed a more fervent desire and enthusiasm toward his weaponry than actor Will Moseley, Dunckley reports. "Even when Andrew was filming

Will's closeups, he would ask for his sword, which would not be seen in the shot, to inspire his performance. It goes back to what Richard says about these props."

"We do believe it's our responsibility to help the actor take on the mantle of the character," Taylor says about the commitment lent to all of Weta's designs. "We're dressing these people. We're supplying them with the hand props that will allow them to play out their characters, and to that end we hope that when they take hold of their sword, they feel like they are embracing not a prop, but a weapon that would determine whether they lived or died, whether they could survive or fall in the world of Narnia."

That corporate philosophy also applied to the miniature sets Weta's talented crew fabricated at their workshop not long after principal photography on the project

LEFT: *Neil Marnane works on one of the castle minatures.*
BELOW AND OPPOSITE: *The miniature sets built by Weta in New Zealand.*

began in February 2007. Weta's miniature-construction crew erected three smaller versions of Roger Ford's enormous castle courtyard set—one at 1/24 scale of the massive twenty-thousand-square-foot build at Barrandov; one at 1/10 scale, and the other at 1/100 scale, which measures sixty square feet (or twenty meters).

The miniature sets were then disassembled and trucked over to another stage in Miramar, where two-time Oscar® winner Alex Funke (*The Lord of the Rings: The Two Towers, Return of the King*) spent over three months filming the sets to incorporate into the main film footage.

"Andrew is a big fan of trying to put whatever is real in the frame," visual effects supervisor Dean Wright chimes in. Miniature sets "make it more real or organic within the frame and the story. Not to amaze the audience. The 24th scale of the castle is a huge miniature built by Weta in New Zealand and shot by Alex Funke and his minia-

ture team that did all the work on *The Lord of the Rings* and *King Kong.* Shooting miniatures is real and tangible. In this case, it will help enhance this very cool-looking castle. When you have a well-lit miniature, you again fall into this world of believing everything you're seeing, and that's what we wanted to do: suck you into the story and the movie."

Through these films, Taylor and his Weta artisans "wanted to reflect in our work what Andrew felt about the books, what his childhood memories of the books were, and how they had enriched his life. To do something like the world of Narnia, you've got to enter it with your heart. You have to willingly embrace the world that C. S. Lewis wrote, and embrace the dreams and fantasies that reading induced in you as a child to bring a beautiful product to the screen. In Andrew, we heard that. And that empowered us to want to go on the journey with him in both these movies."

THE AURALISTS

The Sound . . . and the Music

Movies are a visual medium. Sound did not come into the picture for two decades after the birth of the American cinema.

Today, it would be hard to imagine a movie without sound, be it dialogue to propel the story or music to add ambience or emotion to a moment or scene. Both add immeasurably to the effect a piece of film has on its audience.

The next time you watch a horror film, note not only what you *see* the instant you jump out of your seat at a particularly frightening moment, but what you *hear* as well. It might surprise you that the horrific effect works because of the combination of the sight and the sound.

The same applies to how a filmmaker uses music to define a character, a scene, an emotion. There are so many examples to illustrate the power of a movie's score, but one that comes to mind is 1980's *Chariots of Fire*. Vangelis's powerfully moving title theme is almost a character in the story. Some might say the score was the main reason the film walked off with four Oscars®!

In creating the sound and the music for a motion picture, be it a large-scale production like *Prince Caspian* or an intimate story like *Cinema Paradiso*, hundreds of artists contribute to the film's soundtrack—what ultimately becomes a film's dialogue and score.

While we cannot profile everyone in this department who worked on this movie, we would like to introduce you to the film's sound mixer and composer, both of whom were recognized by industry peers with award nominations for their contributions to *The Lion, the Witch and the Wardrobe*. Both returned at Andrew's invitation to spin their aural magic once again on *Prince Caspian*.

UP TO SPEED

Sound mixer Tony Johnson (or T. J., as he is known to colleagues on the set) returns to the world of Narnia following his Academy Award®-nominated work on the first film, *The Lion, the Witch and the Wardrobe*, which marked his very first Oscar® nomination. He shared the citation with two Los Angeles–based re-recording sound mixers, Terry Porter and Dean Zupancic, both of whom are on staff at the Walt Disney Studios in Burbank, California.

You may be familiar with the Hollywood catchphrase "Lights! Camera! Action!" but "Rolling . . . speed . . . action . . . cut" are the actual directives used when filming is under way.

To announce that the operator has turned on the camera, the first assistant director (here, the veteran, K. C. Hodenfield) begins each take by yelling out, "Rolling!"

The movie's sound mixer next signifies that his recording equipment (a multitrack hard drive) is on by shouting "Speed!" or "Speeding!" depending on the mixer.

That is followed by the director yelling "Action!" at which time the cast begins their work. The take concludes once they hear "Cut!" which signifies the scene is complete.

The motion picture sound mixer (call him an "auralist") is one of only a handful of crafts up for Academy Award® consideration that do not receive what the industry defines as "above the line" credit on the film (those crafts, like cinematography, costume design, film editing, and production design that are noted in the credits at the beginning of the film). Sound mixers receive their credit in the collective credit roll at the end.

One of New Zealand's finest sound craftsmen, Tony has been recording movie sound for almost twenty years. His beachfront home outside Auckland is adorned

with an Australian Film Institute (AFI) trophy for the acclaimed 1993 drama *The Piano*, and a New Zealand Film and TV award for the 1996 Kiwi production *Broken English*.

During filming of the first *Narnia* feature, he had just earned his first Emmy® nomination (as well as a Cinema Audio Society [CAS] nod from this American fraternity of mixers) for the 2004 TNT television movie *Ike: Countdown to D-Day*, which starred Tom Selleck and filmed entirely on location in the Auckland area. In addition to the *Narnia* movies, Tony also recorded the sound for two more recent Walden projects—*The Bridge to Terabithia* and *The Waterhorse*, both filmed on location in his homeland.

The first *Narnia* project also proved educational for the veteran soundman. He met both his postproduction counterparts (Porter and Zupancic) when he flew himself to California to sit in on their sound re-record sessions of his original tracks after filming had concluded in early 2005.

"When I saw the finished movie, I was blown away at how well Terry and Dean had mixed the soundtrack," Johnson relates. "It was also educational for me to sit in with them, as I learned what they needed to adjust in post, which gave me an idea of what I had to watch for on this film."

A native of Wellington (New Zealand's capital), Tony had always aspired to work as a sound recordist. He learned his craft at the now-defunct National Film, a government-sponsored training program. He began his career doing postproduction sound editing before segueing into freelance work on the set, first as a boom (microphone) operator, which he admits he hated. "I did only two projects as a boomman and was told by both mixers that I was awful at it."

OPPOSITE: *Sound mixer Tony "TJ" Johnson.*
THIS PAGE TOP: *Cameraman Greg Lundsgaard films Skandar Keynes.* MIDDLE: *Boomman Roman Rigo.*
BOTTOM: *Filming outside Aslan's How.*

One of only a handful of native Kiwi mixers who work on international movie productions like the *Narnia* films, Tony has seen his craft progress over the years. Back in 1990, when he mixed his first movie, he used a now-obsolete recording machine called a Nagra. In ensuing years, the Nagra gave way to a digital audio tape, or DAT. In this age of computer technology, the old audio tape systems have now advanced to more expensive and sophisticated hard drives, which Tony admits adds a lot to his daily workload on the set.

On a typical workday, Tony's crew comprises three people. Tony operates the actual recording equipment (worth over $100,000) that captures the dialogue and ambient sound on the stage or exterior location. He works with a boomman, the person who holds the microphone that feeds the sound to his recording devices, and a third person who is a utility, or cable, assistant. The assistant works with a second mic and serves as a general aide to Tony on the set.

In many cases, like this movie, much of the dialogue is captured on hidden wireless microphones that have been carefully planted under actors' costumes by his team. "When you have five wireless mics going at the same time, it is a challenge to mix all those into a smooth track. You have to watch the script pages so you know who says what and when," he comments.

Tony says his most challenging scene on *Prince Caspian* involved the Stone Table at Barrandov's cavernous Stage 6, "where there was a council of eight speaking roles. The set had a fire ring burning for the whole scene, which produced a crackle and hiss all through the sequence. All the actors had personal (wireless) microphones as well as the boom mic operated by my colleague, Roman Rigo."

"That made for very difficult sound mixing," he continues. "So many microphones at once over five days. Trying to keep the sound consistent over the lengthy time frame when the microphones have to

TOP: *Filming the Telmarine canoe from a river platform.*
MIDDLE AND BOTTOM: *Filming on location in Slovenia.*

come on and off the actors at the end of every day. The critical thing is to make sure the mic goes on in exactly the same place every day so that when the scene is cut together, the audience should not detect any difference in sound quality."

Working on exterior locations also comes with sometimes insurmountable challenges. For instance, when filming at the Kamiencyka Gorge in Poland (a scout that he did not attend), he arrived at work to discover a cascading waterfall maybe 100 feet from where Andrew staged a dialogue-driven scene involving the four Pevensies and Trumpkin.

"Sound often does not become a priority when scouting locations," Tony admits, "as 'the look' is the big and more important criteria. One such situation I faced was the gorge location in Poland where Lucy sees Aslan for the first time. The script described a deep gorge or ravine, but when we arrived, it was right next to a waterfall, which meant two pages of dialogue will have to be replaced."

Tony confirms there is nothing you can do to elimi-

nate or filter a noise that is as loud, if not louder, than the spoken word. In such instances, the entire scene might have to be replaced. Dialogue that cannot be salvaged from production tracks must be re-recorded in a process called "looping," or automated dialogue replacement (ADR), whereby the actor, after filming wraps completely, watches the image repeatedly while listening to the original production track on headphones as a guide. The actor then performs each line to match the wording and lip movements.

Andrew also knew that Tony's dialogue tracks would be compromised at the gorge location and was prepared to replace the sound, something he confirmed when watching dailies of scene 48 and struggling to hear the dialogue over the ambient waterfalls. "Even though it is frustrating, one has to acknowledge the bigger picture in these situations. No department is bigger than the film itself," Tony adds.

Those are the days when Tony's job requires serious concentration in order for the veteran soundman to stay up to speed.

"... AND THE MUSIC" —
Harry Scores Again

When production designer Roger Ford and costume designer Isis Mussenden and creature creator Howard Berger first sat down to begin envisioning the physical world of Narnia for their respective contributions to these movies, these visualists had some pictorial material from which to draw inspiration: Pauline Baynes's simple pen-and-ink drawings that illustrated author C. S. Lewis's books.

When listening to composer Harry Gregson-Williams's beautiful and evocative musical score from *The Lion, the Witch and the Wardrobe*, an equally significant artistic contribution to the overall endeavor, one wonders what influenced his composition of the film's music, as a book contains no aural reference. Like his colleagues, whose

work is long done when Harry enters the picture, he *did* turn to the source material—the books.

"The fact that I had read the books as a youngster and loved them certainly helped me shape the music for *The Lion, the Witch and the Wardrobe*," the composer states. "When I read the book as a child, I particularly remember being transported into this fantasy world where anything could happen at any moment!"

In his re-reading of the book, that feeling, that emotion, helped Gregson-Williams write what he felt was the most important piece of music for that film: the moment when Lucy first enters the wardrobe. "That scene for me was filled with so much awe and wonder," he says, "and I drew from those feelings when I sat down to write that piece of music, which was the very first theme I wrote for the movie. When I needed further inspiration, I would always go back to that particular piece of music."

Like its history in the evolution of motion pictures, music has always been a significant part of Harry's life. This accomplished composer, conductor, arranger, and

orchestrator studied voice, piano, and violin as a child growing up in London. "Both my parents and all of my siblings were constantly playing and singing music as I was growing up, so it was completely natural for me to follow in their footsteps," he says. "At a young age, I spent a huge amount of time experimenting with various instruments, so playing music became a way of life to me. By the time I was a teenager, it was clear that music was going to *be* my life."

As a youngster, he performed throughout Europe, toured with the choir of St. John's College, Cambridge (where he earned a scholarship at age seven), and played as a soloist for numerous recordings as well as for television. Going from one musical scholarship to another, Gregson-Williams eventually studied at the distinguished Guildhall School of Music and Drama in London.

A position at the Amesbury School in England led to jobs teaching music to children in Egypt and in the Rift Valley in Kenya. "Music is something that can enrich, challenge, and focus young people," he emphasizes. "It is a universal language in which one can express personal feelings either with or without other people's input."

Although satisfied with his teaching career, he did dabble with composing during those days in the 1980s. "I started writing music for fun when I first started teaching . . . experimenting with a piece of choral music." His father's input eventually led him to focus on his own music. His father encouraged him to contact British film composer Richard Harvey, who persuaded the young composer to take a job as an assistant. Gregson-Williams left the classroom for the studio and spent the next five years working closely with Harvey on several projects.

That association led to introductions to a pair of legendary film composers—Stanley Myers and Hans Zimmer—with whom he started his film career as an orchestrator and arranger. Gregson-Williams's arrangement on a particular piece of Zimmer's music for the 1992 film *Cold Heaven* led the pair to realize that they had discovered a burgeoning talent.

Relocating to the United States, Gregson-Williams

spent the rest of his film-scoring tutelage with Zimmer at Media Ventures (now called Remote Control Productions), working on projects such as 1996's *The Rock* and 1998's *The Prince of Egypt* while composing his own full-length movie scores for two 1998 features: *The Borrowers* and *The Replacement Killers*.

During his affiliation with DreamWorks (*The Prince of Egypt*, *Chicken Run*, *Antz*), Harry met director Andrew Adamson for the first time. The studio and filmmaker

*M*y *work is to help Andrew to realize his vision for his movie and perhaps to bring another dimension to this vision.*

were looking for a composer to bring a unique sound to their story of an ogre who falls in love with a princess, "a very different theme because our hero was not your typical fairy-tale character," Adamson says.

The film was called *Shrek*, Harry composed the music (along with longtime ally John Powell), and the film went on to win the very first Academy Award® for Best Animated Feature. Harry himself shared an "Annie" Award with Powell for Best Musical Achievement in Animation. In addition to the well-deserved honors, a partnership was born between Harry and Andrew, one that led to the blockbuster sequel, *Shrek 2*, and both *Narnia* movies.

"You cannot listen to a movie's music and say, 'That's probably a Harry Gregson-Williams score,'" Andrew observes about the musician's diversity in his compositions. "Like authors, composers can develop a certain style. I've always found Harry to display a certain creative flexibility."

That would certainly be evident in the three scores he composed in 2005: Ridley Scott's historical epic, *Kingdom of Heaven*; brother Tony Scott's gritty contemporary biopic, *Domino*; and Adamson's fantastical fairy tale, *The Lion, the Witch and the Wardrobe,* for which he earned a Grammy nomination.

Gregson-Williams's approach to this trio of diverse stories and projects? "I try never to repeat myself when I sit down to write a piece of music. If I can describe my style or approach, it's that of a musical chameleon," he notes.

When he began his work on the first *Narnia* movie, he initially sought a "signpost," as he calls it, to bring him musically into Lewis's make-believe world. He found it in the emotional arc of the four children who venture beyond the wardrobe into the adventure of a lifetime. "As seen through the eyes of the four children, it is important that the music reflects their journeys, both physical and spiritual, in Narnia," he says.

As he began his own journey into Narnia, "I watched the film over and over again, getting to know the characters involved, and from that a musical idea, a theme, was hatched," he explains. "I try to find something extra that the music can say about a character other than what is immediately obvious on-screen. While each of the four children had their own themes, I focused my music more on them as a family unit, which I think worked out well."

"To him, the music comes first, and then he almost finds the application," Adamson told the *Hollywood Reporter* in their May 2007 profile of the prolific composer, who has written over sixty scores to date. "On the 'Narnia' series, when we started with that—before he'd even seen anything—he told me he had 'this big heroic theme that I'm imagining at a coronation or something.' He sat down and played it for me on piano. It was beautiful, and it became one of the strongest themes in the film. He has a very intuitive approach to film music."

Gregson-Williams enjoys his ongoing association with director Adamson because "Andrew likes to be part of the entire musical process," he observes. "Because Andrew plays guitar, he learns each music cue as I play it for him. Our artistic partnership is a collaborative one. My work is to help Andrew, or any director, to realize his vision for his movie and perhaps to bring another dimension to this vision, to show him something about his film that he didn't even know through the use of music. Andrew wants to know about the effect of the music on every frame of film."

Gregson-Williams tackles each score (which he calls "pieces of a puzzle") differently. Sometimes, he can begin writing by turning to the source material, like a book. With director Tony Scott (for whom he has scored his last six films dating back to 1998's *Enemy of the State*), he comes in at the ground level, the script stage, says the filmmaker. In other instances, like on *The Lion, the Witch and the Wardrobe,* he watches the rough edit several times for inspiration.

And he doesn't necessarily write an entire score before entering the recording studio. "It can be quite a challenge to write 120 minutes of music for a movie all at once," he says. "I sometimes do it in phases, writing thirty minutes, then recording that, before going back and composing another segment, then repeating that process."

The composer admits that recording his scores offers the most enjoyment. "There is a lot of angst in composition," he confesses. "When you finally set foot in the recording studio, there is a sense of relief and destiny. I have always found that portion of the process remarkable."

His favorite recording studio is London's Abbey Road (especially its historic Studio 1), which he calls "just magnificent, with a great and long history." While he recorded the score for the first *Narnia* movie at the Todd AO Studios in Los Angeles, he did return to London's famed studio (where he has completed orchestrations for at least thirty of his soundtracks) for *Prince Caspian*, which he began in January 2008.

After watching the new film for the first time in late September 2007, Harry immediately noticed how different *Prince Caspian* was from Adamson's first venture through the wardrobe. While he admits that he hadn't written a note before seeing this early cut, he hinted at what his score for the new movie might contain. "It is a much darker film, which immediately led me to think of unusual solo instruments that might augment an orchestra and choir and lend interesting colors to the overall tapestry."

"I found the Telmarines to be quite menacing, so that will certainly affect the music I write for them," the composer continues. "And the hero, Caspian, who reminded me of Orlando Bloom's character in *Kingdom of Heaven*, will have his own theme, one inspired by the character's sense of destiny in the story."

Of course, before venturing from his Los Angeles home back to his homeland in England to visit with Andrew and begin discussing the score for *Prince Caspian*, he did read the screenplay and re-read the book, this time to a captive audience. "It became the bedtime story for my two kids, ages six and eight, for weeks," he smiles.

Too bad he didn't sing them a lullaby as well, maybe one that would hint at another rousing theme to come.

V isual effects has now got a little home in just about every department. We are part of the art department, part of costumes, part of Howard's team, prosthetics, and so on.

THE ILLUSIONISTS

The Special Effects of Narnia

DEAN WRIGHT AND WENDY ROGERS
VFX Supervisors

After the last shot is rolled, after the castle is torn down, and most of the crew heads home for a well-earned rest, for some, the work is only just beginning to get interesting.

"The Illusionists" is a look at the visual effects (VFX) supervisors and their skilled and dedicated crew. While their contributions are on display in nearly every frame of the film, we decided to spotlight two distinct examples of their work to show how they can make the fantastical seem real.

First, we'll explore how the complicated Castle Raid sequence, one that didn't exist in the book, came together, as the VFX wizards incorporated the craftsmanship of every other department on the film; second, we'll meet one of the story's new CGI characters, Reepicheep the mouse—certainly not your average household rodent.

Our guides through this complicated journey are Dean Wright, a veteran of the last trip into Narnia (and an Oscar® nominee for his work) and Wendy Rogers, who first worked with Andrew on 1995's *Batman Forever* and has collaborated with him several times since. As visual effects supervisors, Wendy and Dean led a team of hundreds of technicians and craftsmen to create these and many, many other essential, imaginative elements of *Prince Caspian*.

OPPOSITE — TOP: *Overview of the Telmarine Village set on Barrandov's backlot.* MIDDLE: *Howard Berger, Dean Wright, and Mark Johnson.* BOTTOM: *Wendy Rogers and crew.*

THE RAID

"One of the many cool things about the night raid in the castle was that it really encompassed all the magic tricks," says special makeup artist Howard Berger. "We had actors, obviously, and extras playing Telmarines and Narnians. The scene featured all our creature suits (satyrs, Minotaurs) and prosthetic makeups (fauns, centaurs), which were integrated with a lot of digital creatures and augmentation, like with our centaurs. And giant flying griffins, which are amazing. The mechanical special effects department rigged explosions and fire and these big air rams. Add to that Allan's stunt department, where there's just stunt after stunt after stunt."

Berger and his creature makeup department, which numbered close to fifty members, brought at least eighty Narnians to vivid life during the thirty-night shoot.

Isis Mussenden's costumers handsomely dressed the human characters played by some one hundred Czech extras. Richard Taylor's Weta Workshop put the lethal weapons in the warring factions' hands. Stunt coordinator Allan Poppleton choreographed the action of not only the creatures and soldiers, but the film's key cast also. Gerd Feuchter's mechanical effects crew rigged the physical effects like fire and wind that added dramatic ambience to the entire scene.

Roger Ford's massive art department and construction crew built the canvas on which Andrew (and second unit director, John Mahaffie) would paint the exciting scene: Miraz's spectacular castle courtyard. And Walter Lindenlaub created the brilliant lighting design, making Roger's iconic set build resemble a sports stadium aglow for a spectacular nighttime battle.

It all began with Rpin Suwannath's previsualization staff, which first conceived of the raid's look and created the very first visuals of the castle raid's design based on Andrew's notes about how he foresaw the action unfolding.

Rpin notes that there wasn't a finished script when his team of artists began pre-vizing the film in March

2006. There weren't even storyboards at this early stage in preproduction. "Most important, the castle raid scene did not exist in the book," he points out. "So we animated this many times over, which in essence served as inspiration for the screenwriters, who were writing based on what we showed them in the computer."

For the visionary director whose long background in movie effects made him the perfect choice to visualize Narnia on the big screen, previsualization is absolutely vital to his ability to mount films of this nature. "It just helps you see pieces of the puzzle that aren't there on the day you direct these types of scenes," he confides. "I can't imagine not using pre-viz for a movie like this."

After filming all the action that could be realized "live" inside the cameras, the whole enterprise came to vibrant life through the special talents of VFX supervisors Dean Wright and Wendy Rogers. Dean oversaw the overall sequence, and Wendy supervised the birth of one of the scene's heroes, Reepicheep. Wendy was responsible for all the CGI character work in the film based on her

previous supervisory experience on computer-animated features like *Flushed Away* and *Shrek*.

"It's a symbiotic relationship," Wright explains. "Otherwise, it would not work. For instance, there's a natural working relationship between the camera department and visual effects because they shoot everything that we need to have later. Visual effects has now got a little home in just about every department. We are part of the art department, part of costumes, part of Howard's team, prosthetics, and so on."

"For Narnia!" raged Peter Pevensie, saber drawn, as he charged across the majestic courtyard of Miraz's castle on Barrandov's backlot. So began scene 98, the castle siege by the Narnians, on the night of April 24, day 43 of the lengthy 136-day shoot.

It was almost a month of night work for the company to film the first huge battle sequence of the movie, which occurs about halfway through the film. The scene was fabricated for the film because "unlike the first movie, at the beginning of this movie we had to start epic and then get more epic," Andrew explains.

Adds writer Chris Markus, "We wanted to get the Pevensies and Caspian in action together prior to the final fight, to give them more of a functioning relationship based on actual incidents. The same holds for them in relation to Miraz. Because he was a more human, fallible villain than the White Witch, it didn't seem right for him to be hidden away in his castle. Getting him up and into the action, letting our good guys get a real, firsthand sense of him, seemed right.

"Also, he and Caspian needed to meet and interact," Markus continues. Those familiar with Lewis's second novel in the series know that Caspian really has no contact with his uncle in the book. He finds out Miraz killed his father and wants to kill him but really never has a chance to act on that knowledge. "To give him the opportunity to maintain or lose control, in his childhood home, against the man who raised him, seemed too good an idea to pass up," writer Markus adds.

William Mosely rightly points out that the night raid serves as a backdrop to illustrate the friction between Peter (Narnia's High King) and Caspian (the rightful heir—but still only a prince). Peter is gung ho about capturing Miraz, but Caspian has his doubts.

"I think it's interesting that the filmmakers played on that rivalry between Peter and Caspian," says Will. "Both have their own issues to deal with," he adds. "When neither is willing to compromise, there's bound to be friction, and that's what happens. The entire story, and this sequence in particular, also deals with humility. They both have to learn humility. A great king needs to be humble and listen to his people. They start off as angry teenagers and become kings in the end."

"The whole thing was very dramatic," raves Anna Popplewell, whose Susan gets to show off her action chops in the scene. "It goes from being three or four characters creeping around the castle to this clash of two races, of the Narnian creatures and the Telmarines."

Adds Andrew, "I got to do some things that I didn't have time to do in the last film, particularly with action. Because of the way the last film was structured, action

was really at the end of the film, whereas in *Prince Caspian*, it is more inherent to the story. There are battles all the way through."

To illustrate his point, Andrew notes that through the magic of CGI graphics, "we'll take griffins and Minotaurs and centaurs and have them fight against human soldiers within the confines of our castle courtyard. These are the kinds of images that we haven't seen before, so it was fun for me to get a chance to play with those kinds of images."

The sequence (comprising scenes 98 to 115 in the script, which equates to approximately ten to twelve

THE SETTING

Surely the filmmakers wouldn't conceive and construct this enormous castle courtyard for just the night raid . . . would they?

"It's true!" exclaims production designer Roger Ford. "It was designed specifically for this scene. In fact, the whole castle, really, was planned around it."

Ford knew what size he wanted for the biggest set he has ever created for a film after Andrew saw Pierrefonds, the castle in France. Once they decided that Pierrefonds would be their inspiration for the castle design and builds, the company turned to Suwannath to animate portions of the thrilling sequence using previsualization, his stock-in-trade.

Suwannath's pre-viz allowed Ford's concept artists, scenic designers, and builders to "give Andrew much more of what he wanted for the action," Ford states. "All the stairs throughout the castle were specifically designed for the action, all purposely built for the film. And everything you see in the final sequence happened the way it was all planned out. The set was designed and built to suit the film, rather than just having to compromise the script and the design to an existing location."

Ford sets the stage for the epic confrontation by explaining that the introduction to the castle storming takes place not on the courtyard floor, but in various other locales around the massive, twenty-thousand-square-foot structure. The early shots were filmed on disconnected sets built inside Barrandov's assorted soundstages. When edited together with the courtyard battle, they will appear absolutely seamless to audiences, as if all the action were staged right on the backlot set.

"The Narnians first arrive very high up in the castle, on towers that we built as separate sets inside the stages," Ford explains. The griffins, who will be rendered entirely in CG, drop the human characters silently atop the parapets, which sets into motion the complex machinery of the mission.

minutes of screen time) combined the efforts of virtually the entire crew to pull off, beginning with Suwannath's previsualized interpretation of an outline provided by Andrew and writers Markus and McFeely that began the massive enterprise a year before the cameras would actually roll on the castle set.

"It's a surprise raid at night," the production designer continues. In the sequence, the Narnians are trying to capture Miraz. First, Reepicheep the mouse and his cohorts gain entrance to the castle through the drains and up the chains and make their way into the gatehouse (on a set built on the studio's new Stage 10). There, they manage to open the drawbridge and the portcullis.

Simultaneously, Edmund, who's on top of a tower with his torch (having been deposited there by a giant griffin), signals to the Narnians that they can start to attack because the gates are now open. And the raid begins. They all pour in through the portcullis. When Susan enters the courtyard, she finds her way up onto a balcony, from which she slays the opposition using the bow and arrows given her by Father Christmas. (Her stunning proficiency with the bow was also the product of the VFX wizards.)

For Susan's vantage point during the night raid, Ford designed a staircase leading to a balcony "where Susan gets herself into a position where she can start using her bow and arrow. We changed the design, put in another doorway, based on Andrew's notes, so Susan could get into position as quickly as possible. And that's just an instance of how the set took shape, specifically for the requirements of the script. And the shot of Susan on that balcony shooting her arrows down at the Telmarines is just fantastic."

THE ACTION

If the castle set is the canvas, and the actors, sets, creatures, stunts, CG characters, weapons, animals, and so on, comprise the palette, then Andrew and the VFX wizards become the painters who outline, color, and shade this masterpiece slowly and painstakingly before it unspools on the screen.

"This is one of the biggest visual effects films ever made," claims VFX co-supervisor Dean Wright, who oversaw all the CGI effects created for the castle raid sequence, along with several other key VFX scenes throughout the film. "After the last film, I think Andrew was bound and determined to up the ante this time. For instance, we started off with at least twice the number of VFX shots compared to the start of *The Lion, the Witch and the Wardrobe*." In fact, he and Rogers have begun their CG journey on *Prince Caspian* with the exact number that Wright finished with on the previous film: sixteen hundred CG shots!

"In the end, we nearly had a shot for just about every scene in the film," Wright notes about the first movie. "On *Prince Caspian*, we'll probably end up somewhere in the neighborhood of eighteen hundred to two thousand shots, certainly making it one of the biggest visual effects movies ever made!"

As in the first film, virtually every moment and scene in the film has been touched by a VFX shot of some sort. Even the very first scene of the Pevensies back in World War II London contains a visual effect, a matte painting of Trafalgar Square, as that moment was filmed on location in modern-day Prague.

For the castle raid sequence, Wright partnered with two colleagues: Greg Butler from London's Moving Picture Company (MPC) whose team oversaw the action and character effects created for this sequence, and Guy Williams of Weta Digital in New Zealand, which created the environments for the scene.

Together, Wright estimated some three-hundred-plus VFX shots will have been incorporated into this pivotal

(and human Telmarines) affected the illusion that there are many more characters and creatures involved in the raid than the number of extras employed for the scene. And, of course, Andrew's use of miniatures enhanced the physical setting erected by Ford's construction crew.

"The work in the castle raid scene, one of the biggest sets I've ever stepped into, was beyond anything we did on the first film," Wright asserts. "Still, the set we worked in was only about one-third the size of the real castle that you will see in the finished film. Roger built a six-story set, maybe sixty feet high. The castle walls were enhanced through matte paintings and the use of a 1/24 scale miniature to affect something two hundred feet high. The castle, with towers all around it, sits on top of a hill, with a bridge over the moat that drops off one thousand feet to a river down below. We have towers surrounding the whole place. And this was just one courtyard that sits inside an entire palace!"

"The castle itself gets extended very high up," adds Butler. "There's high towers all around it. It will be a very impressive-looking environment when seen in the film. It was already impressive as a real location. Once it gets extended and filled with additional creatures, it will become a really exciting place."

In relaying the scope of not only the entire film, but the castle raid itself, Wright details the types of CG imagery required to bring the sequence together: "It's not just the number of shots we create. More important, it's how integrated we are with the entire structure of the film, from the drama, in terms of creating integral characters all throughout the film, to completing the environments, and obviously, completing the whole armies of creatures and Telmarines."

When the fauns, satyrs, and Minotaurs join the rest of the Narnian army in the castle attack, each creature will have its own individual look, says Wright, which represents one of the challenges of the visual effects on *Prince Caspian*.

"That's the complexity of the VFX role this time," Wright explains. "We may not double the amount of

scene in the film, with Butler's crew handling approximately 130 and another two hundred from the Weta wizards.

What types of shots? Suffice it to say that they used a virtual glossary of VFX practices to bring all the elements together that could not be shot "live" over the thirty nights it took to complete the film's first big action scene.

Leg replacement (a CGI practice first perfected in the film *Forrest Gump*) covered the green-screen spandex pants worn by extras portraying fauns, centaurs, satyrs, and Minotaurs. The addition of multiple CG characters shots, but the overall enterprise is 50 percent more difficult than the last film. Andrew is making these characters and creatures organically. Each character has to be very individual. We're not creating a squadron of fauns with two or three different variations. Every faun will have its own unique look, as will all the other creatures, as well as the Telmarine soldiers."

Regarding the integration of Howard's special makeup and the VFX augmentation of these unique characters, Wright emphasizes that "it made this film really challenging for us based on Howard's idea to bring more of a variety to the characters we have. In this film, Howard played with ages and genders. Old age fauns and heavy set characters. Also, African-Narnian centaurs. That created work for CG because we had to build that into our library of digital characters. It will look realistic and won't be cookie-cutter. It won't look cookie-cutter. There will be variety."

Wright notes that Andrew also wanted to break the CG barrier on this one by having real people merge more realistically with the CG characters. This approach is on fine display when Lucy hugs Aslan irresistibly when they meet for the first time; when the mighty griffins hold the Pevensies and Caspian in their claws as they approach the castle from the air; and when Susan jumps atop the back of Glenstorm the centaur to escape from the raid—all sequences where one or more of the "actors" in the scene isn't physically present.

"That presented a huge challenge for us to make it all look real," Wright stresses. "Striving for stuff that looked like it belongs in the frame, not something that

takes your eye away from the action unfolding in the story. I'm a big believer that VFX not dominate the story. These films are about the kids and their journey, and we cannot distract from that or we've hurt the film, not helped it."

He also points to the creation of the mythical griffins for the film, especially those moments that set the castle raid in motion. "The battle starts with the griffins. That effect upped the demands for us to put the humans and the CG imagery closer together, intermix them if you will, to help create one world of characters, a human-CG mix."

The footage showing Peter, Edmund, and Caspian being carried onto the upper towers of Miraz's castle was filmed months after the actual castle raid was done . . . and not inside the castle courtyard set, but on one of Barrandov's new stages.

With the walls of Stages 8 and 9 painted a shade of blue normally used as a VFX backdrop (the effect was akin to being in a fishbowl), Ford's art department designed a castle roof set so Andrew could stage the action that launches the castle raid—when the Pevensies and Caspian are dropped onto the castle tower from the claws of the griffins.

This effect was also augmented, a few days later, by shooting the actors hooked into an uncomfortable harness connected to a motion control camera (basically a giant robotic arm that can repeat precise movements) on the same Barrandov stages. Swinging around in the air, the actors were mimicking the movements of their flight onto the castle walls, borne by griffins. Enormous, deafening fans were on hand to simulate the wind as they flew through the air, and Andrew directed

That decision would mean months of technical design, research, and development with the assistance of motion control expert Ian Menzies. His knowledge of the types of camera moves necessary to successfully mount the sequence would bring the VFX team to build computer control rigs "capable of moving and photographing the kids in a safe environment," Wright says. "It was driven completely by animation approved by Andrew. And it had to look real! The advancements in this type of technology have come a long way, and that ensured our goals in creating this exciting sequence."

Wright emphasizes that the VFX teams all over the world had to work in perfect synchronicity in order to pull off this eye-popping effect perfectly. "We had the animators at MPC in London create the pre-viz for each shot," Wright continues, "plotting the path the kids would fly into and through the castle. This footage was then fed to the MPC animators, who supervised the intricate moves on-set in Prague."

Once completed, the digital files for the shots were sent down to Weta Digital in New Zealand, where "matchmakers" would convert the files for Alex Funke's miniatures crew.

Funke, in turn, filmed a camera test on the 1/24 scale castle model to make sure it all worked. Any required changes were then passed on to the on-set animators, who incorporated the new camera moves into their animation before finally sharing it with Menzies' team. He took the information and fed it into the computer control griffin rigs connected to the motion control cameras to shoot the blue-screen photography of the actors only hours later.

Months after the actual castle raid sequence was completed on location in Prague, Wright found himself back in New Zealand, where he lived for several years producing the VFX on the second and third *Lord of the Rings* films. There he joined Funke, one of the industry's best miniature effects directors, who spent three months shooting footage on several miniature versions of the castle built at different scales.

the actors and the action via a microphone and a public address system just to be heard.

"We had griffins in the first film, and we really loved them as characters," Wright enthuses about the decision to somehow include them in *Prince Caspian*. "When we were designing the castle raid sequence, we came up with the idea of having them carry the kids, Caspian, and Trumpkin—either in their claws or riding on their backs—into the castle for this stealth raid, which will be very cool."

"The 1/24 scale is a huge miniature," says Wright about a set one could actually walk into. Not to mention the 1/100 scale miniature that encompassed a thousand buildings and took in the entire castle and Telmarine village. Only a small portion of the village was erected on Barrandov's backlot on construction coordinator Malcolm Roberts's watch.

"We built these at Weta Workshop in New Zealand," Wright says about the miniature castle sets. "The miniatures were shot by Alex Funke and his miniature team, which did all the work on *The Lion, the Witch and the Wardrobe* and *King Kong*. They're Peter Jackson's team, so they were on loan to us, sort of. They were responsible for shooting something real and tangible that helped create this very cool-looking castle."

Besides the fact that Andrew likes to use miniatures, the use of such movie trickery comes about, says Wright, "because of the very naturalistic building environments in this case. The actual castle was built using architecturally known substances, which are not easy to reproduce digitally. If we wanted, we could probably take little

sections and create them digitally. But to do the whole castle would have been a huge endeavor.

"And when you can get a camera really close to something and shoot it and get the detail there, it just looks real. And it feels real," Wright explains. "And you don't question it. Every time you work on something in CG, you are essentially trying to replicate the natural lighting, make the lighting look as real as the photography you're trying to put it up against. That's something you're constantly battling. With photographic elements, shooting miniatures, it looks much more natural."

We then handed that over to the digital version of her on Glenstorm's back, and then the whole [sequence] becomes digital as we pan across and they leave. So that's multiple effects all in one shot, all of which were challenging on their own."

Butler, whose support team on the raid sequence included Martin Hobbs (VFX producer), Clwyd Edwards (CG supervisor), Adam Valdez (animation director), Charley Henley (2D supervisor), and Richard Stammers (castle raid supervisor), also hints at the challenge of creating the character of Glenstorm, embodied in the movie by English musical theater star Cornell S. John. John endured a lengthy makeup application to transform his face into that of a centaur. When shot full-length in-camera, he donned green or blue spandex leggings that Butler's team digitally removed and supplanted with the body of a horse.

"And there was a horse cast to play the bottom half of Glenstorm," Butler explains. "The horse's name was Califa. A beautiful horse. When we had to do a shot of Glenstorm, we'd get a pass with Cornell, the actor playing Glenstorm, possibly on power risers, those action stilts. We then had to replace the part below Glenstorm with this digital version of Califa."

To complete such a CG image, Butler's team always tried to get a shot of the real horse for reference, "of exactly how that horse should look in this environment," says Butler. He would also have a plate shot (a background image) of everything that was happening behind Glenstorm, "in case we found out later that we couldn't actually use the actor's plate performance for timing, and we had to complete the shot fully digital. We had to shoot that shot a couple of different ways just to give us flexibility later."

Although Butler says that almost anything can be done in a computer, he doesn't have time to do everything. "For every setup or camera and lighting position or action moment, we try to take reference shots mostly for lighting. For that, we put out gray and chrome spheres, which capture the lighting environment around them."

It was Butler's challenge to make Susan's jump onto the back of the centaur Glenstorm look as real and natural as possible when enhancing the thrilling moment at the end of the castle raid.

"There's a pretty difficult shot we had to do where Glenstorm rides by and grabs Susan on the way out of the castle," says Butler, months later in his VFX lair in London. "Susan had to be a digital double. The real actress jumped up 'live' before the cameras.

Wright touched upon the use of these VFX balls in his chapter in the companion book for *The Lion, the Witch and the Wardrobe*. "The silver or chrome ball references light intensity, while the gray one contrasts or defines light and darkness, or shadows, when you bring the shot into the computer world," he explains. "The use of these tools aids in matching the on-set lighting when creating and lighting CG characters later in the computer."

Both Wright and Butler also refer to a gizmo called the high-dynamic-range (HDR) cam, a camera that simultaneously captures multiple photos and multiple exposures that can all be added back together to give you this high-dynamic-range image of the environment being used on the set.

"The HDR cam is a huge contraption that looks like a *Voyager* spaceship," Wright muses. "It's got four eyes with four digital cameras and takes photographs with a wide exposure lens. Its high technology allows us terrific images that help clarify where the light is on the set, as do the silver and gray balls, which have been used for years. VFX writes software to suck that material into their pipeline. When we turn the film over to them, they combine it with this software, and the CG characters pop in as if they belong in the frame. Also, they can adjust the light as a cinematographer would to make it look better and real."

Adds Butler, "We can get more information about that light captured through HDR than the film has any

VFX assistant Charlotte Hayes holds the ubiquitous silver and chrome balls that help the VFX artists reference light intensity for a scene.

ability to. Once we're in the computer, that means we can use those lights at varying intensities and still have what the colors and intensities were at shoot time."

Butler also utilized a network of video cameras, which he calls "witness cameras," planted strategically around the set (and manned by a series of VFX techies called "data capturers") to augment the view of the film cameras. He calls the innovation one of the new strategies in recent VFX animation.

"In order for an animator to get the right animation to match the actors upper half and get the legs working on these Narnian creatures, it's advantageous to have other ways of looking at that same moment in time," Butler notes. "It gives you another angle on the scene and a better view of what the performer did for the movie cameras. But not just another angle—a very specific technical angle. Whereas the film camera might be doing these crane and swooping shots and have various levels of focus, our witness camera is a very boring, dry, locked-off moment just watching, observing, capturing what's going on in the set. And we do that for multiple angles so that later on, when we're trying to animate a scene, you can look at that scene from multiple angles and really work out what was going on at the time."

All of this was for one twelve-minute scene in a two-hour movie.

REEPICHEEP

Step aside, Mickey. There's a new mouse in town. Standing 22 inches high, he's as gallant, noble, and honorable as the finest knight, and, in his creator C. S. Lewis's words, wields a "tiny little rapier," which makes him a force to be reckoned with.

"I grew up on these *Narnia* books and Reepicheep was definitely one of my favorite characters," Andrew Adamson reveals. "He was very ingrained in my imagination."

It's not hard to see why. In Chapter 6 of *Prince Caspian*, Lewis introduces us to this unusual warrior: "A Talking Mouse, the last thing that Caspian expected. He was, of course, bigger than a common mouse, well over a foot high when he stood on his hind legs, with ears nearly as long (though broader than) a rabbit's. His name was Reepicheep and he was a gay and martial mouse. He wore a tiny little rapier at his side and twirled his whiskers as if they were a moustache."

Armed with this description, the concept artists began

drafting possible designs, which were eventually handed over to the VFX companies in production, who went about constructing the mouse anatomically inside the computer. However, the character itself, the walking, talking manifestation, was proving elusive. Even into filming, the filmmakers were still looking.

"The trick here is finding the right voice," Andrew revealed in September. "Too dapper and he comes off as fey. Not strong or noble enough, and he becomes too posh. He's been difficult to find so far."

By the time filming concluded on August 31, the filmmakers still had not selected the actor they truly wanted for the voice recording. Their search reminded us of the same circumstances they encountered on *The Lion, the Witch and the Wardrobe* in their pursuit of a suitable vocal talent for Aslan.

As editor Sim Evan-Jones labored over the first cut of *Prince Caspian* that Andrew would screen for the studio executives, and the trio of VFX vendors simultaneously toiled at their computers to create all the digital magic that breathes life into these big-screen ventures, Andrew

The development of Reepicheep, the swashbuckling rodent.

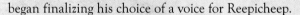

began finalizing his choice of a voice for Reepicheep.

Andrew explains how he approaches the pursuit of a voice actor, having vast experience working on such endeavors on both *Shrek* movies.

"With all your ideas about the character, you record an actor and that reading can inform everything about the character, even uncover things you did not see about him," Andrew explains. "The exciting part of the film-making process is the evolution, having something in your head that becomes a guide track that steers you in the direction that leads you somewhere else.

"I love working with actors for that reason, to discover the character," he continues. "I may write a character I have in my head, then start to talk to the actor playing him, and he then informs my idea of the character, and it evolves from there. Next, you get it on film, or in this case, on an audio file, then possibly change it again in the edit. In the end, you finally get to know the character that you've met only at the beginning of the process."

A character like Reepicheep must also be physical-ized onscreen. That responsibility fell to longtime

Adamson colleague Wendy Rogers and her counterpart at London's Moving Picture Company, Greg Butler, who together oversaw the birth of the gallant mouse for the film. Still, without an actor, there's only so much they can do.

"It's not the fact that the animated character resembles the actor playing him," she explains. "It's more about the voice, because the actor brings so much personality to who the character becomes. We know what attributes Reepicheep has without thinking of a particular voice. We know he's chivalrous, honorable, and proud. He finds it a bit tiresome that others don't take him seriously because of his size. But how he sounds is who he is, and that's the crucial part about casting the right actor, who brings so much to the character. So while we've been able to explore body mechanics and look develop-ment for Reepicheep, the character development can't be finalized until we have that voice cast!"

She also points out that the actual studio voice-recording session by the actor brings more to the character than the actual dialogue tracks.

"For someone like Reepicheep, while saying his lines, the actor may do some mannerisms or a physical flourish, like wave a sword," she describes. "We have lipstick cams at these recording sessions to capture that. That helps our exploration of who the character is. Really valuable to us. Without those specifics, we can interpret Reepicheep in a number of ways—comedic, broad, Errol Flynn–like. The actor's voice and mannerisms can help us narrow who the character is and will become on-screen."

Once Andrew chooses the actor to play Reepicheep, Rogers, Butler, and the designers, technical directors, and animators will begin physicalizing the character, both for his key scenes in the film, where he is the focus and has dialogue, as well as those moments when he stands in the background of a shot that features the human actors interacting with these CG characters. Of course, the key dialogue scenes mandate that the VFX magicians bring forth the character succinctly so the audience gets to know who he is.

In other words, like any actor, Reepicheep has to be true to his character, and his motivations and thoughts need to be visible to the audience.

The longtime visual effects expert (who perfected her VFX character animation expertise during a lengthy tenure at DreamWorks Animation) also points out the fact that "Reepicheep will be a big mouse. Some twenty-two inches tall. That will take some suspension of disbelief. It's not explained in the film

Reepicheep's stand-in on location.

why he is so big. It is in the book. At that size, we still have to make him feel like he's a mouse. We have to find the correct balance between anthropomorphizing Reepicheep and maintaining the fact that he is a real animal a— a mouse. Otherwise, you won't believe he's a real physical creature."

While colleague Dean Wright did copious research for lions in creating the CG version of Aslan in the first movie, "there isn't any research available for twenty-two-inch mice," Rogers quips while pointing to a DVD library on her office shelf profiling virtually every other animal that's been captured by documentary cameras. "We still must create the character realistically. That way, you will accept those things they do in the story that may not be real as applies to such an animal in their actual environment (e.g., walking on hind legs and talking)!"

"Of all the Narnian characters MPC had to create for *Prince Caspian*, Reepicheep was the one requiring the most art direction and overall attention to detail," says Rogers's colleague at MPC, Greg Butler. "This involved a core team of ten artists off and on for all of 2007. Starting from some early sketches given to us from the film production's art department and referencing many photos of mice and other rodents, we began to produce concept artwork for Andrew to review."

Leading this design effort was MPC art director Virginie Bourdin, who first created "mood panels," says Butler, that assembled various images that might be suitable for an aspect of the character, such as the ears, hands, fur style, and color. These were presented to Andrew for his input.

"One of the first challenges that became clear was that a very big mouse would be hard to keep looking "'mousey,'" Butler notes. "We wanted to make sure Reepicheep didn't end up looking like a rat. We also had to work out an anatomy that was based on a mouse, but still allowed him to sword-fight, wear armor, and walk on two as well as four legs. Although the initial design process was done entirely in 2-D, using drawings and digital paintings, we involved our animation director, Adam Valdez, from the very beginning. It was his job to make sure the character that was designed could perform his role in the film."

Once the concept art developed by Bourdin was approved by Andrew, Butler, and his MPC colleagues moved the design into 3-D. Giles Davis, the project's lead modeler, worked with Virginie Bourdin and James Stewart, creature supervisor, to create a subdivision surface model in Maya, one of the frequently used computer programs for CG imagery.

Rogers points out that Maya is probably the most well-known computer program used for VFX character animation.

"Getting the head shape right was the first step," Butler relates. "This was aided by anatomical references of mouse skulls. With a realistic skull as the basis, Giles built the surface up, always referring back to the approved artwork. The final 3-D model had to look right from all directions, not just the one angle visualized in the concept piece."

In addition to Davis's modeling design, the creation of Reepicheep also required such CG techniques as texture painting (Philippe Gaulier) and grooming (Jean Pascal LeBlanc); look development (Stephen Murphy); rigging (Waikit Wan); and animation character studies (Julio Hernandez, Daryl Sawchuk, Robb Denovan, Greg Fisher).

As postproduction began, Reepicheep was still undergoing some design work. The large mouse is described in *Dawn Treader* as being almost black, Wendy recalls. "That would have made him more 'ratty.' We were still developing his fur color at this late stage, making it more of a darker reddish-brown on his back, with a lighter stomach."

At the time of this writing, Wendy and her crew are undergoing an even more intense flurry of activity, because . . . Reepicheep has been cast! After lengthy conversations, Andrew chose the wry British comic Eddie Izzard, best known for his incisive stand-up performances, to put his unique spin on Lewis's diminutive hero. The process now shifts into an even higher gear, as recording dates are negotiated, sound studios rented, and Andrew and Eddie work together to find the soul of the character you'll see on-screen. The animators and character designers then have their work cut out for them: to make the character on-screen embody the character's vocal performance. And when all this is done, this is still only the beginning for the mouse.

"This story is Reepicheep's introduction," Andrew states about one of the film's supporting, but certainly memorable, characters. "*Dawn Treader* will be his story. My job here was to set him up, and I didn't really get to exploit him like so many other characters. But this character is so worthwhile and interesting. So what we've done was set him up and establish him for the next Narnia adventure."

MORE MAGIC

Which leads us to the creation of some of the other CG characters in the story like Aslan, Trufflehunter, Pattertwig, and Bulgy Bear, all of whom come to dazzling life under the watchful eyes of co-supervisor Rogers.

There is the huge climactic battlefield sequence outside Aslan's How that employed some four-hundred-plus extras during filming (playing both Telmarine soldiers and Narnian creatures). It will be enhanced through the magic of Wright's and Rogers's visuals to appear as if

tens of thousands are charging across this verdant prairie.

And there's the inventive River God sequence filmed on location in Slovenia. It was a huge VFX endeavor, says Framestore/CFC's VFX supervisor, Jon Thum, whose company will deliver a full load of visuals, including two of the most heavily featured talking creatures in the movie—Aslan and Trufflehunter.

Thum and his key staff on the film (Robin Saxen, VFX producer; Mike Mulholland, CG supervisor; Kevin Spruce, animation supervisor; Mark Hodgkins, effects supervisor; Mark Bakowski, compositing supervisor; Kevin Jenkins, matte painting supervisor) will summon the River God in their computers by creating the illusion that this entity "comes to life by sucking up the river water in a huge vortex, rising 120 feet in the air as the water cascades back down into the river, forming his features," Thum explains.

At this writing, Thum adds that "his design is very much still in progress to determine how much we can decide on his features from free-flowing water that is sucked up and then let go again. The choreography of the scene was determined in pre-viz."

There's also the moving trees . . . the dryads in Lucy's dream . . . Lucy's first encounter with Aslan . . . and so much more.

"Having Andrew in the director's chair is a godsend for us," says Wright, praising his director and collaborator. "As visual effects professionals, we want to be pushed. I think all the innovation that comes from visual effects comes from a director pushing you further than you ever thought you could go.

"Andrew wanted to make this film bigger than the last, which meant throwing more complicated stuff at VFX," the effects supervisor continues. "Not to amaze the audience, but to make it more real or organic within the frame and the story. If we can make the CG feel more real, you'll forget they're visual effects and enjoy the film that much more.

"When kudos go out for visual effects, there should be an honorary place for the director," Wright adds with sincerity. "He's the one who usually comes up with 95 percent of the vision of what you're going to create. You're there to help it and enhance it. We are making a film here as if there were no visual effects. We're just here to fill in the gaps. Andrew's got the story, he's got the cast, he's got the set. Once he shoots those elements, we know what we can do to finish those shots. And to be able to bring that to the film and be able to produce that, and then have you watch it, and forget that we were ever there, that's the ultimate goal."

OPPOSITE: *Trufflehunter*. THIS PAGE —TOP: *Aslan*. RIGHT AND BELOW: *Concept art of The River God, and The Trees*.

A Day in the Life
August 25 (Day 131)
Barrandov Studios, Prague

I will never forget the very first film I did back in 1988. A lackluster comedy, it was my first freelance experience as a production publicist (after many years in the studio ranks) and my very first extended stay away from home and family. While the film faded from memory quickly, the experience of the journey never has. I've always looked back fondly on the time spent making that film in this exciting environment called the movies.

When a movie shoot comes to its finale, that last day can be tinged with melancholy. It was for me on that debut project two decades ago. One day, you are on a vibrant set with the people with whom you have worked closely for several months, with whom you've certainly become acquainted . . . if not downright friendly. This tight-knit unit simulates a family, as I suggested at times throughout this book. After the last shot, the traditional decree heard daily from the assistant director, "That's a wrap," is heeded one last time, signaling the film's finality. The lights have been dimmed. The curtain has come down.

While you anticipate seeing the fruits of the filmmakers' labor up on that big screen months down the line, for the moment, you are in a strange void, devoid of everything but the memories of the experience as the finish line approaches, not unlike a long-distance runner after a marathon. There's a simultaneous sense of accomplishment and relief that it's over. Those recollections as

Publicist (and author) Ernie Malik with longtime friend and colleague– Howard Berger.

you bid good-bye to the people and the project can be bittersweet.

Sound mixer Tony Johnson describes the feeling best by saying, "It is time to go, but you don't necessarily want to leave."

I have just finished five arduous months of filming in Eastern Europe, mostly in Prague and the Czech Republic, where approximately 90 of the production's 136 shooting days (including the New Zealand portion, which now feels so distant and part of another movie) were completed. Prague is a lovely and historic city. I'm so glad to have had the privilege of living here for five months. (I have Andrew, Mark, and Philip to thank for that.) Even though, like any location away from home, after such an extended period of time it becomes quite familiar. In actuality, Prague is quite extraordinary.

But I am saddened to leave this home-away-from-home, my grandparents' birthplace. I am even sadder to say good-bye to many of the people, colleagues and allies all, whom I have met on this journey through two continents, two hemispheres, and four countries over a period of seven months. There's too many handshakes and hugs to share. I regret not being able to mention everyone I saluted on my way out the door.

Ben Barnes gives me a warm, heartfelt embrace as I bid him good-bye. His final words to me as I take my final bows: "Will I see you on the *Dawn Treader?*" God willing (and maybe with a little help from his agent, whom I joke should put me in this future star's contract).

Anna Popplewell's crystal-blue eyes, the color of the Tasman Sea, reflect a hue of sadness as I reach past Ben in her set trailer to bid my farewells. I've gotten to know Anna much more this time around. *Lovely* is the word I think best describes her smile, her manner, her beauty. She thanks me for looking after her and the rest of the cast so well. Her appreciation touches me in a way I cannot express.

While I catch up with Will Moseley the next day, I would be remiss in not mentioning how this handsome Englishman has matured since I last saw him in late 2004. In the first *Narnia* movie, Will's character of Peter grows from a boy to a man along the journey. While I haven't seen Will in over two years, this rural English lad has done just that—shed his boyhood for manhood in those ensuing years. Too many adjectives spring to mind when trying to pinpoint what best describes this polite, gentle, gracious, humble, and kind young man.

I remember Skandar Keynes's reaction to meeting me on the first movie. When I was introduced as the film's unit publicist, he immediately replied, "You're the PR guy!" That's what we all like about this young rascal, who was always into everybody's business on the first project like a youngster sticking his fingers in the cake batter when Mother looked away. Now at almost sixteen, he's rock 'n' roll. Whether he's toting around his guitar like a troubadour or greeting crew with his unique, multilayered handshake, he's just such a fine young man . . . and a darn cool kid, all rolled into one.

While the youngest of the quartet, Georgie Henley, wrapped the week before me (I was away on her last day and missed my good-byes), I must mention how she has changed since I last saw her. I'm not sure she knew what to make of me on the first movie. She was a nine-year-old acting novice being asked to sit in front of groups of press to talk not only about her character, but also herself. At that age, she handled herself with the maturity of someone twice her years. Now approaching adolescence, she continues to blossom like an elegant flower, one you relish seeing in its full bloom.

Veteran cameraman Greg Lundsgaard extends a warm salutation about our time together, both on-set and during those casual meals after hours. He also courteously offers kind remarks about this book, passages of which he has reviewed when references to his craft

were included. It had been fifteen years since Greg and I last worked together. I hope another fifteen doesn't pass before this privilege comes around again.

Before the last van ride back to my hotel with one of the dependable Czech drivers (whom I always addressed in their native tongue, much to their amusement and appreciation), I share a final half hour with producer Mark Johnson. His genuine gratitude toward my publicity contributions, as small and insignificant to this part of the process as they may be, never goes unnoticed. The congenial, committed filmmaker makes me feel like a rock star in the presence of a true fan. Isn't it supposed to be the other way around? We part with a hug and the promise of booking passage together on the *Dawn Treader*.

In between filming on Barrandov's Stage 9, where he is overseeing blue-screen motion control shots of Skandar flying in the claws of a CGI griffin, Andrew Adamson graciously inquires about my next project and about the progress of this book as we shake hands goodbye. He's always smiling, and I thank him for the time he has contributed to the publicity campaign. The success of my job on-set rests with the interest and cooperation of the director as he discusses the project with visiting media. I could not have been blessed with a better collaborator or spokesperson. Cheers, Andrew.

And so it goes with the farewells, too many to mention—cinematographer Walter Lindenlaub (snapping photos for his scrapbook of everyone donning one of Howard Berger's many creature wigs); the prosthetics genius himself, Howard Berger (whom I've known now for twenty years); makeup artist Paul Engelen (one of the industry's true gentlemen); Kiwi Tim Coddington (over a glass of his debut 2006 Chardonnay); producer Philip Steuer (the quiet American); Andrew's lovely assistant, Alina Phelan (the green-screen queen?); co-producer David Minkowski (without whom this film could not have been made); and Joe Dunckley and Rob Gillies (the capable and committed Weta armorers who helped the cast bring a heroic nature to their characters with their vast supply of weaponry). On a project this size, the list of good-byes is virtually endless, the emotions ceaseless.

This would be the appropriate place to tell you that everyone involved in *Prince Caspian* worked exceedingly hard to bring you the best of moviegoing experiences. There are many you've met on the journey through these pages, and many more you have not. While the film is very different from *The Lion, the Witch and the Wardrobe*, as you've heard from the assorted voices scattered throughout the book, the untiring commitment from these dedicated professionals has not waned since the last movie. We say good-bye to you in these last pages with pride and the confidence that we indeed will entertain you as you sit back in your local cinemas in 2008.

Filming continued for another week beyond my departure. My role had come to an end on-set (no more press visits scheduled), and the next job beckoned in the very near future. Maybe I'll chronicle it in another "making of" book.

Until then, thank you for the privilege of showing you around this set and for introducing you to the wonderful people who made the film. And thank you for reading these words, which I sincerely hope reflect what the experience of *Prince Caspian* meant to all involved.

See you at the movies!

AFTERWORD
Ben Barnes

As I write this, we are coming very close to the end of the seven-month shoot on *Prince Caspian*, and I feel sad that the cast and crew will soon leave Narnia to return to the real world. As Caspian says to Susan in the final scene, "I wish we had more time together."

It was such a privilege for me to be cast as the prince that I grew up idolizing. I learned how to gallop horses through the woods in a few short weeks. The feeling of fighting ten men with sword and dagger and confidently wielding crossbows and pikes was incomparable. I feel I earned the right in the end to wear Miraz's jeweled crown. But I have to say that the real honor has been to visit all the places and work alongside all the people you have been reading about in this book.

I was not surprised when I found out the location for shooting my first scene was actually named Paradise. It truly was an enchanting place. I had two weeks of horse training and Spanish lessons there with my wonderfully encouraging teachers when we first arrived. I have never seen sunsets like those on the South Island of New Zealand, and I could not believe that one day on the set with the second unit in February we had to stop filming because snow began to fall. In the summer!

My initial encounter with a Pevensie was a shot riding through the forest with Anna on the back of my horse. I felt chivalrous and heroic . . . until she nearly fell off. Thankfully, Anna has a wonderful sense of humor, and she actually found it amusing that she had an imprint of my chain mail on her cheek from holding on so tight. And, to walk on set and see my double, Andrew Cottle, fully dressed in my armor rehearsing a stunt sequence, was surreal, to say the least.

My first dialogue scene was with Warwick Davis in Trufflehunter's Den. The two of us sparred, joked, and made fun of each other from the first moment and did not relent throughout filming.

Every day on the set uncovered fresh challenges working with our one-thousand-strong crew guided by Andrew Adamson. The talent, focus, enthusiasm, and kindness of everyone I met was truly overwhelming, from sitting on the How in silence with my professor, Vincent Grass, to battling hundreds of Telmarines with William, Anna, Skandar, and Peter at my side. I have tried to savor every moment. The first time I walked onto the set of the castle, my heart skipped a beat. When Sergio Castellitto leveled his gaze at me during our first rehearsal, I was truly in awe.

I was filled with pride when stunt coordinator Allan Poppleton gave me a thumbs-up after watching my first fight sequence. I have never high-fived anyone as much as I have with Skandar Keynes. I have never laughed as much with anyone as I have with Peter Dinklage.

Andrew Adamson's warm, caring, calming, and comforting manner encouraged me through my daunting task, and I will forever be thankful to him for giving me the opportunity of a lifetime—and for giving me a sword that was just slightly longer than William Moseley's.

Thank you so much to everyone who worked on the film and everyone who watches it. It has been an honor. My appreciation may be best reflected in these words:

The proper rewards are not simply tacked on to the activity for which they are given, but are the activity itself in consummation.

C. S. Lewis

ACKNOWLEDGMENTS

While there may be only one name affixed to the cover of this book, I only sculpt the words that come from the ideas, experiences, and vision of many connected to this enterprise called *Prince Caspian*.

To borrow a line from filmmaker Frank Capra in his classic 1946 film, *It's A Wonderful Life*: "No man is a failure who has friends."

If this book has proven a successful venture, there are too many individual "friends" who deserve proper thanks and credit for their support, guidance, and inspiration. Those listed below (whether they know it or not) contributed in some small way to the words and ideas in this book.

To these friends and colleagues, and to acknowledge the lands in which we filmed, I say 'thank you' in four languages — *Dekuji vam* (Czech), *Podziekowania dla Wszystkich* (Polish), *Hvala vam* (Slovene), and *Tika Hoki* (Maori).

Victoria Acosta

Kimberly Adams

Andrew Adamson

Damián Alcázar

Alexa Alden

Kevin Alexander

Oren Aviv

Ben Barnes

Howard Berger

Brian Bouma

Phil Bray

Kerrie Brown

Greg Butler

Christine Cadena

Josh Campbell

Sergio Castellitto

Ira Cecic

Mark Ceryak

Rich Chapla

Ryan Chingcuangco

Lida Claussova

Murray Close

Tim Coddington

James Crowley

Ricardo Cruz

Rico D'Alessandro

Judy Dale

Gareth Daley

Warwick Davis

Peter Dinklage

Cynthia DiTiberio

Joe Dunckley

Paul Engelen

Sim Evan-Jones

Pierfrancesco Favino

Gerd Feuchter

Mark Forbes

Roger Ford

Rob Gillies

Martina Gotthansova

Harry Gregson-Williams

Vincent Grass

Doug Gresham

Jána Hrbkova

Georgie Henley

Helen and Mike Henley

K.C. and Roxie Hodenfield

David Hollander

Greg Irwin

Silvia Janculova

Cornell S. John

Mark Johnson

Tony Johnson

Skandar Keynes

Zelfa Hourani and
   Randall Keynes

Eddie Knight

Jiri "Effa" Kotlas

Tami Lane

Veronika Lencova

Jennifer Lewicki

Karl Walter Lindenlaub

Greg Lundsgaard

John Mahaffie

Paul Martin

Chris Markus and
   Steve McFeely

Wayne Martindale

Marjorie L. Mead

David Minkowski

Chris Mitchell

Perry Moore

Jenny Morgan

Samantha Morley

William Moseley

Julie and Peter Moseley

Isis Mussenden

Duncan Nimmo

Jeff "O" Okabayashi

Alina Phelan and
   Mark Ballou

Allan Poppleton and
   erika Takacs

Anna Popplewell

Debra Lomas and
   Andrew Popplewell

Shane "Sweet As" Rangi

Malcolm Roberts

Wendy Rogers

Marianna Rowinska

Sarah Rubano

John Sabel

Peter Schakel

Ashley Seabright

Katka Silna

Ryan Stankovich

Philip Steuer

Rpin Suwannath

Lauren Swearingen

Tilda Swinton

Richard Taylor

Jon Thum

Barbara Toennies

Marketa Tom

Cindy Vance

Charlie Visnic and
   Jenny Nicol

Tatiana Vomackova

Mike Vosburg

Frank Walsh

Tom Williams

Dean Wright

Diego Zanco

Finally, a very special and heartfelt thanks to Jane, Daniel, and Lauren, whose love and inspiration in the real world have helped me achieve my dreams in this reel world called the movies.

Photo and Art Credits

HOWARD BERGER: 114, 126 (*inset*), 138, 139 (*bottom*), 140, 141 (*top*), 142 (*2nd down*), 143, 144 (*top*), 145 (*top right, bottom left, and bottom right*), 147 (*bottom*), 149, 150, 154 (*bottom*), 199, 206

PHIL BRAY: vi, x, 2, 6 (*bottom*), 7, 9, 13, 15, 16, 18, 19, 21 (*top*), 22, 23, 30, 32, 35, 36, 38, 40 (*full*), 41, 42, 43, 44, 46, 50, 62, 64 (*top*), 68, 73 (*2nd and 3rd down*), 80 (*top*), 81, 82, 98, 106 (*right*), 108, 109 (*top left*), 113, 117 (*top and bottom*), 118, 120, 122 (*bottom*), 146, 147 (*top*), 155, 177 (*top*), 178 (*top*), 207 (*middle*), 208 (*top*), 209 (*bottom*), 211

RICH CHAPLA: ix, 34

ERIC CHARBONNEAU: 175, 180, 182

MURRAY CLOSE: vii, 4, 6 (*top and middle*),10, 11, 12 (*top and bottom*), 20, 24, 25, 29, 45, 49, 51, 52, 53, 54, 57, 58, 60, 61, 64 (*bottom*), 65, 66, 69 (*top*), 69, 70, 72, 73 (*top and bottom*), 74, 76 (*top and bottom*), 77, 78, 80 (*2nd and 3rd down, and bottom*), 83, 84, 86, 87, 88, 90, 91, 92, 94, 95, 96, 100 (*bottom*), 101 (*bottom*), 102, 104, 107, 109 (*right*), 110, 111, 112, 123, 125 (*bottom*), 126 (*full*), 128, 129, 130, 131, 136, 137, 139 (*top left, top right, and middle right*), 141 (*bottom*), 142 (*top left, middle right, and bottom*), 144 (*bottom*), 145

(*top left*), 148, 151, 152, 153, 154 (*top*), 156, 157, 158 (*top*), 159, 160, 161, 164 (*bottom*), 165 (*bottom*), 167 (*middle and bottom*), 170, 171, 174, 176, 177 (*middle and bottom*), 178 (*middle and bottom*), 179, 183, 184, 187, 188, 189, 190, 191, 192, 194, 195, 196, 198, 202, 207 (*top and bottom*), 208 (*middle and bottom*), 209 (*top*).

RICO D'ALESSANDRO: 23

FRAMESTORE CFC/TOASTIE PRODUCTIONS: 204

CHRISTIAN HUBAND/ TOASTIE PRODUCTIONS: 132, 133, 134, 135

TOASTIE PRODUCTIONS: 26, 27, 205

MIKE VOSBURG: 21

WETA WORKSHOP: ii, iv, 125, 132 (*full*), 162, 163, 164 (*top*), 165 (*top and bottom*), 166, 172 (*top*), 197

JOHN WHEATON/KNB EFX: 100, 106

TOM WILLIAMS: 14

DEAN WRIGHT/TOASTIE PRODUCTIONS: 172, 173, 197